REALITY WEDDING

REALITY STAR BOOK 3

LAURA HEFFERNAN

SAY 'I DO' - OR ELSE

Life as reality royalty rocks: Jen's bakery is booming, Justin's got his dream job, and they're saving for a wedding. Then the producers call with an offer Jen can't refuse: hold the wedding on national TV, or they'll make sure Justin loses his job.

Oh, well. It's just a few weeks, and the wedding will be paid, so how bad could it be?

Dumb question.

The producers don't want a show about love, they want ratings and drama. From a wedding "dress" made of body paint to vegan cake, they've chucked Jen's wishes out the window. Worse, Justin's stuck in Florida, and the producers want the show to go on without him. Walking away from the show means a $100,000 penalty. If she can't find a way to make her own ratings smash, *Jen & Justin's Big Day* may turn into *Jen's Financial Fiasco.*

PRAISE FOR LAURA HEFFERNAN

SWEET REALITY

"If you like sweet contemporary romances with a reality show theme, then you are going to enjoy Heffernan's Reality Star series...Jen and Justin.are likable and relatable characters....Heffernan does a wonderful job with character development and painting vivid scenes. There are also some cute and funny moments that makes this book a worthwhile and entertaining read. If reality shows are your guilty pleasure, give Heffernan's *Sweet Reality* a try."

- RT Book Reviews

AMERICA'S NEXT REALITY STAR

"Smart, witty, and really freaking good, *America's Next Reality Star* is a fun read that has you cheering from the first paragraph through the last page. Laura Heffernan spins an entertaining tale, expertly mixing the main character's real life events with the reality show's challenges. With enough drama to not only satisfy fans of reality TV shows, but readers who thrive on a good story with humor and romance, this book is a perfect read." —Kerry Lonsdale, *Wall Street Journal* bestselling author

"Reality TV fans, this is your book! Laura Heffernan captures all the drama and over-the-top craziness in this fun and flirty romance."

—Amy E. Reichert, author of *Love, Luck, and Lemon Pie*

"*America's Next Reality Star* is one sweet, sexy brain-candy read! You won't be sorry you indulged." —Leah Marie Brown

BOOKS BY LAURA HEFFERNAN

The Reality Star Series

America's Next Reality Star

Sweet Reality

Reality Wedding

The Oceanic Dreams Series

Time of My Life

The Gamer Girls Series

She's Got Game

Against the Rules

Make Your Move

Push and Pole Series

Poll Dancer

The Accidental Senator

Finding Tranquility

Anna's Guide to Getting Even

CHAPTER ONE

THE NETWORK
requests the honor of your presence
at the Wmarriage of their stars
AMANDA LEE HUNTLEY
and
BRADEN ANDERSON
Saturday, the tenth of June
in the year two thousand seventeen
at one o'clock in the afternoon
at The Marrying Kind mansion
Black tie
Invitation required for admission
Reception to follow

Unlike most brides, nearly every milestone of my relationship with my future husband, Justin, had been captured on video and broadcast to America as part of season one of *The Fishbowl*: our growing attraction, our first fight, our first kiss, the proposal. So I shouldn't have been surprised when I answered my phone in the middle of a lull at work to find my favorite reality show producer asking if we wanted to get married on TV.

Shouldn't have been surprised, but Connor's question stopped me in my tracks. I stared at my phone, watching the timer tick upward. Five seconds seemed an eternity. Then ten seconds passed. The bustle of the bakery continued around me, but all I saw was my phone. That timer ticking.

"Jen?" His voice sounded tinny. Far away. With effort, I returned the phone to my ear and found my voice.

"Hold on," I said, ducking through the kitchen and out the back door for some privacy. I didn't want anyone to overhear this conversation. "You want us to get married in Los Angeles? On what, a special episode of *The Fishbowl*, season three?"

"No, no, no. That season doesn't start filming until July. We want to give you your own show. *Jen & Justin's Reality Wedding. J&J's Big Day. Becoming Mrs. Taylor.* The title's still a work in progress," he said. "Anyway, we'll film everything: cake tastings, dress fittings, meetings with the officiant. Then we'll film the ceremony in a two-hour special. The viewers will eat it up, and it'll be a great lead-in for *The Fishbowl*'s new season."

While theoretically, having your own reality show sounded awesome, this wasn't my first rodeo. I wasn't sure how I felt about having every last detail of my wedding broadcast to the world. This seemed more personal than solving puzzles or taking a cruise. The stakes were higher. I didn't want the Network interfering in my relationship again.

"Being on TV last time almost broke us up."

"And being on TV the first time brought you together," he said. "You'd never have met if not for the show."

That was true, but when Justin proposed, we both swore to leave the reality TV community behind forever. No more pop-up appearances. No more reality fun runs. Maybe a fundraiser or two for the right charity, but absolutely, positively No More TV Shows.

"I'm sorry, Connor, but we can't. Justin and I have retired our reality show personas."

"Are you sure?"

"I'm afraid so. But I appreciate the thought. And you and Ed better still come to the wedding when we have it." My best friend Ed, *The Fishbowl*'s official runner-up, lived with Connor in Los Angeles, where he'd built a successful stand-up career after our appearances on two reality shows.

"We wouldn't miss it for anything. You sure I can't get you to change your mind?"

"If you want, I can ask Justin to be sure, but I'm guessing the answer is no. I'm sorry."

"What if we offer to pay for everything?"

My ears perked up. "Everything?"

"Including the honeymoon."

Now that was tempting. Sweet Reality, the bakery I co-owned with Justin's sister, Sarah, was doing fine, but we wouldn't be able to afford a real vacation any time soon. People thought we had loads of money because we'd done a reality show, but that couldn't be further from the truth. Most of my *Fishbowl* winnings went into launching the business. The second show we did, *Real Ocean: Caribbean*, was only a week. We made almost nothing beyond the free vacation.

Justin was still a first-year associate at his law firm, and we'd spent most of our incomes in the past year on his parents' medical bills and paying down his student loans. To call our wedding budget a shoestring stretched the bounds of the English language. We were on a dental-floss budget, unless we wanted to wait three years to get married. And we could. We could wait for the big, fancy wedding. Or we could have a small ceremony now, and a big, fat vow renewal on our tenth or twenty-fifth anniversary. There were many options. The world was our oyster.

Then another thought struck me. "Wait a sec. The honeymoon? I mean, you're not asking to film the honeymoon, right? Because that would be a hard no."

He laughed. "No, of course not. But we will send you on a two-week tour of Europe, all expenses paid, if that's what you want."

The balloon of hope that had been growing inside me deflated as the reality of those words sank in. "Unless you're also paying someone to run Sweet Reality for me while I'm gone, that could never happen."

It had been bad enough when I'd ducked out for a week to film *Real Ocean* right before our opening last year, though I'd made it back for the big day. Now, the bakery was thriving, but until we hired a full-time manager, I couldn't disappear for several weeks to film a show and then take a luxurious honeymoon.

Sarah needed me. Sweet Reality needed me. I couldn't walk away from my business less than a year after it opened. Not when we were starting to turn a profit.

Connor sighed heavily into the phone. "Okay, look. I'm not supposed to tell you this. Promise you won't mention it?"

"Mention what?"

"I'm in a bind here. Remember Braden from the cruise?"

"Sure." Braden had come in third in a baking competition Justin and I helped judge on the show. He'd starred in some dating reality show where he'd winnowed a pack of beautiful women down to one bride, who I hadn't met. We weren't exactly friends, but he'd seemed nice enough.

"Well, this was supposed to be *his* wedding," Connor said. "The Network has already scheduled everything, and most of it's paid for. He and Amanda broke up last week, so now there's a hole in the TV schedule. I need someone for a wedding-themed reality show, and I haven't been able to come up with anyone else. Besides, you and Justin are perfect. You're reality stars, and you met and got engaged on Network shows. The public has followed your relationship since the beginning."

"I appreciate that, but that's exactly why we'd like some privacy now. We want to start our life together as a married couple away from the public eye."

"I completely understand, Jen, absolutely." He took a deep breath. "But *Braden & Amanda's Big Day* was my shot at being first associate producer instead of a cameraman or assistant. This is my show. All eyes are on me. If I can't come up with another couple, I'm fired."

A pang of guilt hit me. I didn't want to ruin a friend's career any more than I wanted to ruin my own life. Connor had been a good friend over the past couple of years, but I wasn't sure if his career needs were more important than the health of my relationship. Then a thought hit me. Justin and I weren't the only couple that hooked up on *The Fishbowl* and stayed together.

"Why don't you and Ed get married? You've been dating as long as me and Justin. Longer, actually, since we never snuck away on the show to make out. And America loves Ed. He's hilarious."

Connor sighed. "I wish. The first gay couple getting married on live TV? It would be amazing. I pitched it, but Leanna shot me down hard."

"Leanna's running this show?" My voice moved toward a range only dogs could hear. "When were you going to mention that?"

He must be desperate to ask me to get involved with that woman again, after she arranged for me to miss the cruise ship from Jamaica, leaving me stranded with my ex-boyfriend while Justin sailed away with my archrival. She only agreed to bring me back aboard after I promised to create more drama. Drama that nearly broke up me and Justin for good.

"After you agreed," he said sheepishly. "But, I swear, I will be your only contact with the network. We've set up the whole thing. You won't see or talk to her at all. She's the show runner, meaning she'll be in the background the entire time, but she'll be dealing with everyone else."

"Right. Of course she will. Let's go back to you and Ed. Are you guys getting married?" Nothing would make me happier than seeing my friend and twice costar make a lifetime commitment to the man who cherished him and had encouraged him to follow his dreams. After moving to LA, Ed rode the fast track to stardom, becoming the most famous (only famous?) former member of *The Fishbowl*.

"Eventually. When the show said no, I decided to take time to plan the type of proposal he deserves," Connor said. "So, back to you. We're going to film the show over ten days, so you won't have to be gone from the bakery for too long."

"The Network pays for everything?"

"Everything. Picture the dream wedding you always wanted."

Unbidden, an image of Kate Middleton, Duchess of Cambridge, swam before my eyes, pulling up to the church in a horse-drawn carriage. Walking down the aisle in that gorgeous white dress. Not puffy or overwhelming, classy. A simple veil down her back. Carrying a bouquet of white flowers before driving off with her prince while the crowd cheered. I'd watched the entire wedding with my mom, and we'd gone through half a box of tissues.

Some small part of me wanted that. I never would have thought myself the type. I always figured I'd have a fairly low-key wedding. On a beach, at sunset. A simple, lacy sundress. Flowers braided into my hair.

Or no flowers, since I shaved my head on the cruise after losing a bet. Six months later, my hair was still pretty short. Extensions weren't exactly in our budget, but the Network had much more to spend than me and Justin. My excitement started to grow. I never thought I wanted a princess wedding until Connor said I could have anything.

Reality burst my bubble as I pictured the producers at my wedding, interfering. I shook my head. Justin and I didn't need a fancy wedding. It didn't matter whether I had long hair, short hair, or no hair. All we needed was each other, a marriage license, witnesses, and someone ordained by the state of Florida.

Connor must have recognized my silence as indecision. His words tempted me, although I wished they didn't. "Please think about it?"

"When do I have to decide?"

"Tomorrow. No pressure."

A bark of laughter choked me. "Right. No pressure at all. One more thing: if I do this, I am under no circumstances consuming any food I did not physically see being prepared, unless it comes from Ed. Neither is Justin."

"You think we're going to drug you?"

"I don't know. I didn't expect anyone to give me pot brownies while filming *Real Ocean*, did I? Or cupcakes with breast milk in them?"

"Fair point," he said. "Deal. I'll get Ed to move into the house with you for the duration. He can be your personal chef."

"In that case, yes, I'll think about it. Let me talk to Justin."

"Thanks, Jen. You're the best." He hung up.

Leaning against the brick wall of the building, I nibbled one thumbnail while I debated whether to call my fiancé before heading back inside. I should say no. We didn't need to get married on national television. Sure, it would be nice not to go into debt to fund our wedding, but we were never going to do that. When we first got engaged, Justin's mother had been suffering from cancer, so we'd expected to have a short, quick ceremony, possibly at her bedside. The plan never had been to spend a lot of money, and that was fine with us.

My future mother-in-law had miraculously gone into remission in January, so she could now join us anywhere we tied the knot. But did we want to get married in Los Angeles? And not needing to get married quickly didn't automatically translate to spending a lot of money. Did we *want* a big, fancy wedding? The poufy white dress, a dozen attendants, all that jazz?

My phone buzzed with a text. An image filled the screen. The same picture of the Duchess of Cambridge I'd already formed in my head. A smile spread across my face as I pictured myself in that gown. Connor knew exactly how to tug my heartstrings.

Aw, man. I did want *My Beautiful Princess Wedding*. Or whatever they decided to call it.

Sure, we didn't need a big wedding. But we could also let the Network pay for it. We could have everything we ever wanted, now. If his mother's cancer returned, she'd have the joy of watching us get married before she got sick. Possibly over and over, watching us get married On Demand. Every mother's dream, right? My mother would certainly be overjoyed.

My phone buzzed again with another image. This one of Kate with her sister/bridesmaid, both in their white dresses. The text came seconds later. *You and Sarah? You and Rachel? We'll fly in whoever you want.*

I promise, I'll talk to Justin. We'll call you tonight, I replied.

The phone went back into my apron pocket as I went inside and dove back into the bustle of the bakery. The rest of the morning flew, but as lunchtime approached, I thought more and more about Connor's offer. Finally, about twenty minutes before my lunch break, I pulled Sarah aside.

Her mouth dropped when I explained the offer. "Holy crap, that's huge. They're going to pay for everything? Like, including my maid-of-honor dress?"

"I told you, you don't have to buy an expensive dress."

"Of course I do. Especially if the Network's buying." She winked at me.

"We can afford to close for a week while you come out, right?"

"I don't need an entire week. You know me and reality TV. I'll just come out for the wedding." Her response came as no surprise. Sarah and I met during my audition for *The Fishbowl*, when I found her crying in the bathroom because Justin talked her into trying out for the show with him. She'd never wanted to be on TV, even after seeing how the experience changed my life.

"But you'll still be in the wedding, right? Even though it's televised?"

"I wouldn't miss it for the world." She held my gaze, strong and steady. "Does this mean you're considering it?"

"Depends. Can you make it for a couple of weeks without me?"

At the front of the store, a cashier took and filled orders for a growing line of customers. If anyone else walked in, she'd need to grow a second set of hands. Back in the kitchen, Sarah's assistant iced cupcakes. Someone needed to mop and sweep the floors, and a stack of phone orders waited for Sarah by the back sink. Running the bakery wasn't a one-person job.

"We'll be fine," she said. "It may be time to promote Betsy to assistant manager and find someone new to cover the front. I've been stalling because I have trouble trusting other people to get the work done when we're not here, but you have to cut the cord eventually."

"You're serious? You don't mind?"

"Of course I don't mind! Hiring more people means we can both take regular days off. Besides, your fame is half the draw of this place! Actually, you're most of the draw."

"That's not true. People come for your cupcakes."

"There are a thousand cupcake places in Florida. We get Internet orders from Fort Lauderdale and Atlanta because of you." She gestured at the walls, which were adorned with reality TV stills, mostly me and Justin and other friends from *The Fishbowl*. "Go. Be famous. Talk up the bakery. Sales will skyrocket, both when they announce the show and when it airs. I don't mind leaving Betsy in charge for a couple of days while I fly out for the ceremony. It'll be a good test to see if she can handle the job full time. When are you leaving?"

"If all goes well, the end of the week."

"That's so exciting!" She threw her arms around me. "Why aren't you ecstatic about this?"

I hesitated. "Because I still have to talk to Justin."

"Oh, right. Justin."

Right. The man who swore on his grandmother's antique engagement ring that we were done with reality television forever. He wasn't going to be happy that I was considering another show.

"I'm going to go to the courthouse for lunch." Justin and I had a standing Wednesday lunch date when he had to appear in court, which was more often than not. The walk would give me time to figure out what I wanted to say to him.

"Hold on a sec." Sarah stuffed a white cardboard box into my hand. "Lemon meringue cupcakes. You might need 'em."

"Thanks."

THE ENTIRE TEN-MINUTE walk to the courthouse, I practiced what I could say to convince Justin to take time off work, fly to Los Angeles, and film another reality show.

Hey, you know how much paying for a big, fancy wedding would suck…? No.

Remember how much fun it was to be on TV? Double no.

You miss Ed, right? Maybe.

I was still musing when I walked up the courthouse steps, not even realizing that Justin stood at the top until he spoke. His voice nearly made me drop his cupcake.

"I got a message from the Network this morning."

My breath whooshed out of me. At least I could skip half the intro I'd been stumbling over on my way here. "Yeah, Connor called me, too."

He blinked several times, the only way he tended to show surprise. "I didn't talk to Connor. Leanna called my boss. I got an urgent message to call him at the next recess."

"Wait, what? The producers called your boss?" That didn't sound good. It also didn't sound normal. Reality TV producers didn't arrange for their cast members to take time off work.

"Yeah. Apparently, she used to date his daughter in college. She got to know the family over breaks. So when she decided that she needed a favor from me, Leanna thought calling Mr. Anker would be the way to get it."

I shook my head. What a ridiculously small world. "Are you serious?"

"Yeah. They must be desperate."

"They are." Quickly, I filled him in on the conversation I'd had with Connor earlier. When I finished, I said, "A free wedding and honeymoon sounds amazing. Sarah said it's okay if I want to take the time off, since the publicity helps the bakery."

He tilted his head to one side. "You asked my sister about our wedding before me?"

"I know, I'm sorry. I figured you'd say no. I wanted to find out if I could afford the time off before bringing it up."

We stood in the stream of pedestrian traffic, so I steered him down the steps, toward a nearby copse of trees shading some picnic tables. My hand went naturally to his waist to pull him close. Our eyes locked, and I saw the strain of working so many hours in the lines beneath his usually sparkling green eyes. He didn't need additional stress right now.

"We don't have to do it."

"But you want to?" he asked.

"Honestly, part of me does," I admitted. "But we're a team. We make these decisions together. I don't care where or when or how we get married. All I need is you."

Going onto my tiptoes, I kissed him. His lips lingered on mine, and the cardboard cupcake box crumpled as he pulled me closer. I opened my mouth, reveling in the feel and taste of him. This wasn't the time or place to get distracted, though. We were less than twenty feet from the entrance to an institute of justice, where Justin worked, not hanging out on the beach.

When I pulled away, our eyes met, his serious green eyes peering into my soul. "I love you. But I don't want to risk our relationship again."

"I don't want to risk our relationship either," I said. "Did you tell them no?" *Without asking me?* I wanted to add, but didn't. One thing at a time. Kissing in public was okay, but arguing stayed at home where it belonged.

"Well, like I said, I would have, if they hadn't brought my boss into it."

My brow furrowed. I must not have heard him right. "What does your boss care? You do pro bono landlord-tenant disputes."

"Sure, I do. But the firm does everything. And, apparently, Mr. Anker wants to branch out into entertainment law."

Queasiness sprouted in my stomach. "And what does that mean?"

"He wants to start signing D-list celebrities, with an eye toward eventually representing all the couples appearing in *Real Parents of Miami* and *Atlanta*. There's some hotshot in the NYC entertainment department who's been wanting to move someplace warmer. Getting the Network's business would be a huge coup, and might stop him from jumping ship and heading for an LA firm."

That uneasy feeling grew stronger. "I don't like where this is headed."

"Neither do I," he said. "If we don't do the show, bring in this business for the firm, I'm fired."

CHAPTER TWO

THE NETWORK
requests the honor of your presence
at the marriage of their stars
~~AMANDA LEE HUNTLEY~~ JENNIFER ANNE REID
and
~~BRADEN ANDERSON~~ JUSTIN CHARLES TAYLOR
Saturday, the tenth of June
in the year two thousand seventeen
at one o'clock in the afternoon
at The *~~Marrying Kind~~ ~~mansion~~* Fishbowl
Black tie
Invitation required for admission
Reception to follow

Justin's words hung in the air, as if attached to a cartoon balloon over his mouth. *I'm fired.*

My ears rang. Fired. They're going to fire him.

No, I must have misheard. My heart pounded. Justin did a

great job. More importantly, he needed that job. Sure, we were doing okay together, but I couldn't support us both with half the earnings from a small bakery. Not when we'd been open for less than a year.

"They're going to fire you? Can they even do that?"

"'Can' is a funny word," he said. "They are doing it. My contract doesn't prevent them from firing me at will. My department already costs the firm money. If I refuse to get married on the show—which seems like a perfectly reasonable request to them, since we're already engaged—then they'll say I'm not a team player. And if I'm not a team player, they don't want to keep me around. I might have a case if we weren't already engaged. Then again, if I sue my employer, it'll be impossible to get another job."

"What if we broke up organically?" I asked.

"You don't think they'd find it odd that we happen to break up hours after they tell me I'm fired if we don't get married on TV? Lawyers don't believe in coincidence."

"Right."

"Also, they'll expand the pro bono department, give me interns, and allow me to help more people."

Even though I'd been considering the show, I hated the Network's heavy-handed approach. Still, we might as well make the best of things. I plastered a smile on my face. "The good news is, we're getting a free wedding, right?"

"That's my girl. Always finding the bright side."

"What did they say? You're sure all we have to do is get married on TV?"

"That's it. One simple 'I do' brings us job security for me, a fabulous wedding, and business for the bakery, hopefully. It's a dream come true." He snorted, betraying what he thought of the Network's offer.

"You know it's not going to be that simple," I said. "They're going to bring the drama hard-core. It's not just a two-hour wedding special. They're making a whole series. They're going to pack months worth of wedding planning into less than two weeks."

"But Sarah's okay with you taking the time off?"

I nodded. "You're really okay with this? You're not worried they'll try to break us up for the added entertainment value?"

"Oh, I'm positive they will," he said. "But I have a plan."

I raised an eyebrow at him and crossed my arms, leaning back as much as I could without falling off the bench. *Thank you, Pilates.* "I can't wait to hear this."

"When we go on the show, we're not us. We're Jen and Justin, actors on a television show. The things we do and say, that's not us. We're playing roles. We're making a show called *My Tacky-Ass Wedding*."

I groaned. "Can't it be called *My Perfect Fairy Tale Wedding*?"

"It could be, and for your sake, I hope it is, but the Network is going to want drama. I'm sure the wedding planning won't go smoothly, at least not until the last minute. We're better off expecting everything to go wrong so we can roll with the punches. Any positive experiences will be a pleasant surprise."

Thinking about the impact of his words brought a smile to my face. "Won't that drive the producers crazy? Every time they try to get a rise out of us, we'll go with it, because the goal is to have the most ridiculous wedding possible."

"Exactly. And it won't matter, because the wedding isn't about us. It's about entertainment. But there's something else," he said. "If we're acting, we're not Jen Reid and Justin Taylor. We're not showing our real emotions, not until the vows, anyway. Nothing that happens can be held against us. If they bring in our exes to flirt with us, that's fine."

He must be thinking of what happened the last time the Network invited my ex-boyfriend into our lives to stir things up. "Would they bring Dominic back a second time?"

"I wouldn't put it past them, but I have exes, too. Some of

them might like to be on television. Be nice to them. If they bring in some hot guy to flirt with you, go with it. We can detach emotionally and watch the drama unfold."

Justin's eyes were sincere. He met my gaze, unwavering, while I chewed my lower lip, considering. I didn't want to kiss anyone else. I didn't want Justin to, either. But I also, obviously, didn't want him to get fired. His having a job was a large part of our plans for the future. I wanted the dream wedding we couldn't afford. And I wanted to know that, at the end of the day, our relationship could withstand whatever the Network threw at us.

"Does that mean you won't get upset this time if some guy kisses me out of the blue?" When a photographer caught my ex pressing his lips against mine on *Real Ocean*, it almost ended our relationship, and I hadn't even kissed Dominic back. I didn't want that to happen again.

He shook his head. "Actors kiss people all the time, right? It doesn't mean anything. Go for it. Do what you need to do. Me, too. We agree, right here, right now, that it's allowed, and it doesn't mean anything."

"Kissing only?"

"Oh, yeah."

Finally, I nodded. "I keep remembering what Janine said on the cruise ship, when I tried to get her not to play the video of Ariana and Dominic."

"Oh, yeah?"

"She said, 'This is *our* story.' It wasn't your story or mine. Not the story of reality TV personalities on a cruise. It's the Network's story. They were allowed to turn it into whatever they wanted. And if we do this show, we're not making our story. We're making theirs."

"We have to remember that. It's their show. We're only playing along. Deal?"

"Deal." We sealed the agreement with a quick kiss.

"I'll even draw up a contract," he said. "A prenuptial agreement. That way, we've got proof later that it's all fine, just in case. And I'm not saying that things will go wrong, or that we should go make out with other people. Just that, if things get out of hand—it's okay. You have permission, and so do I."

"You're a genius," I said. "As long as my acting abilities are up to par."

He shrugged. "You've seen enough reality TV to know that the acting standards aren't terribly high. Just don't swoon in J-dawg's arms, and I think we're fine."

I'd almost forgotten about our nemesis from *The Fishbowl*, a guy who dedicated all his energy to acting as obnoxious as possible the moment he stepped onto the set. Rumor had it he wasn't anything like that in real life, although I didn't care to find out. People can't change their personality at will. If you're awful when you're around me, I don't care how you act the rest of the time.

I squeezed Justin's hand under the table, and he tugged on it, pulling me in for another kiss. My lips parted beneath his. He took his time, cupping my face in his hands while we explored each other with our tongues. By the time we broke apart, breathless, we understood that we belonged to each other, no matter what happened.

"Kiss me like that," Justin said, "and I'll agree to anything. When do they need us?"

"They want us to fly out as soon as possible. The wedding will be a week from Saturday."

His eyes widened. "That soon?"

"You're not getting cold feet, are you?"

"Nope. I am, however, in the middle of a trial. When do I *need* to be in Los Angeles?"

In all the discussion about whether we should do the show or wanted to, I hadn't thought through the logistics of getting married so quickly in another state. "When will the trial be over?"

"Right now, I expect to present the last of my evidence on

Monday. The other side starts their case Tuesday. It should go to the jury Wednesday morning."

"If most of the show is about dress shopping and flower arrangements, I can manage without you until then," I said. "Will deliberations take more than a day?"

"I hope not," he said. "If so, I can send someone else from my firm to the courthouse for a couple of days. It's the least they can do, since they're forcing me to do the show."

"Valid. There's a lot of wedding planning stuff I can do without you: my hair and make-up trial, my wedding dress, the bridesmaid dresses…"

"And decorations and cake tastings and planning the honeymoon and decorating the grounds and writing your vows." His dimples flashed. "Are you sure you need me for this at all?"

"Nah. Ed can probably fill in. He looks great in a tux."

Our eyes met, and electricity jolted down my spine. When Justin looked at me like I was the most delicious treat he'd ever seen, all I wanted was to drag him off to the nearest bedroom. Or dark corner. As if he read my mind, his pupils dilated. A smile spread across my face.

Reaching across the table, Justin took my hands in his. "I'll get there as soon as I can. I trust you to make decisions before I land, and we both know the Network isn't going to care what we want, anyway. I'm more worried about you, on your own, dealing with all the BS they'll do to cause drama."

"Just knowing you'll show up soon, that we're going to be together forever, will help a lot," I said. "I'll insist on Rachel, Sarah, and Birdie as bridesmaids. And Ed will be there. I'll be fine. Besides, I have a Plan."

"Uh-oh. What kind of plan?"

"An absolutely brilliant, capital-p Plan that came to me on the walk over here. A bit of insurance, if you will."

"So, well-thought-out for like nine minutes?"

"More or less," I said. "But listen. I say we get married right now. You and me. Without the show, without all the hoopla."

"Seriously?"

"Why not? We're already at the courthouse. We already took that class to waive the three-day waiting period." The last time Justin's mom got sick, we didn't want to risk her missing the wedding, so we'd done a state-sanctioned marriage course. When she'd gotten better, we decided to wait and plan a less spur-of-the-moment wedding. But the course benefits lasted a year.

My heart twisted a bit at the thought of getting married without most of our friends and family, but this was only the legal ceremony. Everyone we loved—and quite a few people we didn't, probably—would be at the big party in LA.

Doubt filled his eyes. "You don't think getting married on a whim is a bit impractical?"

I shrugged. "Was chasing my limo down the driveway and out of the Fishbowl a bit impractical? Quitting the show in hopes we'd like each other in the real world? Proposing on national television?"

"Well, when you put it that way..." He pulled out his phone and started tapping. "Maybe impractical is our thing."

"I prefer to think of it as head over heels in love." What did that saying even mean? Your head was almost always above your heels.

"That, too." He kissed me briefly, eyes twinkling, then returned to his phone.

"What are you doing?"

"Drafting a quick prenup. We want to memorialize our agreement. You call Sarah and tell her to pick up Mom and get over here. She can call Dad, too."

My heart swelled. He'd addressed the only minor issue I had with the Plan. Bringing Justin's family in would make our wedding feel less cold and impersonal. "That's perfect. I can't wait to become Mrs....well, Mrs. Jen Reid."

He laughed. Justin knew I had no intention of changing my last name after we married, and he didn't want me to. "Nothing would make me happier than to make you *Mrs.* Jen Reid. Let's do this."

CHAPTER THREE

PRENUPTIAL AGREEMENT

- *This document is intended to serve as a prenuptial agreement between Jen Reid ("Bride") and Justin Taylor ("Groom"). The parties agree that this is a full and complete embodiment of their agreement and that it is intended to supersede any prior agreements, written or oral.*
- *While filming the reality show currently known as Jen & Justin's Big Day, and only during the filming, kissing third parties shall not be considered adultery.*
- *Bride and Groom agree that neither will participate in any divorce-themed reality shows without the express written consent of the other. Such consent will not be provided absent a contract outlining the terms. Neither Bride nor Groom shall be responsible should the show deviate from those stated terms.*
- *In the event of a divorce, Groom shall be permitted to buy out Bride's interest in Sweet Reality, the bakery co-owned with Sarah Taylor. This provision will be null and void if Sarah blames Justin for the divorce.*
- *Bride agrees to stop leaving cupcake crumbs in Groom's car.*
- *Groom agrees to bring Bride coffee every time he works late, even if she doesn't ask.*

Our wedding was pure poetry. The groom wore an off-the-rack gray suit with a green striped tie that matched his eyes. The bride wore flip-flops and a hot-pink top with yoga capris. The maid of honor wore black pants with a scorch mark on one knee. The father of the groom rushed to the courthouse directly from his construction job, tightening his belt on his way into the room.

At least the mother of the groom dressed for the part. She'd apparently had time to change before Sarah picked her up. When I spotted Mrs. Taylor—er…Charity? Even when she was sick, it felt weird to call her by her first name—I wished I'd taken the time to run home and change. But we hadn't wanted to call any attention to what we were doing. Going to the courthouse every week for lunch was one thing. Showing up at the courthouse dressed to the nines with Justin's entire family in tow looked suspicious. As it was, I hoped no one recognized Sarah from her brief appearance on *The Fishbowl* or knew what Justin's parents looked like.

Charity looked fantastic in a blue silk suit that set off her green eyes and blond hair. She looked more like Justin and Sarah's older sister than their mother. She'd probably purchased the suit before Justin and I were born, but I didn't have the heart to suggest that my future mother-in-law take out the shoulder pads before walking to her seat in the front row.

So it wasn't an exact replica of Kate and William's wedding. So Sarah would be dropping chocolate sprinkles in front of her because we didn't have rose petals. So my bouquet was plastic flowers Sarah yoinked from one of our displays at Sweet Reality on her way out the door and I kept tugging my hair in a futile effort to cover my ears. I was about to marry my best friend, and I wouldn't have it any other way.

We stood in an empty courtroom, presided over by a new judge who worked at Justin's law firm before being elected to the bench. I waited near the doors with Sarah and Justin's father, preparing to take the plunge. I wished Mom and my brother, Adam, could've been there to watch us get married, but there wasn't time. We needed to do this today so I could pack and shop and fly out Friday morning. Besides, if everything went well, no one would ever know that the wedding my family attended—the one hosted by the Network and filmed for live television—wasn't the only ceremony. We just wanted some added insurance, a way of cementing our bond before filming started.

"You ready?" Greg asked, breaking into my thoughts. For some reason, while I had trouble addressing his mom as Charity, Justin's dad and I had always been on a first-name basis. I barely remembered my dad, so I embraced the idea of a new father figure. One who wasn't a deadbeat. "You sure this is the wedding you always dreamed about?"

"The Network is going to give us my dream wedding," I said, although I was anything but sure of that. More likely, the final show would turn into more of a high-school prom drama than my perfect fairy tale wedding. Not getting drenched in pig's blood seemed the best I could hope for. But Justin's family didn't need to worry about the Network. The decision was made, the Network already emailed the contracts, and Justin and I would deal with whatever happened.

All his parents needed to know was I loved Justin with all my heart, I wanted to marry him, and I'd devote the rest of my life to making him happy. My eyes met his met across the court-room, and a massive grin split my cheeks. Everything was going to work out for the best. I couldn't wait to marry him. Part of me had known he was the one for me ever since the first week on *The Fishbowl* when we found ourselves geeking out over the same vintage commercial.

"Yes, this is what I want," I said. "Just the two of us and our family."

"Yay! I'm so excited." Sarah hugged me and held out her hand. "Give me the ring."

"Oh, right."

We hadn't bought our wedding rings yet. I'd planned to use my engagement ring for the ceremony. To our surprise, Justin's mom had brought a set of rings with her—his and her wedding bands, originally belonging to Justin's grandparents. Simple, timeless. Perfect.

"Okay, then." Greg held out his arm, and I took it.

Sarah went first, humming "Here Comes the Bride." Beside me, Greg sang the words, his deep voice filling the courtroom. He tried to set the pace, but when Sarah cleared the gate separating the spectator area from the front of the courtroom, my excitement took over. I bolted past the rows of benches, straight to Justin, practically dragging his father through the little wooden door.

"Hey, beautiful," he said.

"Hey yourself." I popped onto my toes and kissed him, almost coming out of my flip-flops. "What did you want to do for lunch today?"

"Oh, I don't know. Thought maybe we'd get married."

"Sounds good." Grinning broadly, I took Justin's hand and turned toward Judge Fahr.

"Ready?" We both nodded. "Ladies and gentlemen, we are here today to join Justin and Jen in marriage. Thank you to the family for attending on such short notice. This is my first wedding ceremony as a judge, but even if it weren't, it would be unique, as I've had the pleasure of watching this couple from the beginning. My wife is a huge reality television fan, and she couldn't be more thrilled that the two of you asked us to be here today."

A few feet away, the bailiff smiled and waved. Mrs. Fahr had to sign a confidentiality agreement Justin drafted on his phone, but we didn't have the heart to exclude the judge's wife after hearing how much she loved our shows.

"When Justin chased Jen down the driveway at the end of *The Fishbowl*, tears sprang to my eyes," Judge Fahr said. "And like millions of other fans, it warmed my heart when the two of you became engaged. As someone who saw Justin grow throughout law school and watched the two of you blossom as a couple on television, being asked to do this means a lot to me. They say you never forget your first, but I'm truly honored to be here."

Don't cry, don't cry, don't cry. I couldn't look at Justin. If I did, these tears of happiness would explode, and I wouldn't be able to say my vows.

"Do each of you come freely and unattached before me, seeking to be married of your own free will?"

"I do," we said together.

"Excellent," Judge Fahr said. "Now, each of you has prepared a few words to say. Jen, you're up first."

I pulled a sheaf of notes from my back pocket, scribbles made while waiting for everyone to arrive. "I love you so much."

"That's very sweet of you, Jen, but I'm already married, so perhaps you should speak to Justin," the judge said.

My cheeks grew warm as everyone chuckled. At least I no longer felt on the verge of tears. When I turned away from the judge to face Justin, the smile on his face melted away my nervousness. I took both his hands, not caring when my notes got crushed. Whenever I'd thought about my vows, they never quite sounded right. I'd expected a lot more time to come up with something. But when I looked into those warm green eyes, finally, I knew what to say.

"Justin," I said. "The two years since we've met have been unreal, despite the reality shows. I never dreamed I would meet someone who understands me the way you do, whose family embraced me the way yours did, who made me feel as loved and special as you. There's no one I'd rather laugh with, no one I'd rather have comfort me when I'm sad. You're the person I want to fall asleep next to every night, and the first person I want to see when I wake up in the morning. I love you."

He grinned, mouthing, "I love you, too."

I continued. "I know these aren't the vows that will be recorded, but to me, that makes them even more special. After the entire country witnessed so many highs and lows of our relationship, I'm glad we have this private ceremony. And I promise you this: I will love you, cherish you, remain faithful in my heart, and not let anything the Network throws at us interfere with our relationship. No matter what happens on this show, I will never lose sight of the one thing that matters, and that's you and me. Jen and Justin forever."

He dabbed at his eyes before responding. I struggled to maintain control of my emotions.

"From the moment I spotted you at that first audition, I knew you were special," Justin said. "You had this amazing energy. You still do. I love your unique perspective on the world, the way you make the best of every situation, the way you care about other people. I love your heart, Jen, and I love you. When I found out we both made the show, I cheered. I couldn't believe how lucky I was. Through it all, we've only become stronger. We're a good team, and it's a team I am ecstatic to be on for the rest for my life."

He kissed me, and Judge Fahr cleared his throat. "Not so fast. I believe we have rings?"

Sarah handed me a platinum band.

"Jen, place the ring on Justin's finger, and repeat after me. I, Jen, take you, Justin, as my lawfully wedded spouse. To love and to cherish, in sickness and in health, until death do us part."

Although I'd heard the words about a hundred times, both at real weddings and in the movies, I'd never felt their weight so strongly. My heart was full as I spoke the vows, my eyes never leaving Justin's. The ring slid snugly onto his finger, cementing our bond.

He repeated the gesture, the warm metal sliding into place on the third finger of my left hand. Then he leaned over and kissed me again before Judge Fahr stopped him. It was a long, slow kiss, full of tenderness and love. All the promises we'd made to each other were sealed by our lips against each other's. And when we parted, I knew, absolutely knew, that getting married before going on the show was the right move.

"I now pronounce you husband and wife," Judge Fahr said. "Usually, this is where you'd seal the deal with the kiss, but the two of you seem to be a bit ahead of me."

I giggled, then leaned over and placed another quick, soft kiss on Justin's lips.

"Ladies and gentleman," Judge Fahr said to the room, "I am happy to introduce you to Mr. Justin Taylor and Mrs. Jennifer Reid!"

Hand in hand, we walked up the aisle as "Happy" played behind us. After recording the ceremony on her phone (which we grudgingly agreed to allow upon penalty of death if she showed it to anyone, ever), Sarah had switched to her music app.

She followed us, practically jumping up and down with excitement. "I can't believe my best friend and my brother are married! And I don't even have to give a toast at the reception. It's perfect!"

"Not so fast," Justin said. "You're down for a toast at the big reception. The one on TV."

Her face turned white, and I nudged him with my foot. "That's not funny." To Sarah, I said, "He's kidding. Ed and Rachel will be giving the toasts. He's hilarious, she's poised, it'll be awesome."

"In that case, I won't withdraw my support and sell this video to *Entertainment Tonight*," she said. "I can live with being a regular bridesmaid, not maid of honor."

"You'll be co–maids of honor." I hugged her, and she whispered another congratulation in my ear.

Going out for a huge celebratory meal would have called attention to us, and Justin had to get back to his trial after lunch, so we ducked into a corner of the courtroom for a kiss goodbye. Before leaving, we removed our rings. I tucked them into a zippered pocket of my purse, where they'd stay until we put them on again during the Fishbowl ceremony. The rings were a symbol, and they were important, but not as important as the promises we exchanged. We kissed again, then Sarah drove me back to the bakery, both of us babbling and grinning the whole way.

That evening, everyone went to Justin's parents' house for dinner. Charity went all out, cooking more than she'd done since I'd met her. We sat down to an array of our favorite foods. Sarah brought a small chocolate, banana, and peanut butter cake from Sweet Reality for dessert, adapted from one of our most popular cupcake recipes.

Maybe it wasn't the most traditional wedding, but it was the perfect day. Justin and I were married, and nothing the Network did could come between us now.

CHAPTER FOUR

Shocking Entertainment News Online

ONE-HALF OF ROYAL REALITY COUPLE LANDS IN LOS ANGELES
But where's the other? And why the rush?
by Talky Ted

Ever since *The Marrying Kind*'s Amanda announced that she was leaving Braden to join the Peace Corps, we've wondered what would happen to their show, scheduled to start filming at the end of May. Now, thanks to some astute Instagrammers, I've got the inside scoop.

Jen Reid, half of the famous "Jen and Justin" from *The Fishbowl*, landed in Los Angeles this morning sporting gorgeous long hair begging for an updo. Fans may remember that the couple met on one of the Network's shows and became engaged on another, making them an obvious choice for a last-minute replacement. As recently as March, the couple had reportedly not set a date.

But is there another reason for the quick, secret trip? Jen, is that a baby bump or did you enjoy too many free cookies on the flight?

A spokeswoman for the Network said, "The show will go on," but refused to elaborate. Jen did not return several voice mails. Justin could not be reached for comment. I managed to get ahold of his twin sister Sarah at her place of business. In response to my question whether Jen and Justin could expect their very own bundle of joy soon, she replied, and I quote, "Bite me."

When does that girl get her own show?

Related Stories:

- **He Went Down On One Knee, and You Won't Believe What Happened Next**
- ***The Fishbowl* Star Ariana Sassani, 26, Passes Away After Long Illness**

Brandon Martinez to Jen Reid:
You've never going to believe this, but I can't get a week off work to appear in a reality show about making your wedding.
Jen Reid to Brandon Martinez:
Yeah, I hear Ninth Circuit justices are super unreasonable about giving clerks time off for show biz. :-(
Brandon Martinez to Jen Reid:
You're not upset?
Jen Reid to Brandon Martinez:
I'm unsurprised. Disappointed, though. Can you still come to the wedding?
Brandon Martinez to Jen Reid:
As long as I don't do any confessionals, and they don't show my face on TV.
Jen Reid to Brandon Martinez:

I'll take what I can get. But you can't be a groomsman if you're not filmed.

Brandon Martinez to Bridezilla:

LIFE IS SO UNFAIR.

Brandon Martinez to Bridezilla:

Thanks for understanding. I'll sit in the audience and throw tomatoes at my replacement.

Jen Reid to Brandon Martinez:

Aim for Ed. He's used to it. ☺ Love you! See you next week!

Connor had warned me that changing my hair wouldn't prevent the media from recognizing me if spotted in LA. But I wanted extensions before the wedding, I didn't want to pay for them, and I didn't trust the Network anywhere near my head. So I'd told him people would be less likely to recognize me with longer hair, and they wouldn't waste a day of filming me sitting in a chair. Win, win. He didn't sound like he bought it, but he wanted us to do the show, so he'd set up the appointment. Justin and I had spent the rest of the day going over our ideas for the wedding with the producers. We didn't have a lot of time, but we wanted to make sure the wedding contained things that mattered to us.

Returning to the Fishbowl almost two years after I drove away felt like returning to high school after starting college. I still remembered my first view of the dazzling glass house, with the sweeping driveway, the dragon fountain out front, and the millions of tiny stones lining the walkway. But somehow, without my other eleven Fish, it felt smaller. Quieter. Less imposing.

Before going in, I took a selfie with the house in the background and texted it to Justin. *RETURNING TO THE SCENE OF THE CRIME...HOPEFULLY WITH LESS DRAMA.*

DON'T BET ON IT, HE RESPONDED.

Connor met me at the door for a tour before everyone else arrived. The first thing I noticed was those awful glass walls, polished to invisibility, daring me to spend the next week bouncing off them like that first summer. My brilliant plan to mark each one with lipstick had been foiled by the Network's cleaning crew, so I knew better than to try that again. Hopefully they hadn't moved the walls in the past two years.

"Why are you giving me a tour?" I asked Connor. "Aren't you too big and important for this job now?"

"Probably, but I volunteered to show you around. It's not every day my second-favorite reality star comes to visit. Or one of my favorite people."

I grinned at him. "I'm just glad to see you and not Janine."

During *Real Ocean: Caribbean*, I'd thought the tall production assistant named Janine seemed nice enough, until I found out she'd concocted the plan to strand me in Jamaica. Then, when Justin and I finally patched things up, Janine stole a video I'd made of Ariana and aired it on national television. Sure, I shouldn't have made the video, but I hadn't expected anyone to see it. If Ed hadn't helped explain to Justin what happened, this wedding wouldn't be possible. Janine was literally the last person I wanted to see, anywhere, ever again.

"Well, don't get upset, but she's here." My gut urged me to turn and go, but I clasped my hands together and pasted a smile on my face. Even though I knew this was a possibility, I'd allowed myself to hope she wouldn't come to the house. Connor said, "Not right this minute, but she'll be around. She's Leanna's assistant now. I'll run as much interference as I can, but I need this job. Until an opening comes up with the Discovery Channel or LOGO, the Network owns my ass."

The living room hadn't changed a bit, down to the plush green cat tower–looking couch, which provided several levels of seating. I rubbed one side, remembering all the hours I'd perched on the top while plotting to stay on *The Fishbowl*.

When I moved in with Sarah, we'd spent weeks scouring the

Internet and furniture stores for anything remotely similar. Unfortunately, custom-made furniture hadn't been in our budget, so we'd settled for something a little more economical, less of a conversation piece: a regular couch. At least it was also green.

Something about the kitchen seemed different. It took me a minute to realize they'd moved the fridge to the wall between the kitchen and the living room. I laughed and nodded at the new glass wall above the counter space. "No more hiding in the laundry room?"

Although there were cameras in the tiny space beyond the kitchen, early in my stay on the show, Birdie found a spot that couldn't be seen from the rest of the house. With the window created by moving the fridge, that corner now stood visible to anyone standing at the counter. Ah, well.

Connor laughed and nodded before taking me through the rest of the house.

Upstairs, the guys' bedroom hadn't changed a bit. Rows of twin beds lined the space, a pirate's trunk standing at the foot of each. It seemed like a lot more beds than necessary for the wedding party.

"How many people are staying here?" I asked.

"Here? You, Birdie and Rachel, sleeping upstairs. Sarah, once she arrives. Brandon, Ed, Justin, and Justin's roommate."

I shifted from one foot to the other, then back. "Then why so many beds?"

"This is already set up for Season 3. We're not using all the beds for your show. Everyone else lives nearby or is staying at a hotel. They'll only be here if needed for filming and for the ceremony. After the rehearsal dinner next Friday, we'll take you ladies to the hotel. You'll sleep there, have a spa day, then get ready onsite. A limo will bring you back."

"That sounds amazing," I said. "What about my family?"

"We figured your mom would be more comfortable at a hotel. She flew in this morning; Adam and Lynne get here

Wednesday. They're also staying at a hotel. Your brother's girl-friend didn't seem too interested in the show."

"She doesn't speak much English," I said. "Born and raised in Quebec. They met when Adam was in college in Montreal. I'm just glad they're coming."

"Well, we've got an interpreter on standby for her, if need be."

We continued the tour through the giant bathroom, designed to be shared by thirteen people. I wondered if the smaller, private shower stall still ran only cold water, the Network's transparent attempt to force us to pile into the larger group shower to get clean. (Which just meant showering took forever; people almost never went in together.)

Upstairs, a thick rug covered the once all-glass floor of what would be my bedroom. They'd made a few minor changes since my season. Blue and green curtains draped two rows of twin beds, each beside a white dresser with starfish- and seashell-shaped handles. One of the beds was surrounded by sheer white curtains. A sign reading "Bride" hung off the end.

"I'll leave you here to rest and unpack," Connor said. "When you're ready, head down to the old School Room. We're calling it the Chapel now."

I chuckled. After spilling all my secrets in the School Room and the Guppy Gabber, I'd wondered what punny name they'd come up with for the show's confessional.

"Sounds good. I'll check in after I get a nap," I said. "Where's Ed?"

"He's finishing packing, picking up groceries, and he'll meet you here at six. I'll see you then. The PAs are taking you to a spa in about an hour. We've got a full day booked for you and your mom: waxing, exfoliation, nails, everything."

Oh, that sounded amazing. I squealed at the thought.

Laughing, Connor hugged me and left.

Although I'd lived in this house for eight weeks two summers ago, I'd never spent even a second alone. I spread my arms, flung my head back, and twirled in a circle, because I could. They'd probably started filming the second I walked in, but it didn't matter.

When I finished, I turned my face to the camera in the ceiling by the closet. "Home sweet home!"

BEFORE I FINISHED UNPACKING, the front door slammed downstairs. I was debating whether to see who had arrived when a familiar voice screeched up the stairs. "Jennifer Reid, get your perfect ass down here! Don't make me waddle up these stairs. #Pregnant."

Laughing at the way my old friend still spoke in hashtags, I left my open suitcase on the bed and pelted down the stairs where a familiar freckled face peered up at me from under red bangs. One of my favorite former co-competitor's warm brown eyes crinkled with laughter.

With my own whoop, I shot down the remaining steps, arms outstretched. I hadn't seen Birdie since the day she asked us to eliminate her from *The Fishbowl* because she broke her ankle and couldn't compete in the remaining challenges.

"It's so good to see you!"

Her arms enveloped me. I pulled her close, but her bulging belly got between us. I pulled back. "Sorry. Am I squishing the baby?"

"Don't be stupid. A hug can't squish an O'Brien. Let's go catch up. I can watch you drink coffee and cry about my lack of caffeine. Oh, and let me see that ring in person."

She led me into the kitchen. It's one thing to get texts from your friend that she's having a baby and to see pictures online, but another to see her in person at more than seven months pregnant. At five feet tall, Birdie's stomach swallowed her.

"I'm so glad you're here," I said. "I was worried you wouldn't be able to make it."

She shrugged. "I have seven Los Angeles ob-gyns programmed into my phone, just in case. But I'm not due for another few weeks."

"You shouldn't be here if you're that close."

"Shut up. I wouldn't miss this for anything. I'm still pissed I had to find out about the proposal on TV with the rest of the world. You couldn't have called me?"

"Nope. Confidentiality. You should've come on the cruise."

"Sure I should. America would have loved watching me throw up for a week. #MustSeeTV." She wrinkled her nose at me, but her eyes twinkled. "So what's the deal? Can we find me a bridesmaid muumuu by next Saturday?"

About an hour later, Birdie went to nap while the Network whisked me away for the first of seemingly a zillion planned activities. Inside the limo intended to take me to the spa, I found an ice bucket chilling a bottle of California-made sparkling wine. Someone had been listening when I said champagne was too stuffy. Bouquets scattered around the interior filled the car with a sweet scent. The buttery leather seats felt like leaning against a cloud. On *The Fishbowl*, the contestants had been blindfolded and herded into vans when we needed to go anywhere. I could get used to this treatment.

Two production assistants sat across from me, both having steadfastly refused to give their names. Apparently, the Network had been cracking down on staff interacting with "the stars." (I still couldn't think of myself as a star, even after three reality shows, one of which was entirely about me and Justin.) I blamed Ed for this change in policy. The Network hadn't minded his relationship with Connor as long as they kept it quiet. But they changed their tune when Connor helped me retrieve the video of Ariana that Janine had stolen. He'd been on probation for months.

The assistant on the right sat stiffly, her long legs folded under her, hands clasped in her lap. She had flawless brown skin, different colored nail polish on each finger, and perfect black curls. My own hair never held a curl well, but I suddenly wondered what possibilities these extensions opened up for me.

The PA on the left was shorter, slight, dressed all in black, and so pale I wondered why he lived in LA. He wore chipped black nail polish on most of his fingers and a stud in his nose. Without names, I dubbed the female PA Great Hair and the male PA Chin Dimple.

Although Birdie and I didn't get as much alone time as I would've liked, I couldn't wait to see my mom. When I lived in Seattle, we got together every Tuesday night to watch our favorite reality shows. But I hadn't seen her in ages. Mom spent the holidays in Montreal with her new boyfriend René, who she met when visiting Adam. I wondered if René would be attending the wedding. His kids were too young to be on TV without parental consent, but I'd included their names on the guest list, just in case.

Apparently, traveling back and forth from Seattle to Montreal agreed with her. When I entered the waiting room and spotted Mom sitting on the couch, I almost didn't recognize her. She looked ten years younger. She'd lost at least thirty pounds since I moved away, blond hair dye covered her previously gray strands, and…

"Mom? Did you get Botox?" I pulled her close, peering suspiciously at her unmoving forehead.

"Of course I did! My only daughter's getting married on television. I have to look good for all these Los Angeles people."

"You're beautiful," I said. "Before and now."

Together, we stepped up to the front desk to check in for our appointment. The receptionist didn't even do a double take at the cameras following us, so either this kind of thing happened all the time in Los Angeles, or she'd been paid not to react.

The receptionist handed us each a fluffy robe and directed us to the locker rooms to stow our clothes. When we returned to the waiting room, two women dressed in black yoga pants and fitted black tops appeared as if by magic. Both had long black hair tied back into buns at the napes of their necks, brown eyes, and identical, serene looks.

The shorter attendant spoke first. "Tina Reid?"

"Actually, it's Tina Carter," Mom said. "I went back to my maiden name after the divorce."

"Very well. Right this way, please."

"Wait a minute. We're not going together?"

"No, I'm afraid the Network has booked separate treatments for you. You'll be able to rest and relax together in the lounge between services or when you're done."

Mom laughed. "Yeah, I told them there's no freaking way I'm letting them wax anything. You go and have fun. I'll be enjoying my facial."

The other attendant stepped forward. "I'm Sofía. I'll be helping you today."

I shook her hand. "It's nice to meet you. Sorry about the cameras."

She waved one hand as if to say, *Whatever, it's LA.* Chin Dimple followed my mom down the hall, and I hoped he had some idea what was and wasn't appropriate to actually capture on video. Great Hair trailed me and Sofía down the hall to a small, dark room. The moment I entered, tension faded from my shoulders. Lavender scent made me relax even more. Speakers in the corners filled the air with low, soothing music.

My emailed schedule called for a mud wrap, then a massage, including a scalp massage, followed by a mani-pedi. After my early morning six-hour flight, and the excitement of the last few days, topped off with the joy of getting to see Connor, Birdie, and my mother, I was exhausted. I turned into a puddle of goo before I finished rinsing off the mud wrap and climbed onto the heated table for my massage.

By the time Sofía asked me to roll over so she could do the front of my legs, drops of drool formed a ring on the floor beneath the face pillow. I flipped over, scooted down so my head rested on the table, and was out before she replaced the sheet.

Falling asleep during the day always gave me weird dreams. The Network had hired dogs to do an exfoliation, and they were slowly licking me all along my legs and torso. I groaned and stretched, coming awake slowly.

"Don't move," Sofía ordered. "You'll ruin it."

Ruin what? The massage?

Her hands were moving in long strokes down my body, which partially explained the dream, but she thankfully wasn't using her tongue. And why wasn't she rubbing more? It was more of a…brushing.

I opened my eyes, coming fully awake when I saw Sofía and a stranger running brushes down my body while Great Hair filmed from the far corner. I jolted upright. "What the hell are you guys doing? This isn't a massage."

"The massage ended over an hour ago," Sofía said. "I explained, but you were sleeping. Now we're painting on your wedding dress to see how it'll look on the big day. Like a fitting."

What?

Although I understood each of the words she used individually, my half-asleep brain couldn't piece them together in any way that remotely made any sense. Then I looked down. And shrieked.

When I'd fallen asleep, I'd been naked, lying under a sheet. Now, I still didn't wear any clothes, but I barely recognized my torso. White paint covered my entire front, coming up and outlining my breasts. They'd also painted the lower halves of each arm and my fingers to replicate gloves. Intricate silver detailing swirled around my upper body, outlining my belly button, tracing my nipples. The stranger held a brush full of white paint near my left leg; my thigh held a few brushes of color, as if she'd been working on it before I stopped them.

It almost looked like I was wearing a dress. Except I was naked.

Oh. No.

"No way," I said. "Absolutely not. Who told you I was wearing a dress made of body paint?"

"The producers said this was the hottest new thing. All the big stars are doing it. You'll be featured in magazines worldwide. An overnight sensation."

"I'll be *naked*."

Okay, Justin and I agreed to go with whatever the Network wanted, and maybe it was too early to make waves, but this couldn't happen. I needed to draw a line somewhere, and nudity on national television was it. I could not and would not get married wearing nothing but paint. What if I started sweating? Was body paint waterproof? If it was, how did I get it off?

"What if it rains?" I asked.

Great Hair smirked from the corner. "We're in Los Angeles, sweetheart, not Florida. It won't rain. Especially not in June."

Ugh. Swinging my legs off the table and clutching the sheet to my chest, I scrubbed one hand across my face, hoping this would all turn out to be part of my dream. "Nuh-uh. No way. I don't care. Get me Connor on the phone. I'm not wearing this. I want a real dress."

"Connor's not the show runner. He may be First Assistant Producer, but this is over his head. You need to talk to Janine."

"You mean, Pure Evil Janine? Janine, the one person I said wasn't allowed anywhere near me if I were going to do this show? That Janine?" I didn't even have to play up my exasperation for the cameras. "I'm not talking to her. In fact, I don't even want to see her. Let me talk to Connor."

They wanted a show, I'd give them one. Let them air this scene. Or not, I didn't care, as long as someone found me clothes for the ceremony.

"You signed a contract." Great Hair spoke as if I were a very small, unintelligent child. "You agreed to let us make the show. And Janine is in charge of the show. If you want to complain, you need to complain to her. Your friend's boyfriend can't help you."

"Sure, I signed a contract. And I know exactly what I agreed to do. But I didn't agree to do any of it naked." Maybe I'd agreed not to cause drama, but I wasn't the only one here who'd think this idea sucked. Jumping off the table, I headed for the door, wrapping the sheet around me.

"Where are you going?" Sofía asked.

"I'm going to find my mom. She didn't sign anything. She's going to have a lot to say about this, and no one messes with Tina Carter."

CHAPTER FIVE

Tina: Oh, there was no way I was going to let the Network put my little girl on television wearing only paint. I don't care what contract those kids signed. I didn't sign nothing, and you don't become one of the top r\Realtors in Seattle without learning how to bring people around to your way of thinking.

Ed: I can't wait to see the footage of Jen waking up to them painting her. I mean, I knew she would hate the idea as soon as Connor told me about it, but I had no idea she'd sic her mommy on the producers. That had to be awesome.

Growing up, my mother had been my greatest champion. When I was ten and the class bully put slugs down the back of my shirt, she called his dads. When the high-school cheerleaders mocked me for being good at math and science, she busted them for paying another kid to do their homework. Tina Carter did not let people mess with her kids.

Since Justin and I swore to roll with the punches and not cause excess drama on the show, I needed reinforcements.

Rachel would have stepped up if she'd been around, but Mom was the best person to fix this situation.

She didn't let me down. She moved into the other room, so I only caught snippets of the conversation. Something like, "If my daughter doesn't wear a dress to her wedding, neither will I!" Possibly a description of her stretch marks. I loved my mom.

Less than five minutes after I handed over my phone, I'd been given the all clear to wear a regular dress, as long as the Network approved it. Anything was better than body paint, and the contract already gave them the right to pick my dress. I agreed without hesitation.

Besides, the more control I gave them, the longer I could pretend this fiasco was just *My Tacky-Ass Wedding* and not what was supposed to be the most special day of my life. Then I didn't have to worry about things like how ridiculous they were going to make me look, or the parade of Justin's and my exes they'd probably invite for sport.

Once Mom returned my phone, I took a selfie of the half-finished "dress" and sent it to Justin. It's bad luck for the groom to see the bride in the dress before the ceremony, so obviously, I couldn't use it once he'd seen it. Or something.

He responded instantly with a series of emojis that I took to mean he felt the same way as me about body paint. Or he'd laughed so hard, he threw up.

Mom talked them out of it, I texted.

He responded with three smiley faces with tears in their eyes and two thumbs up.

Laugh it up. Just wait until they put you into a body paint tux.

Immediately, my phone buzzed with his response. Bring it. I'd look awesome in body paint. Very lawyerly.

Returning to the spa for the rest of our relaxing day was no longer in the cards. After I washed the body paint off, Mom and I walked around until we found an ice cream store. Real ice cream, not fro-yo, not smoothies, not that low-carb, low-sugar crap. It took longer than it should have. I got a triple cone and sat on a bench outside, luxuriating in the sunshine.

"You're not worried about fitting into your dress with that?" Mom asked.

I shrugged. "If I gain weight before the wedding, I guess we'll revisit that body paint idea."

She snorted. "Over my dead body. My daughter will be *clothed* on her wedding day."

Suddenly, my cone didn't look so appealing. I wanted to tell her that this wouldn't be my wedding day, that Justin and I got married two days ago. The third finger on my left hand burned beneath my engagement ring. But she'd be crushed not to have been invited, not to have at least been conferenced in via video so she could watch the exchange of vows. She'd be mortified that I got married in flip-flops. Not to mention hurt that Justin's family got to attend. She probably wouldn't be mollified by me pointing out that she could have watched, too, if she'd only been willing to learn to use FaceTime.

Which meant I wanted to make my fake wedding day the stuff of her dreams, too. This was, after all, her one and only chance to shine as mother of the bride. Possibly wearing nothing but body paint, if I heard her correctly when she was on the phone with Janine.

Rather than giving everything away, I changed the subject. "Are René and the kids coming?"

"Adam, Lynne, and René are flying in together on Thursday. The kids aren't going to make it. Their mother refused to hand over their passports, I'm afraid."

"That's what you get for dating someone who isn't American."

"Hey, we all need a contingency. What if I want to move to Canada?"

I laughed. "I'm sorry I won't get to meet them, though. We'll have to plan a trip to Montreal later this year."

"We'd like that," she said. "Especially since I *am* planning to move there in September."

"Seriously? You're moving to Canada?"

She nodded, beaming. "I was going to wait until René got here to tell you, but we're getting married!"

My jaw dropped. In the nearly two decades since my father left, Mom hadn't seriously dated anyone. Sure, she went out once in a while when I was younger and wasn't totally clear about where she was going, but she'd never brought a guy home. And now she was going to marry someone I'd never met.

I swallowed those mixed emotions. "Mom! That's so amazing. I'm so happy for you!"

She bounced on the bench, looking almost like a teenager. "You're not mad at me for stealing the thunder of your wedding with my big announcement?"

"Don't be ridiculous. This is fantastic news. I can't wait for Justin to get here so you can tell us again on camera."

"Oh, no." Mom laughed. "This reality show thing is for you kids. I plan to stay off camera as much as possible. I don't need the attention."

"Well, you're going to get it! I can't wait to see your pretend surprise face when René gets down on one knee. You better start practicing."

Mom hadn't had time to go shopping before flying to LA, so after we finished eating, the driver took us to Rodeo Drive to find her a mother-of-the-bride dress. Great Hair followed us in and out of stores. People in LA must be used to people filming all the time, because for the most part, no one even looked at us.

We found the perfect dress in the third store. Light blue, flowy, flattering. Mom questioned the cost, but Great Hair ended the debate by handing over a network credit card.

On our way out of the store, two girls about my age stood on the sidewalk, whispering. One was tall and lanky, with curly brown hair and tattoos covering her bare arms. The other was shorter, with close-cropped black hair and cat-eye glasses that almost made me wish I needed lenses. The taller girl pointed at us from behind a raised hand.

"They're pointing at us," Mom said. "Do you get this a lot?"

"Almost never," I said honestly. "But we've never filmed while walking around in a big city like this. *The Fishbowl* set was completely closed off, and *Real Ocean* took place mostly on a cruise ship. We did meet-and-greets with the fans, but most of them were respectful of our time outside the public events."

"Don't people recognize you?"

"A little, mostly when I'm at Sweet Reality. It's been a long time since anyone recognized me out of context," I said. "I guess people in Miami aren't as conscious of TV personalities. Or maybe they don't care."

"I'm so proud of my little girl, the big reality star!"

"I'm not a star." My friends all thought one appearance on reality TV made you super famous, but given the total number of shows and people on them, most people didn't care unless they knew you.

"Looks like you are." She nodded at our audience.

The girls continued to stare, watching our whispered conversation. My face grew warm, both at the unexpected attention and at Mom's praise. She was so proud of me.

We were blocking the door into the store, so I steered Mom a couple of feet away, which brought us closer to our audience. "Should I go say hi to them?"

"Do you have anything to autograph?"

I shook my head. Before I could say anything else, the girls approached. The one with the tattoos spoke first. "OMG, we are such big fans! Can we get a picture with you?"

"And I *have* to get an autograph," Glasses said. "Please? My friends back home are going to be so jellyfish!"

With a smile, I dug into my bag. "Let me see if I can find a pen. What are your names?"

"I'm Brittany, and this is Chloe," Glasses said. "We're from Peoria, Illinois."

Beside her, Chloe clapped excitedly. "I can't believe we got to meet one of the *Real Housewives of Beverly Hills*! This is so exciting."

Wait, what?

For the first time, I realized the girls stood tilted toward Mom; they spoke to her. She stood between me and them, which had seemed like some kind of thoughtful buffer, but they didn't recognize me. It wasn't me they were excited to run into on the street; it was my mother. My lips twitched at the realization, but I managed to keep from laughing.

"I found a pen for you," I said before she could correct them. "Do you have something she can sign?"

Mom shot daggers at me with her eyes, but I could tell she was trying not to laugh, too. Behind the camera, Great Hair's shoulders shook silently. I wondered if this scene would make it into a bloopers reel someday, or if she'd ask them to sign waivers so they could appear on the show. Other people were starting to look and point, too. This could be a long day if Mom started signing autographs for a line of "fans," but I wouldn't begrudge her a single second of it.

I texted Sarah where Mom couldn't see, asking her to create a new baked good based on my mom. The False Idol or something.

Brittany shoved her phone at me. "Would you take a picture of the three of us together?"

"Maybe a picture of the four of us would be better," Mom said. "I'm sure our camerawoman here wouldn't mind."

"No offense," Chloe said, "But we don't want some rando stranger messing up our picture."

"I completely understand," I said, my knees weak with suppressed laughter.

They stood on either side of Mom, wearing identical broad smiles. Mom looked a little shell-shocked at the unexpected attention, but the picture came out beautifully. She signed a receipt Chloe found in her purse, and they disappeared into the sidewalk traffic.

Mom leaned against the building, laughing until tears flowed down her cheeks. I collapsed beside her. Several moments passed before I got enough control of myself to speak.

"I can't wait until they decipher your signature and start to wonder who Tina Carter is," I said.

"They won't," Mom said. "I signed it Lynda Carter. For today only, I am Wonder Woman!"

Her comment set off another bout of laughter, but people were still looking at us, so I led her down the street, toward where we'd left the car. We made it about twenty feet before Mom planted her feet on the sidewalk and pulled me to a halt.

"What's wrong?"

"Nothing's *wrong*," she said. "We're here."

I looked around, but didn't understand what she was talking about. "Where? You already got a dress. I can't look at more without my bridesmaids. The show's doing an entire episode about it."

"Not dresses," she said. "We're *here*. Tiffany. It's time to register for gifts."

I blinked at her. "Tiffany's, the jewelry store?"

Mom laughed. "Tiffany sells everything, dear. Sure, they have jewelry, but there's so much more. Crystal, decor, picture frames, stemware… You name it, they've got it. I can't believe you've never explored a Tiffany."

She seemed so excited, I hated to put a damper on her fun. But registering for gifts wasn't on my to-do list. "Oh, I don't think so. We don't need gifts. It's enough that people are flying out to watch us get married. Justin and I don't even have a house yet. I wouldn't begin to know what we need, or how much space we'll have. Plus, I can't register on my own."

"You can, and you will. Justin's not here yet. You'll both be busy when he arrives, and people can't be expected to wait until a day or two before the wedding to buy you gifts. Besides, do you honestly think he'll care what dishes you wind up with?"

"With the hours we both work, we don't need fancy dishes," I said. "Does Tiffany sell his and her matching porcelain takeout containers?"

"Stop arguing. I don't get to help pick out your dress. I just pretended to be a celebrity for you. My role as mother of the bride is essentially to stay off screen unless I'm creating drama. You're doing this for me."

A pang hit me. When I'd lived in Seattle, Mom and I had been super close. Then, I'd gone on *The Fishbowl*, and everything changed. I moved away, we'd naturally started talking less frequently as the bakery demanded more of my attention, and I hadn't even consulted with her before agreeing to do *Real Ocean*. To my knowledge, Justin never spoke to her about our getting engaged before he proposed—which was fine by me, I'm not my mother's property. But Mom might have appreciated a phone call.

Justin and I hadn't talked about what our parents would think of us getting married on national television—not that we had a choice. But, still, she was right. Mom didn't get to help me pick a venue. She wasn't helping me with the flowers or the catering or the cake or anything. She could come with me when I tried on dresses, but even that would be only one day, not the multiple visits so many of my friends made with their moms.

Going to register for gifts with my mother was literally the least I could do for her, especially after she saved me from being naked on national television. Even if Justin and I didn't need gifts, it's not like anyone we knew would buy anything from Tiffany. It would be fun to wander around this ridiculously expensive store and dream about how the super-rich lived.

I turned to Great Hair. "What do you think? Do we have time for this today?"

"I'm scheduled to follow you around until dinner. Ed's cooking, so you don't need to be back until almost seven."

"You think I should register?"

She shrugged. "There will be a gift table at the ceremony. If there are some real presents mixed in with the empty gift-wrapped boxes, it means less work for the crew."

It was like she and Mom conspired to come up with the best way to get me to agree. I couldn't refuse to go shopping now, knowing if I did it would mean hours spent wrapping empty boxes for the low-paid, overworked production staff.

The giant doors swung outward, and I gestured for Mom to lead the way. She went straight to a sales associate, who introduced herself as Hillary, and proudly let her know we wanted to start a registry. Hillary showed me how to work the scanner gun while Great Hair talked to the manager about filming in the store. Ten minutes later, everyone had signed waivers, and I still had no idea what I wanted.

Before doing anything else, I called Justin on speakerphone to let him know what we were doing. As Mom suspected, he didn't mind not being involved. His only word of advice was, "Get good knives," so we started there.

Just like Mom promised, Tiffany sold basically everything. Before we walked in, I had visions of people judging me for adding diamond earrings to the gift list. But this store was so much more. Hillary led us from knives to candlesticks to crystal beer mugs to…three-hundred-and-fifty-dollar butterfly-shaped straws?

"Does that do what I think it does?" I asked. "It's a drinking straw? For three hundred fifty *dollars*?"

"Never look at the price tag when registering, dear," Hillary said. "I'll put you down for four."

I couldn't even argue. It didn't matter what she put on the registry, no one would pay these prices for any of this stuff. I moved on, adding a gorgeous cake platter that would've left Sarah drooling (a steal at only four hundred dollars!), a cocktail shaker that somehow cost more than my monthly rent, and a gorgeous, swirly blue-and-white vase that made me drool. Even though we could probably find another fantastic vase some-where for less than five hundred dollars, I added it. I even found ridiculously overpriced sterling silver chopsticks. Over my objection, Mom scanned them, too.

"What about your wedding gift for Justin?" Hillary asked when we finished. "Have you picked something out for him yet?"

I shook my head. "With all the hustle and bustle of the show, I hadn't had time to think about it yet. Do we need to exchange gifts?"

"It's traditional," Mom said. "Small tokens, nothing fancy."

"The Network is planning to film a gift exchange after the ceremony," Great Hair said. "If that makes any difference."

"Okay, fine, I'll get him something. But I'm not sure if any of the stuff in here is his style. We're pretty low-key."

"What does he do for a living?"

Unemployed, I thought, if this show doesn't go well.

Out loud, I said, "He's a lawyer."

"Oh, that's perfect," Hillary said. "We've got some great gifts for professionals. Come with me."

The sterling silver business-card case looked nice, but seemed out of place for a lawyer who focused on pro bono work. Too show-offy. Same with the monogrammed cuff links. Justin would never wear a sterling silver belt buckle. I'd nearly given up when I spotted something that might work.

Justin liked to be prepared. He'd been a Boy Scout, would've made it to Eagle Scout if his mother hadn't gotten cancer when he was fifteen. He also lost his Swiss Army knife on the cruise we'd taken together and hadn't gotten around to replacing it. There, in front of me, sat a sterling silver Swiss Army knife. It was way overpriced and ridiculously fancy. But it could be engraved with our wedding date, and it was something my husband would actually use.

"This is it!" I said. "It's perfect."

CHAPTER SIX

<u>Jen in the Chapel, Friday:</u>
Spending the day with my mom was perfect, even with the body paint drama. It's been too long, and with so many people arriving, I'm grateful for the alone time. With that said, I can't wait to see everyone else.

<u>On the Groom Cam, Friday:</u>
Justin: Hey, America! I'll be joining Jen in California in a few days, but until then, the Network gave me a camera so I can keep you posted on what's going on here. My trial is moving right along. We're on track to finish with the evidence early next week. With any luck, I'll be on the five o'clock flight out of Miami on Wednesday, ready to enter the Fishbowl and start filming. I'm excited. I'm marrying my best friend.

<u>Dominic Rossellini to Jen Reid:</u>
I'm so honored to be invited to your wedding, Jen! Thank you! I wouldn't miss it for the world.

Jen Reid to DO NOT PICK UP:

You're not invited.

Dominic Rossellini to Jen Reid:

Am too. I talked to Janine.

Jen Reid to DO NOT PICK UP:

You will attend this ceremony over your dead body. You are not welcome here. I don't care what the Network offers you.

Forward from Jen Reid to Danielle Rossellini:

Um... What the heck is this message? He's not coming, is he?

Danielle Rossellini to Jen Reid:

Oh, noes! I'm sure he's just trying to get a rise out of you.

Jen Reid to Danielle Rossellini:

Thanks. Will I see you at the wedding? You're actually invited.

Danielle Rossellini to Jen Reid:

Of course! Can't wait to see you two. :-*

Dominic Rossellini to Jen Reid:

After receiving a phone call from my ex-wife's lawyer, I've decided that I am unfortunately unable to travel to Los Angeles next weekend, after all. I wish you and Justin every happiness.

message deleted

Driving in and out of the Fishbowl without a blindfold felt super weird after my first stay. Turned out, we weren't as isolated from the rest of Los Angeles as everyone thought. And I wasn't positive, but the house from *America's Next Top Drag Model* appeared to be about four blocks over. Maybe I should invite the cast to the wedding. They'd look fantastic in body paint.

The first thing I heard upon reentering the house was my favorite Midwestern drawl, floating toward me from the kitchen.

"The Network said I could bring a date," Rachel was saying. "They didn't put any stipulations on who that date could be."

My stomach gurgled at her words. I had a sneaking suspicion I knew who she wanted to bring, even without hearing the rest of the conversation. I crept toward the kitchen door, well aware that cameras followed my every move. Inside the room, Ed stood at the island, chopping something, while Rachel sipped wine, her back to me. Ed winked over her shoulder.

Loudly, he said, "Of course they didn't. The Network is here to put on a show, and part of that show means fireworks. They'd stack the guest list with neo-Nazis and Jewish people if it weren't for the cost of insurance. That doesn't mean Jen's going to be on board with this."

That was my cue. I entered the kitchen. "On board with what?"

Rachel squealed upon seeing me and raced into my waiting arms. My face broke out into a huge smile. Rachel was tall, muscular, pretty—basically every girl's dream. She'd even been head cheerleader and class president. The last time I'd seen her, we'd both shaved our heads after losing a bet on *Real Ocean*. Since then, she'd dyed her natural blond hair a vibrant red and kept it close-cropped. She looked amazing. Her brown eyes danced when she greeted me.

"Oh my gosh, I love your hair! Why didn't I think to get extensions?"

"Because you look like a model no matter what?"

"Shush, you."

Ed followed, only half a step behind her. My friend still had the goatee he'd worn during our cruise, and the wavy black hair he'd shaved in solidarity had grown into a buzz cut. No matter what he did to his hair, with his perfect body and easy smile, Ed was one of the best-looking guys I'd ever met. When we'd first met, I'd thought he looked exactly like Rodrigo Santoro from *Lost*.

The three of us jumped up and down, hugging like we'd won the NBA Finals. I'd missed my friends. Being locked in a house with strangers for weeks created strong bonds, and our week on the cruise only solidified our friendship. I was ecstatic that they'd been able to come on such short notice, not just for the wedding, but to spend ten days with me.

"I can't believe you're all here," Ed said. "This is so much better than Braden and Amanda's wedding would have been."

"You were going?" I asked.

"Of course. You weren't?"

Rachel shook her head. "I wasn't. Only met Braden for about thirty seconds on the cruise. I told him I was pissed he hadn't picked Molly, and that was it."

"Justin and I didn't want to take time off without knowing how long we'd be gone for our own wedding and honeymoon," I said.

Before I could ask what they'd been talking about when I walked in, Birdie entered the kitchen, rubbing her eyes. Rachel and Ed rushed to exclaim over her enormous pregnant belly. Finally, we all settled back at the island, Rachel and I sipping wine while Ed cooked.

"It's so great to be back here," I said. "Just like old times."

The only change was Birdie, drinking a glass of water rather than an alcoholic beverage and sitting on a stool instead of helping.

"Funny you should mention that," Ed said, with a sideways glance at Rachel. "Did you want this to be *exactly* like old times?"

"It can't be exactly like old times. Ariana won't be here."

"No, she won't," Ed said. "I never thought I'd say it, but I'm sorry not to see her."

We sat in silence for a minute, remembering our costar. Ariana was the dark-haired bombshell who pretended to fall for Justin during *The Fishbowl*. She'd done everything to keep us apart. When she'd popped up on the cruise in November, we expected more of the same, but she swore she'd turned over a new leaf. After I blamed her for the Network's nearly breaking up me and Justin, I learned Ariana had a terminal illness. She wanted to make peace with everyone. She hadn't been involved in the Network's shenanigans. We'd made up, sort of.

Justin and I had planned to invite Ariana to our wedding, but she passed away a couple of weeks before Connor called me. Instead, we asked the Network to prepare a tribute to air during the first episode. Something that would've made her toss her hair and smirk at the camera.

"Poor Ariana," Rachel said. "Her life was much too short."

"Poor Ariana," Birdie agreed. She lifted her glass. "To living life to the fullest, without regrets."

"To forgiveness," I added.

We all clinked and sipped quietly. Rachel turned to me. "Speaking of forgiveness, there's something I wanted to talk to you about."

I was already pretty sure I knew what she wanted to say, but for the sake of the cameras, I drew it out. "You forgive me for asking you and Sarah to be co–maids of honor when she's not here to do half the work?"

"No, I do not!" Rachel's words came out indignant, but her brown eyes danced with amusement. "We've been friends longer!"

"Technically, that's not true. I met her at the audition."

"You talked for three minutes. That doesn't count," she said. "But I'll let it go, if you say I can bring a date."

"New boyfriend? Tell me more!"

"Oh, she's not looking to bring a *new* boyfriend," Ed said.

"What's the big deal? The invitations gave you all a plus-one, right? Except Ed, because he and Connor were invited as a couple?"

"I got a plus-one," Birdie said. "Shockingly, I even had people offering me money for it. Turns out there *are* people who want to escort an eight-months-pregnant woman to a wedding, if said wedding is going to be on national television."

"How much?" I asked, intrigued.

"Let's not get distracted from Rachel's news. It's not that she wants to bring a date," Ed said. "It's who she wants to bring."

"Rach? Did you sell your plus-one on eBay?"

Of course, she wanted to bring Joshua, the jerk from *The Fishbowl* who insisted we all call him J-dawg. The second week of the competition, the house had unanimously voted to eliminate him after he got caught cheating. He and Rachel clicked instantly for some inexplicable reason. She'd been his only friend in the house and the only one excited for him to return to the show after Justin and I left. They'd stayed in touch.

There wasn't any part of me that wanted to see Joshua ever again. But the guest list was out of my hands. Although the desire to tell her I already knew made my lips twitch, Rachel needed to drop her bombshell for the viewers. I sipped my wine to keep a giggle from escaping.

"Oh, this is no fun at all," Ed said. "She totally figured it out."

"Well, I *am* the Smart One," I said, referring to the way the Network billed us when introducing the show's cast. "And I don't care if you want to bring Joshua as your date. I'm still not calling him J-dawg."

"Really? You don't care at all?" Rachel wrinkled her nose, as if she'd been gearing up for a fight. She probably had, since the Network's fingerprints were all over this invitation. And for that reason, I refused to argue.

"Not a bit. As long as he doesn't try to rap a toast at the reception." For some reason, as part of his reality villain routine Joshua had decided to always speak in rhyme. It was so weird. I assumed he didn't do it in real life. No one had yet corrected me on that.

"Of course not. I'll be rapping the toast," Ed said. "Here comes the bride, taking the Network's free ride. There goes the groom, who's never used a broom. Peace OUT."

I giggled. "What about, 'A toast to the happy lovers. Jen, I hope Justin don't steal the covers.'?"

"Sorry your friend's date's a jerk, but the music's playing, so everybody *twerk*!" Ed said.

Rachel smothered a laugh behind her glass. "You guys are the worst."

"You've got to let us have a little fun," I said. "Since you're bringing someone Justin and I can't stand to our wedding."

Birdie blinked into her glass several times. "Are you drunk? You're okay with *J-dawg*, of all people, coming to your wedding?"

"See, that's the reaction I was expecting," Ed said.

I laughed. "Guys, it doesn't matter. I get to spend the whole week with some of my favorite people. Justin and I are getting married, and we get to share our happiness not only with you, but with the viewers who helped make it all possible. Bring Joshua! Bring whoever you want. I'm just glad you're going to help us celebrate."

"You mean that?" Birdie asked. "Because I'd like to volunteer to personally remove J-dawg from the premises when he arrives, if you're kidding."

"She's been possessed," Ed said. "Or she doesn't remember J-dawg at all. Quick, someone roll the tapes from our season."

"Seriously guys, it's fine."

"And you're not taking any medication?" Ed asked.

"Not a thing."

"Who are you, and what have you done with my friend?" Rachel asked. "Not that I'm complaining, but..."

"Let's say being a bride agrees with me."

Nothing was going to ruin this week for me. Not even the return of my incredibly obnoxious former costar. Justin and I had a Plan, and I was sticking to it. The Network could do their worst. They wouldn't faze us.

After dinner, Ed, Rachel, and Birdie went to the salon for "wedding day prep," whatever that meant. Instead of going with them, the producers called me into the living room to meet my wedding planner.

In this case, the planner was more than someone who put the wedding together. The planner worked for the Network. The producers couldn't just follow me around looking at fabric samples and reading catering menus for a week. So instead, I had a guide, someone who walked me through all the decisions —and who would spoon-feed me information the viewers needed. Part wedding planner, part host, part shit-stirrer, as Connor explained it. But it was all part of the deal. We let the Network turn our wedding into a drama bomb, Justin kept his job. Totally fair trade.

Well, not really, but there was nothing we could do about it.

For some reason, I expected to meet some sweet old lady, or maybe David Tutera. Instead, when I entered the living room, Logan Cassidy sat on the couch.

Five years ago, Logan was a celebutant, famous for being famous. He flitted between Southern California and New York without a care in the world, spending money inherited from his mother's hotel fortune while generally contributing nothing to society. He prided himself on dating celebrities, courted paparazzi, and manufactured scandals everywhere he went. But a few years ago, his mother had drawn the line when he allegedly had a threesome with his friend's eighteen-year-old sister. At twenty-five years old. Legal, but gross. Logan revealed that he suffered from drug and alcohol addiction and went into rehab. When he finished treatment, his mother cut him off until he could prove he'd changed.

After disappearing for a couple of years, he had his own reality show, *Love with Logan*, where he helped rich people plan ridiculously extravagant weddings. Shockingly for someone who'd never shown any aptitude for anything but causing trouble, when sober, he had a knack for calming bridezillas and organizing napkin-folding.

When Logan spotted me, he rose from the couch and extended a hand, flashing the smile that dropped a thousand panties. Chestnut hair cascaded to his shoulders in waves I'd have killed for. He wore exactly enough scruff to make him think he looked manly, which tended to annoy me but seemed to work for him. When I moved closer, his eyes sparkled even brighter than on television. He had to be wearing contacts. A person could lose themselves in the ocean of his eyes.

"Jen, hi!" Logan said. "It's a pleasure to meet you. I've been rooting for you and Justin since the first episode of *The Fishbowl.*"

His statement threw me, as the guy I'd seen on the entertainment blogs didn't seem like a reality TV connoisseur. "You watched the show?"

"Absolutely. Just like you never miss mine, right?" He winked, then leaned forward and whispered. A lock of hair fell across his blue eyes, which twinkled mischievously. "It's TV. Lie. No one will ever know. They'll cut to me coaching you."

When he straightened back up and fixed his hair, I continued shaking his hand, which I'd now been holding far longer than appropriate. I hoped he didn't notice how sweaty my palm was. But I needed to follow his lead before pulling away. "Logan Cassidy! I can't believe it! I'm your number one fan! You're even better-looking in person."

"That's what my grandma says." Man, was he laying on the charm. But instead of coming across as smarmy, his act somehow endeared him to me. It was like the two of us were playing a huge joke on the rest of the world. "Why don't we sit down and have a chat about your dream wedding?"

"I'm a simple girl, really," I said. "I know people might not believe it, since we're doing this dream wedding show, but our original plan was quiet and small. This whole thing happened pretty suddenly. Justin and I were expecting a small, intimate gathering with our families."

"When you're a reality star, the whole world's your family, am I right? I mean, you've had millions of people following your relationship from the beginning. It's only natural they want to share in your 'big day'."

"That's why we're here," I said. "I'm so grateful to all the loyal viewers who will help make our wedding special."

"Absolutely! I completely understand. Wait until you see what I've got in store for you: the gown, a horse-drawn carriage ride the morning of the wedding, the hedge maze rearranged into a heart shape, the ice sculptures, the string quartet..." Logan trailed off with a happy sigh. "It's going to be amaze-balls. I can't wait for you to see everything!"

As he went on and on about his plans, an uneasy feeling grew in the pit of my stomach. Everything had already been decided. Justin and I spent most of Thursday going over what we wanted with the producers, but they hadn't listened to a word of it. We didn't have an iota of input here. I'd known the Network called me and Justin at the last minute because they were in a bind, but I was starting to get the feeling we'd be standing in at Braden and Amanda's called-off wedding. We'd be lucky if someone gave the officiant the correct names.

I mean, okay, sure, we'd already gotten married before leaving Florida, but the Network didn't know that. Justin and I didn't even tell Ed because he sucked at keeping secrets. He'd have pouted around the Fishbowl, complaining loudly that he missed the "real" wedding and asking that I explain for the seventh time why I let Sarah attend in her work pants. No, thanks.

When Logan started to wax poetic about a gluten-free, all-natural vegan cake, I found my voice. "Hold on a sec. I'm not eating flavorless cardboard cake. I want eggs and sugar and flour and butter—all of which, by the way, *are* natural ingredients. Sugar's a plant. Flour comes from wheat, which is a plant. Butter is from cows. All natural. And *tasty*."

"Your cake is going to be totally organic. Free-range, home-grown goodness."

My back teeth ground together as I silently reminded myself to keep my voice even, my smile pleasant. No drama here. "That doesn't even make sense. It's cake. Cake should taste good. People eat it because they like the sugar. I don't care about the calories."

"Your guests will."

"Which guests? My friends and family won't eat vegan 'cake.' We eat real food at weddings. Everyone is expecting to get to try Sweet Reality's signature caramelized banana chocolate cupcakes with peanut butter frosting."

One of the reasons Justin and I agreed to go on *Real Ocean* was so I could get a cupcake recipe from one of the other stars. That turned out to be a total bust, but we also judged a bake-off aboard the ship. Madison, star of *Deaf Teen Mother*, had made these amazing Elvis-inspired cupcakes. When she realized I was in a bind with my own bakery, she gave it to me.

The cupcakes had gotten a ton of buzz after the episode aired, and six months later, they remained one of our top sellers. When Justin and I agreed to this show, we'd asked Sarah to make a cupcake tower for us. Now it sounded like I was going to have to eat something about as appealing as dirt instead.

Logan's smile faltered. "The Network's guests want something healthy. And you can't serve peanut butter to a large group of people in LA. Someone could be allergic."

"Can't that someone not eat the cake, then? Or can't we have an alternative for those people? The beauty of cupcakes is that we can make as many kinds as we want." I realized that part of me had veered from the Plan less than a day after entering the house. Arguing was against the rules, but vegan cupcakes? No. Justin would understand me fighting this one battle.

"I'm afraid not. The order's already in, and the baker's hard at work," Logan said, not sounding remotely sorry.

Silently, I chanted *remember the Plan* while willing a smile on my face. I probably looked like I needed to poo. But I could go along with this. As long as I could get Sarah to bring me some cupcakes on the plane.

He turned to face the cameras. "This seems like a good time for a break. When we return, Jen and I will talk about the thousand fairy lights I ordered to spell out 'Jen & Justin 4-Eva' over the pool."

A thousand lights? That sounded ridiculous. Although, a giant testimonial to our love floating in mid-air might be… No, it would be way too big. Possibly blinding. That was a freaking lot of lights, even small ones.

Still, Justin and I swore to go along with whatever happened. I refused to argue about stuff that didn't even matter. The cake was one thing, especially since I owned a bakery. What would it say if people thought I didn't trust my business partner to make the cake for my own wedding? That needed to be discussed.

But fairy lights? Whatever. It wasn't like they wanted us to eat them. I forced the smile on my face to widen, determined to give this whole thing a chance, and sighed happily. "Oh, that's going to be amazing!"

The smile remained in place until the cameraman said, "That's a wrap!"

"I'd scale back the fake happy sighs a little, but overall, nice job." Logan stepped out of his cheesy wedding planner persona as easily as shrugging off an overcoat. "Sorry about that. Didn't mean to blindside you with everything. I thought the Network filled you in on the deets. They didn't tell you everything's been decided?"

I shook my head slowly. "Do I get to make any decisions at all?"

"You picked the groom, right?"

"That I did. And I can't imagine marrying anyone else."

"Then my advice is, don't sweat the rest of this. It's all for the show. The Network wants ratings. You get a free wedding. And at the end of the day, none of this stuff matters, right?"

His words echoed the Plan. As horrified as I was at not getting a real wedding cake, I needed to roll with the punches, make the show, and save Justin's job. As long as Sarah agreed to smuggle in the cupcakes, I'd be fine. We could hide them in the fridge until after the wedding.

"You're right. I don't care if the cake is inedible crap. I care about marrying my best friend and sharing my joy with all of America." With a little more practice, I'd be good at this. Maybe I could do the Network's spin for a living if the bakery didn't work out.

"That's the spirit! Come walk the grounds with me, and I'll go over the rest of my vision with you for the cameras. All you have to do is smile and look delighted at spending time with me."

Logan headed for the rear doors, and I couldn't suppress a grin. At least enjoying the wedding planner's company should be easy enough. His quick smile and behind-the-scenes comments should make this whole process more fun.

CHAPTER 6.5

<u>On the Groom Cam, Saturday:</u>

Justin: Good morning! Today, I'm on the hunt to find the perfect wedding present for my beautiful bride. Sarah was supposed to come with me, but she's a little camera shy.

I need to come up with a gift that beats a fully paid wedding, with honeymoon. The Network's already outdone me. But I'll figure it out. I've stopped by my parents' house to ask for words of advice.

The camera turns, revealing a wrought-iron table surrounded with four chairs on a small brick patio overlooking the pool. A house sits in the background. At one of the tables is a woman in her fifties with milky, white skin and golden hair, streaked with gray.

Justin: This is my mom, Charity. She and my father will be flying out to Los Angeles at the end of the week.

Charity: We're not staying in an all-glass house, I'm afraid. That would have been lovely during my sorority-girl days, back when I met Justin's father. Back then, we didn't have any problem swanning around the house in nothing but our underwear.

Justin: Mom, I beg you not to share any more.

Charity: Don't be ridiculous. We're all grown-ups here. But I'm sure America doesn't want to hear about a fifty-five-year-old woman's drunken escapades almost thirty years ago.

Justin: Why don't we talk about the wedding?

Charity: I'm delighted that Jen and Justin are getting married. He gave her my mother's diamond ring, you know. Carried it around a cruise ship for a week waiting for the right moment. He's lucky he didn't lose it in the ocean.

Justin: Any thoughts on a wedding gift for my bride-to-be?

Charity: Traditionally, the wedding was the couple's gift to each other. Or the honeymoon.

A middle-aged man with a bald head, deep tan, and a thick, white mustache enters the frame.

Justin: And this is my father, Greg Taylor. What do you think about a wedding present for Jen?

Greg: You're giving her the gift of the Taylor name! What could be better?

Justin: I think I need something she can unwrap on camera. Especially since she's not changing her name.

Greg: Get her an emergency roadside kit. Let her know that, no matter what happens, you'll never leave her stranded.

Justin: Jen doesn't have a car, Dad.

Charity: Oh! Get her a car! One of those cute British ones.

Greg: He can't get one of those. No room for grandkids in the back.

Justin: Cars—and babies—are a bit out of our price range at the moment. Dad, why don't you tell me about marrying Mom?

Greg: Thirty years ago, feels like it was yesterday. Your mother was a real knockout. When the door opened and I saw her waiting at the front of the church, she took my breath away.

Charity: It was the '70s, dear. We all looked so atrocious, I hid the photo albums.

Greg: I liked that tux! Powder blue, ruffled, what's not to love?

Charity shudders.

Charity: The only thing to love is the man wearing it.

She leans over and kisses Greg. Justin clears his throat off camera, but they ignore him. A moment later, the camera swings around and Justin comes back into view.

My parents, everyone! It looks like they could use some time alone, so all I can say is, I hope Jen and I are as happy in thirty years as they are today. You guys are an inspiration.

Charity: Thank you, darling.

Greg: We wish you every happiness.

Together: Congratulations!

CHAPTER SEVEN

<u>Confessions from the Chapel, Sunday morning:</u>

Rachel: Joshua and I have been in contact ever since The Fishbowl ended. He's not at all like the person he portrayed on the show. He was playing a character, trying to be the person he thought the viewers would vote to keep around. Who doesn't love a good villain, right? But we've talked about this, and he understands that he went about it all wrong.

J-dawg: In retrospect, I think speaking all in rhyme was my downfall. From now on, the J-dawg will only share poems when they're natural. Ha! See what I did there? No, I'm serious. I'm just here to repair my image and spend some quality time with Rachel.

Jen: Whatever. I can't even. He calls me fat once, he's out.

[Male producer's voice, off camera: *That's fair.*]

<u>Justin Taylor to My Wife:</u>

Oh, no! You mean I'm going to miss getting to see the J-dawg?

<u>Jen Reid to Justin Taylor:</u>

He'll still be here when you arrive.

<u>Justin Taylor to My Wife:</u>

Do you remember J-dawg? I have my doubts.

<u>Jen Reid to Justin Taylor:</u>

Oh, I would never deprive you of the pleasure of a reunion. If the Network tries to remove him before you get here, I'll throw a fit.

<u>Justin Taylor to My Wife</u>:
No fits. Remember the Plan.
<u>Jen Reid to Justin Taylor</u>:
Shut up.

JOSHUA ARRIVED at the Fishbowl the next morning. To my unending disappointment, he didn't seem to have changed a bit. His blond hair was longer, the top pulled into a man bun. He'd spent precisely the right amount of time in his tanning bed to avoid turning orange. That summed up Joshua: So all-American, his skin was the color of apple pie. He still dressed like he'd stepped off the pages of a J. Crew catalog. He and Rachel made a gorgeous couple. He also still acted like he was running for Jerk of the Year.

When he arrived, Birdie and I were floating in the pool, hanging on to rafts turned sideways. Rachel lounged on a raft nearby, using it properly. Logan sat at a patio table, working on something top secret. Hopefully not a tux made of body paint for Justin, or the officiant, or something even more ridiculous. I wouldn't put anything past the Network at this point, but I hoped Logan could be trusted to temper some of the tacky.

Every once in a while, Birdie glanced over my shoulder at the hot tub she couldn't use for the next month or so and whimpered.

A primal scream ripped through our peaceful afternoon. Something catapulted into the pool. Water exploded around us. Birdie gasped and grabbed her stomach. I abandoned my raft and towed her to the side of the pool. By the time we got there, the water had calmed. Our old nemesis stood in the middle of the shallow end, laughing.

"Man, you shoulda seen your faces," Joshua said. "The J-dawg is baaaaaaaaaaaaack!"

Inwardly, I groaned. Here some part of me had been hoping he'd turned over a new leaf. But Justin and I promised to roll with the punches. *Eye on the prize, Jen.* I needed to deal with whatever the Network threw at us happily so Justin kept his job.

After wiping the water out of my eyes and making sure Birdie was okay, I forced myself to greet him pleasantly, still refusing to use that ridiculous moniker he'd given himself. "Hello, Joshua."

"Hey, Jen! Marrying a lawyer, huh? Way to go! Now you can sue the Network for making you look like such a jerk on *Real Ocean.*"

"Everyone made some mistakes on that show."

"Oh, yeah? Here I assumed it was the editing. Why else would you gang up on the chick with cancer?" My fists clenched, but I bit my tongue. He turned to the only person in the pool area who wasn't glaring at him. "Hey, Rach. Why are you still hanging out with these losers?"

She slid from the raft into the pool and swam toward him. "These are my friends. And you promised to play nice."

"Right, right." He tossed the next comment over Rachel's shoulder. "Jen, Birdie, I'm sorry you guys are total losers. And Birdie, sorry you got so much fatter."

"She's pregnant, you Neanderthal," I said. "And I swear to God, if you're going to act like this at the wedding, you're not invited."

"No worries. I wouldn't be caught dead at a snooze-fest like the wedding. I'm here to liven up the reception."

"Wonderful." I rolled my eyes at him and exited the pool with Birdie. I couldn't control that he was here, but I didn't have to engage. As we passed Logan, I said, "Can you make sure, after he goes to his hotel, that I'm not here when he comes back?"

Logan glanced from Joshua to me and back. "Sure. You two have some kind of history I should know about?"

"Only what you saw on the show," Birdie said. "He treats everyone like that. Except Rachel, for some reason."

"I didn't watch the whole thing, but I saw enough," Logan said. "At least he stopped rapping."

"Thank God for small favors," Birdie muttered. "C'mon Jen, let's go inside."

My plans for the afternoon had involved writing my wedding vows, but running into Joshua ruined my mood and my focus. After about a thousand false attempts, I gave up and texted Justin to wish him luck with the trial. He sent me back a link to "Top 10 Ways to Insult Someone without Them Noticing" and suggested I practice on Joshua.

Feeling a bit lighter after the exchange, I went back outside to work on wedding favors with Logan. Having not been to a ton of weddings, I didn't know what to expect. One friend gave out chocolate candies printed with their initials. Another did donations to a charity, which sounded cool but not the Network's style. Ah, well. No one went to a wedding to receive gifts, right?

Well, in Seattle and Florida they didn't. Maybe in LA they did. Green and blue gift bags littered the table. Logan filled them with stuff that had to cost more than a wedding dress. An actual one, not body paint. Fancy chocolate bars I'd spotted selling for ten bucks each on Rodeo Drive. Engraved Tiffany heart-shaped keychains with J&J plus the date. Coupons that let the bearer into a private party at a hot new sushi place.

"These are the guest favors? What else are you giving them? Gold?" I asked, sitting down and pulling a bag toward me.

He laughed. "This is LA. It's a celebrity wedding. It's got to be big."

"I'm no celebrity."

"Around here you are," he said. "Besides, I am, and all the Hollywood bigwigs will be here. The bags have to be epic.

People should be talking about them for months. I wanted to include new iPhones."

"That's a huge waste of money," I said.

He shrugged. "We're doing iPad minis instead."

"Can I have a keychain?" When he nodded, I stuck one in the pocket of my sundress. Whoever started putting pockets in dresses was my hero. Then I pulled a stack of folded bags toward me and opened them, setting them up on the table in a row.

"You know we've got an entire production staff here to help with this," he said.

"Yeah, but I need to do something with my hands other than wrap them around Joshua's neck."

He laughed. "That guy's a piece of work. I'm surprised you invited him."

"I didn't." I hesitated, wondering how much of the Plan to reveal to Logan. He seemed sweet and open and on my side, but he also worked for the Network. Also, there were more cameras around the pool area than people on my guest list. "If Justin and I were getting married at home in a private ceremony, I never would've considered inviting him. And I wouldn't have let Rachel bring him as her guest. But that's a different world. This is LA, we're on TV, and the viewers like drama. Joshua brings the drama."

"That's a great attitude." He leaned forward, giving me a conspiratorial wink and lowering his voice. "If you think 'accidentally' shoving him into the pool will bring the right kind of flair to your wedding, let me know."

I laughed. His cologne hit me, making my stomach flutter. I didn't know what he was wearing, but it smelled good enough to eat. No wonder Logan managed to make dozens of coeds swoon over him every year. I was torn between wanting to ask what he wore so I could buy some for Justin and never wanting my husband within ten feet of a scent that made every woman in Miami want to rip his clothes off.

Grabbing the next goodie bag, I quashed the sudden weirdness in the air. Surely, he wasn't flirting with me. Or if he was, the Network put him up to it. A wedding planner who hit on the brides probably wouldn't stay in business long. I must be misreading him. There was only one way to tell.

"I'm so glad you're here with me this week, Logan," I said, pushing my shoulders back enough to make my boobs stick out. "I really need a friend right now."

"You know I'm here for you, Jen. Whatever you need." His voice grew thick, and I wondered how he managed that.

"Thanks, Logan. It means a lot to me to have you here." My voice oozed with sincerity. I searched for something utterly bizarre to say to him. "You know, I thought you were some womanizing jerk, but you're actually a big pineapple. A little rough on the outside, but sweet and gooey on the inside."

"You've got me," he said. "But don't tell anyone. If word got out, my reputation would be ruined. Besides, I only turn sweet and gooey for brunettes with big blue eyes."

I forced myself not to roll my eyes. Yup. It's the Network. He's playing me.

"It'll be our little secret," I said, still holding his gaze. "Wild horses couldn't drag it out of me."

Logan leaned toward me. "Does your fiancé know what an incurable flirt you are?"

"It's the thing he loves most about me," I lied.

"Then I guess we have something in common."

Uh-huh. I leaned closer, putting one hand on his arm. "You two have a lot in common. You're both smart, good-looking…"

Logan turned red and shifted in his chair. Uh-oh. Maybe I misread things. Poor guy. Now I'd made him uncomfortable. Maybe I needed to tone it down.

When Rachel, Birdie, and Joshua headed into the house, I kept stuffing bags, enjoying the feel of the sun on my shoulders and talking to someone who understood the need to create drama while secretly reveling in the ridiculousness of it all. All part of the show.

Slowly, completed bags filled the table in front of us.

"Thanks for helping with this," Logan said. "Most brides can't be bothered with the grunt work."

"It's no big deal," I said, double-checking the contents of a bag. "Besides, there's not much for me to do other than ask 'how high?' when the Network says 'jump'."

Logan laughed, but it sounded hollow. "Why won't you look at me?"

The truth was, I felt bad about the flirting. I didn't want to lead him on if the innuendo wasn't a joke for him. If the Network hadn't told him to flirt with me to create drama, I didn't want to alienate someone who could become a friend. The Plan didn't call for me to take advantage of other people. I decided to answer with a bit of honesty. About one percent.

"I thought you were embarrassed earlier when I compared you to Justin, and I felt bad," I said.

"I'm not embarrassed," he said. "There's something between us. I feel it, too. But there's nothing we can do with you getting married at the end of the week."

Logan's eyes met mine. He had the same expression as before, but he widened his eyes a touch too much. His gaze flickered, just a hair, but I caught it. His Adam's apple bobbed up and down, a bit too slowly. He was good, very good, but he was lying. And he needed a breath mint.

Two could play at this game. I summoned up a mental image of Justin, hoping it made my pupils dilate. When my tongue darted out to moisten my lips, Logan's eyes followed. I didn't know what to say, but I refused to look away first. We sat in a silent staring contest, each of us daring the other to make a move.

A voice from inside the house made me jump. "Jen? Where are you? Your dad's here!"

My dad? Who the hell invited him?

CHAPTER EIGHT

<u>Jen in the Chapel, Sunday evening:</u>

My parents divorced when I was a kid. I barely remember them together; I don't remember a time when they were happy together. For a while, we'd visit every other weekend or so, but I haven't seen my father in close to fifteen years. He stopped sending Christmas and birthday cards when I turned eighteen.

Never in a million years would I have considered sending him an invitation to my wedding—I'm surprised the Network even found him, to be honest. Especially on such short notice.

Jen to Mom:

OMG! 911!! The Network brought my father into this?

<u>Tina Carter to My Favorite Daughter:</u>

Impossible!

<u>Jen to Mom:</u>

I'd like to think so, but he's here. What do I even say? I haven't talked to him in fifteen years.

<u>Tina Carter to My Favorite Daughter:</u>

I'm so sorry, honey. The Network said they didn't need me

today, so I'm meeting an old college friend in San Diego. Zoo, then dinner. Do you want me to come back?

<u>Jen to Mom:</u>

No, it's fine. I'm wearing my big girl panties. See you tomorrow. Love you.

<u>Tina Carter to My Favorite Daughter:</u>

You too, sweetheart. You'll be fine.

I DIDN'T KNOW which was worse: that someone had found my father and invited him to the wedding, or the fact that, if he'd walked out of the house to find me himself, our first interaction in years might have been him finding Logan's lips much too close to mine. My father obviously didn't know about the Plan, I couldn't tell him, and I doubted he would understand even if I wanted to try to explain.

"Out here, Rach!" I called, breaking the ridiculously fake tension in the air. I shoved away from the table with more force than necessary, then stood with my eyes closed, willing my pounding heart to slow. My father. I didn't want to see my father. And I couldn't let anyone see how his appearance flustered me. Roll with the punches, that was the Plan.

"Are you okay?" Logan asked.

Not anything I wanted to share with him, but I needed to say something. "My father's name shouldn't have been on the guest list."

"Well, then, let's find out what's going on."

The two of us headed toward the back door. Logan walked a bit closer to me than he should have, his arm brushing against mine. I tripped over one flip-flop, letting my arm graze his hip when I reached out to steady myself. Let the Network dissect these moments. Before we got to the house, the glass door swung open.

Rachel stood in the entrance, as always looking as if she'd

stepped off the front of a catalog. She looked from me to Logan and back. "What's going on?"

Darn it. Rachel was too perceptive.

Since I couldn't explain Logan's pretend interest in me, I ignored her question. "Did you say my father is here?"

"Yeah, they took him straight to the interview room to talk about how excited he is that his little girl is getting married."

I rolled my eyes. "He's barely seen or spoken to his 'little girl' since the judge entered a child support order when I was nine. How do we get him out of here?"

"Oh, hell. I'm sorry, Jen," Rachel whispered. "I had no idea you didn't want him here. You never talk about your dad, but I didn't think about why. Maybe there was some kind of mix-up?"

A withering look was my response. The possibility that this was some kind of mix-up defied all logic and probability.

"Right, sorry."

Part of me wanted to go to the producers immediately, demand an explanation. But I knew what this was really about: drama. And I refused to make a scene on camera for them. So I'd play along. I'd go talk to the man who sired me, but I'd do it on my terms. Which meant he could wait until I was good and ready for him. After I took a long shower and cooled off. But first, I needed to text Justin and let him know that everything was proceeding exactly according to the Plan.

Justin couldn't believe I came on to Logan by comparing him to a pineapple. By the time we finished texting, tears of laughter streamed down my face. The conversation gave me the strength I needed to face my father, but I still didn't see any reason to hurry down the stairs. After all, I'd been waiting on him for more than a decade.

Once I felt a bit more together, I popped into the Chapel for an interview, hoping that by the time I finally made it to the living room, all the men in the Fishbowl other than Ed and Connor would have vanished from the face of the earth.

No such luck.

When I entered the living room, a dark-haired man stood with his back to me, looking out over the grounds. He was shorter than I remembered, only a few inches taller than me. But I suppose when you're nine, all adults seem tall, the same way all thirty-year-olds seem ancient until you're like twenty-nine and three hundred sixty-four days.

My heart pounded in my throat as I stood silently. My eyes devoured him as he watched the pool ripple in the breeze. If I didn't say anything, hid in my room, would he walk away again, turn and leave this house as easily as he left me, Adam, and my mother? Or would he stay, fight for a second chance to prove himself?

I didn't know the answer, and I didn't know which I preferred. It never occurred to me that my father would attend my wedding. When Justin and I had been in charge of the planning, his name hadn't been uttered once. I'd planned to surprise Brandon by asking him to walk down the aisle with me, but that wouldn't work since his job wouldn't let him appear on the air. Still, making the walk alone, a grown woman walking toward her new husband, was better than being "given away" by the man who tossed me aside as a child.

But then my father turned around, and the same blue eyes I saw in the mirror every day focused on mine. My resolve to hate him wavered. His face broke into a smile, and he stepped toward me, arms open for a hug.

My heart swelled, and I blinked back tears. Part of me felt like that little girl who just wanted her father to come back and love her.

The adult side of me remained pissed. I moved backward, away from his embrace. "What are you doing here?"

"Is that any way to greet your father?"

"I'm sorry. Hey, so, how's that child support you never paid?" My reaction surprised me. If someone had asked what I wanted to say to my father given the chance, I probably wouldn't have started with an accusation. But the Network ambushed me.

He blanched, moving backward as if struck. When I said nothing more, his outstretched arms dropped, and he flopped onto the couch. "I should have known you wouldn't be happy to see me."

"I would have been thrilled to see you," I said. "At ten. On my thirteenth birthday. At the father-daughter high school dance. At my high school graduation. Or college. What I'm not thrilled about is the way you disappeared from my life for about fifteen years and mysteriously turned up again just when I've got my own TV show. How much is the Network paying you?"

Part of me hated myself for saying these things. Not because I'd promised Justin not to get shaken up, but because none of it made any difference. Whether he showed up of his own volition or for the cash, that didn't make it better. Even if he wanted to make up, I didn't.

Forget the Plan. The moment I saw my father, all those years of pain came flying out of my mouth. The Network wanted drama, I'd give them drama. I was happy to tell this man—Patrick Reid, not Dad or Daddy or even Father—exactly what I thought of him before telling him to get the hell out of the house and disinviting him from all future events and reality shows I might participate in.

After more than two years of appearing in the media or on television, I was used to all the crap the Network constantly threw at me, but there was no way this man would get anywhere near my mother, which meant he needed to leave. She'd suffered enough. Her new boyfriend was on the way, they were planning to get married, and I wouldn't allow her daughter's wedding to be ruined by the appearance of an uninvited, unwelcome ex-husband.

"What are you talking about?" Patrick asked.

"Well, I assume you didn't come to celebrate your joy at

seeing me and Justin happy together," I said. "What are you doing here?"

"You know what they say about assuming, right? I was thrilled to find out my little girl was getting married."

"Yeah, right. Tell me another one."

"Fine, I will. I've got a lot of stories for you, Jen. There's a lot you don't know about what happened between me and your mom. If you'd give me about ten minutes and let me apologize, I'll tell you all about it."

I hesitated, nibbling on a thumbnail Rachel had painted earlier. She'd throw a fit if she saw me. On the one hand, I didn't have any interest in seeing or talking to this man. On the other hand, it *would* make great TV. I could hear the promos.

After almost fifteen years apart, Jen finds herself face-to-face with her father for the first time! Will she forgive him for disappearing? Will he approve of Justin? What will Jen's mother say when they meet again?

Patrick's voice broke into my thoughts. "Please, Pumpkin? You don't have to sit. Just listen."

Something in me stirred at his tone and the old nickname, a name he'd lost the right to use years ago. I was torn between wanting to hug him and wanting to smack him. Keeping my warring emotions off my face took willpower I didn't know existed. "I'm listening."

"I never wanted to leave you and your brother, but I was a total mess," he said. "Your mother was absolutely right to throw me out. I'd go out, get drunk, stay all night in bars. I'd get a DUI, go into rehab, come out, get drunk, repeat. Tina gave me one chance after another, over and over, but I couldn't get my act together."

This was all news to me. My mom never said a negative word about my father. I knew he wasn't paying support because I saw how she struggled to pay the bills, especially before she got her Realtor's license. The rest of this...almost sounded scripted. As if the Network told him what to say to get back into my good graces. Did he mean any of this?

I probed deeper. "So what's changed? Why are you here?"

"I've changed, Pumpkin. Thirteen years ago, I got arrested for my third DUI. In Washington, that's a felony. The judge took one look at my record and put me away for three years."

"Wow. I had no idea." That explained why he vanished.

"Of course you didn't. I begged your mother not to tell you kids."

"I'm sorry. Really." Maybe he didn't deserve my empathy, but three years in jail didn't sound like a picnic. Maybe it changed him, but he was too ashamed to reach out.

"Don't be. It was the best thing that ever happened to me. I got healthy, haven't had a drink since the day I went in. I've been doing AA for almost ten years now, and I'm here to make amends."

My heart sank. I didn't know why I let myself even hope he was here to see me, or why it still hurt to find out he wasn't. "So that's it? You're here as part of some twelve-step program?"

"I'm here because I got a call extending the olive branch. One of the producers told me that my only daughter was getting married, that I'd regret it forever if I wasn't here. She was right."

Something about his words sounded off. His story still sounded too perfect. I didn't trust it. "How do I know you're even my father? Maybe you're just some actor hired by the Network to tug on the audience's heartstrings."

"You think so little of me?"

"I think so little of *them*. Television producers have done worse things for ratings," I said. "Tell me something they wouldn't know. Tell me a story."

"I'll do better." He pulled his wallet from his back pocket and pulled something out, offering it to me. "Look, Pumpkin. You and Adam, back when you were little kids."

My hand shook as I reached for the picture. There I was, seven or eight years old, dressed as Bella Martinez for

Halloween, never dreaming that one day I'd go on a reality show and she'd be the host. My brother Adam stood behind me, wearing ripped jeans and a fake studded leather jacket, holding a pair of drumsticks. I hadn't thought about that night in ages.

"This was the first Halloween we let you two go out on your own," he said. "I made you give me all the candy to 'check' before letting you eat anything. Remember?"

"You did! And then you stole all the gummy bears from both our sacks." For years, I'd believed Adam and I were both allergic to gummy bears.

He chuckled. "Your mom ate most of them. I wanted the chocolate bars. Luckily, you had so many, you didn't notice a few missing."

The memory brought a smile to my face. I wasn't quite ready to forgive, not yet, but it wouldn't hurt to talk to him.

"Thanks," I said. "I guess, since Mom's not here, you can stay for dinner. I don't want the two of you fighting. I'd rather you steer clear when she's around. Where are you staying?"

"I can't stay here?"

I glared at him and crossed my arms, lips pressed together stubbornly.

"Just kidding, Pumpkin. I'm at a hotel. Not the same one as your mom. Don't worry, I'm not in a rush to see her, either."

"Let's be one hundred percent clear, here: I am completely on Mom's side. I won't listen to anything negative you have to say about her."

"Understood," he said. "It means so much to me that you're keeping your name, after everything we've been through."

Ugh. My decision to keep my name hadn't even taken my sperm donor into account. "That wasn't about you. I've been Jen Reid for twenty-seven years. I like my name, and I like who I am. You don't change your name just because of one asshole who shares it. Besides, it's not like I'm Jen Manson or Jen Trump."

"Ouch." He gave me a wounded look.

"I hope you're not waiting for me to apologize."

"No, I deserved that," he said. "Now, can your old man buy you dinner? Let's get away from these cameras and catch up."

"The cameras are coming." I still didn't trust this man. I didn't want to spend time with him. But at least I could try to salvage some of the Plan by going along with what the Network set up for the evening. "But dinner sounds good."

"Great! Do you still like burgers with chocolate milkshakes?"

"Doesn't everyone?"

CHAPTER NINE

Shocking Entertainment News Online

I Promise not to hate you?
Awkward Notes Found that Appear to be Bizarre Wedding Vows
by Talky Ted

The Network has been tight-lipped about what type of reality show they're planning now that Braden and Amanda 4-Eva has disappeared from the fall lineup. A small clue may have been uncovered, however: The Fishbowl's Jen Reid was spotted shopping at Tiffany & Co. on Rodeo Drive. A search of the company's online wedding registry revealed nothing, but surely Jen's clever enough to have registered using a fake name? There's definitely something going on here.
A source working with the Network found what appears to be wedding vows in the trash cans outside the fishbowl-shaped house where Jen and Justin originally started their relationship. But is there trouble afoot for our couple already? From "thanks for not being an obnoxious douche" to "I love that you don't constantly speak in rhyme," the snippets we found suggest our green-eyed lawyer may not be at the forefront of Jen's mind

while planning this wedding. Is she having a lover's tiff with another man? Or is something else going on? What is the Network planning to air in September? Where is Justin, anyway? Sources spotted the groom in a bridal shop in Miami with a gorgeous blonde, trying on wedding dresses. Justin, is there something you'd like to tell the rest of us? As storms brew off the coast of Florida, this reporter can't help but wonder if there are thunderclouds in our couple's future, too.

Jen cannot be reached for comment while she's in the Fishbowl, and Justin appears to be allergic to answering his phone. Texts requesting comment went unanswered.

The lovely Sarah Taylor, Ms. Reid's business partner and Mr. Taylor's twin sister, did answer the phone at Sweet Reality, but her comments were less than helpful. If Ms. Taylor is to be believed, Jen intends to marry the Loch Ness Monster before Justin joins them for a three-way honeymoon on Pluto. That pretty and funny? Remind me again why this girl doesn't have her own show? Perhaps the answer lies in her parting comments to me: "Why can't you people leave us alone?" Oh, Sarah, if only you weren't quite so entertaining. I can't wait to visit Sweet Reality next time I'm in Miami to talk to this enchanting woman in person.

Related Stories:

- **The Fishbowl Season 1 stars quietly gather in Los Angeles**

The next morning, Birdie, Rachel, and I piled into the limo for a trip downtown to find the perfect wedding dress. Mom and Logan waited for us outside the store. Mom flashed questioning eyes at me, but I didn't want to talk about my father.

I still needed to figure out how I felt about having him back in my life. If I wanted him around after he vanished for so long. One thing I'd made clear at dinner, though: Patrick Reid would not, under any circumstances, be walking me anywhere. Especially not on my wedding day. I'd traverse the aisle alone, thank you very much. Depending on how the week went, he might or might not be allowed to attend the ceremony. The producers hadn't argued the point with me yet, although I expected them to push back if I banned him. More likely, they'd invite him anyway, and there wouldn't be anything I could do about it.

Logan must've called ahead, because the store owner greeted us outside a locked shop with two sales assistants. One carried a pink cardboard bakery box full of doughnuts and the other held a carafe of coffee. Other than us, the store was deserted. The owner told us to dig in, waved at a plush couch in the middle of the room, then went to pull some gowns for me to try on.

My eyes bugged out at the first dress. Thousands of layers of tulle made up the skirt, leaving the impression of a cake covered in whipped cream. The train extended at least fifteen feet. Two associates had to help keep it off the ground. As much as I liked cake, the dress was ridiculous.

"Nuh-uh," I said. "No way. That dress will swallow me. I'm only five foot four."

She waved one hand. "You may need some heels."

I shook my head. "Bring another one."

"You haven't even looked at the top," she said. "At least try it on so we can see if the shape flatters you."

It wouldn't, and I'd need stilts to pull off the skirt, but arguing wasn't going to get me anywhere. It was much easier to step aside for a "private" camera interview where I lamented not wanting to look like a Christmas tree topper, then take the stupid thing into the dressing room. Mom followed to help.

I'd been so dismayed by the skirt, I didn't even look at the front of the dress. Nothing but sheer lace, the neckline plunging to my belly button. Now I looked like a doily sitting on top of a Christmas tree. A doily with nipples.

"My daughter is not wearing that on television," Mom said.

"Oh, hell no."

"Actually, I'd prefer you didn't even wear it out to show the others."

"I have to. It's in the contract."

Not bothering to put on shoes, I lifted the skirt as high as I could and tiptoed out into the main room, trying not to trip. Bonus, my hands held the front of the dress over my half-naked top. Unfortunately, when I got to the dais placed in front of several mirrors, I had no choice but to drop the skirt and let everyone see this monstrosity.

"That's amazing," Logan said.

"No, it's not." I turned to Rachel. "Can we please make him leave?"

"It's not that bad," she said.

"Not that bad?" Birdie cut in. "She looks like my grandmother's afghan fell into bleach, then got attacked by rabid dogs. #EpicFail."

In that moment, I could've kissed Birdie. I'd missed her—and her way of saying what other people were thinking—so much. With a laugh, I headed back to Mom and the dressing room to see what else the Network had in store.

The next dress looked a thousand times better. A strappy sheath, also topped with lace, but lining kept it from being pornographic. The neckline dipped to a vee, revealing a hint of cleavage. The fabric hugged my body all the way down to my knees, where the skirt flared around my feet. Lace scallops hovered over the ground, and the train didn't extend halfway to Mexico like the first one. It was summery, light, elegant, and perfect.

Mom followed me into the room to get everyone's reactions. When I spotted myself in the three-way mirror, a smile split my face in two. I pictured the look on Justin's face when he spotted me walking toward him in this dress, and warmth spread through my belly. I never wanted to take it off.

"I love it," I said.

"This is the one," Birdie said. "You look beautiful."

"It's exactly like I pictured your wedding day, sweetheart," Mom said.

Logan shook his head. "Not nearly sexy enough. Bring more like the first one."

My jaw dropped. "No. No way. This is perfect."

"Don't be ridiculous. You're not getting the second dress you try on. For one thing, we need a montage for the episode."

"Fine," Rachel said before I could reply. "She'll try on a dozen more. She'll hem and haw at the end and pretend to be incredibly torn. But can't you at least tell the sales associate to keep this one nearby until we're done filming?"

Logan glanced from the firm set of my mouth to Rachel's concerned look to Birdie, who looked like she wanted to tweet the entire exchange. She'd been forbidden, naturally.

"The sooner we get this over with," I said, "the faster we can move on to the bridesmaids' segment."

Finally, Logan's face softened. "I'll think about it. Try on a few more. But I want at least one bridal meltdown before we get through the day."

Of course he did.

SINCE WE'D FOUND The One and I was only trying on more for the show, Mom left with a promise to meet me at the house later. I didn't know where Patrick would be, so I sent a quick text to Connor before removing my perfect dress and starting on the rest of the less-wonderful gowns they had pulled for me.

Keeping my promise to Justin in mind, I tried to be a good sport. I really did. I wanted to fulfill my end of the bargain with the Network and I wanted to create a show that would entertain the viewers while going with the flow. They brought out white gowns, ivory gowns, and off-white gowns; ball gowns, mermaid gowns, and Empire-waist dresses that would fuel the pregnancy rumors started by that tabloid jerk; sleeveless, long-sleeved (in June!), cap sleeves, and strappy gowns. For more than two hours, I tried on every single dress presented, and I did it without commentary or complaint. Sure, at one point, I insisted they bring me another donut before I continued, but this was exhausting work.

But when the owner helped me into a dress with a skirt that poofed out to my knees in the front, with a long train in the back, I almost fell over laughing. I looked like the bride in that super long music video from the '90s. The bride whose dress is held up as the model of horrible bridal gowns. This one was made even worse by a four-inch-wide glittery belt around my waist and a gauzy, one-armed white "jacket" to go over the top. The skirt belled out, nearly filling the dressing room. The owner had to squeeze out the door to help me get into it. I couldn't move without turning into the proverbial bull in a china shop.

When I finally managed to compose myself and walked out to show the others, Rachel's eyes widened. She tried to turn a laugh into a yawn, and I glared at her.

"That is the mullet of wedding dresses," Birdie said.

With an impish look at Logan, I feigned surprise. "What? You don't like it? I think it looks awesome! This is definitely the one, guys. At least for the ceremony. We'll need another one for the reception. Just like Kate Middleton had."

Rachel snorted. "The only similarity between that dress and Kate Middleton's is, they're both made of fabric. They're not even the same shade of white."

"Liar," Birdie said. "I will give you a thousand dollars to walk outside in that monstrosity."

Logan stepped forward. "Okay, fine, you guys win. Jen, you don't have to try anything else. But I do need you to at least pretend to be indecisive."

"Fine. Let me go change."

Two minutes later, I returned to the room, back in my

sundress and flip-flops. The shop's owner brought out the dress I wanted and the original doily dress. For a good five minutes, I glanced back and forth, eyes shining, before Logan told me to stop hamming it up.

"Okay, you're done," he said. "Let's move on."

"We're going with the second one, right?"

"Yeah. Let me just get a couple more reaction shots from the store. You don't have to put it back on. They can fake it. Just stand on the dais."

Obediently, I moved back to the center of the room. I stood on my toes in my flip-flops, held out the corners of my sundress, and spun around in a circle that nearly had me falling into the leftover doughnuts. "What do you think? Isn't it perfect?"

Logan stuck his tongue out at me. "Very funny."

Rachel gasped, then looked up and waved one hand in front of her face, blinking rapidly.

Birdie watched her for a moment before turning to me. "I think what she's trying to say is, it's perfect. #BeautifulBride."

One hand on her chest, Rachel nodded. Then she formed a heart with her hands.

"Perfect! Now, on to accessories." Logan said.

"Oh, hell. We have to do this again?" Birdie said. "#Weddings are such a pain."

"It's okay," I said. "Accessories are fun."

Despite my confident words, choosing accessories went much the same as the gowns. We weren't picking what I wanted. We were making a TV show. My friends and I were having fun with the experience, but on the air, I couldn't criticize anything made by one of the show's sponsors or talk too fondly about anything made by a competitor.

Logan insisted I try on at least two dozen veils of every color, length, and style. At one point, the stylist brought out a pillbox hat with a veil, like what widows wore in the Old Days. When Logan insisted I try it on, I started to wonder if the Network was paying him extra to make me look ridiculous. His "favorite" headpiece looked like someone had crumpled up toilet paper atop my head and let it trail down to my butt. It even had long pieces of fabric on either side with giant beads tied to it.

"Absolutely hideous," Rachel announced when I turned to show everyone.

"One of the ugliest headpieces I've ever seen," Birdie said.

Logan let out a wolf whistle, which somehow didn't seem creepy coming from him. He must've practiced. "Oh, Jen, you're stunning! It's perfect."

My hands found their way to my hips as if of their own accord. "You're joking, right? Or are you blind?"

"She's not wearing that," Birdie said.

I swung my head back and forth, letting the beads smack my nose. "This is a problem. Also, ow."

Logan shrugged. "Fine. We remove the beads. But otherwise, this is it. It's exactly what I envisioned."

"I thought we were friends, Logan."

His eyes met mine, and I gave him a dazzling smile. He grinned back, reminding me why he was one of the most desired bachelors in the state. Possibly in the world, since William and Harry were both taken. It wasn't fair for a Network shill to be so charming and good-looking and delicious-smelling.

Logan said, "I like you, Jen, but the Network pays my salary."

"Are they paying extra to make her look like a fool?"

Once again, I adored Birdie for voicing my thoughts. Silently, I blew a kiss at her behind Logan's back. With this thing on my head, it didn't matter how I styled my hair. No one would see it. I could've left it short.

"We don't have to decide right now, do we?" Rachel asked, ever the peacekeeper. "Why don't you take them both back to the set and see what your mom thinks?"

"This one's paid for." Logan insisted. "I'm the wedding planner, I hold the credit card, and the Network is footing the bill. This is it, and that's final."

Ugh. With a groan of frustration, I ripped the awful veil from my head and dropped it to the ground. It wasn't like anything I did could possibly make it look worse. Then I stomped back into the dressing room to put on my regular clothes.

Time for me to sit, sip a glass of wine, and watch my friends subjected to the same torment I'd just been through. Hopefully, it would be more enjoyable to witness.

Then again, if I had no say at all in the final choice, which became more apparent by the minute, maybe I should go next door, order a drink, and call Justin to talk about my father's sudden appearance. Tempting, but my friends were here, and they expected me to stay until the bitter end.

Back in the viewing area of the shop, I settled onto the plush couch, crossing my legs away from Logan toward the dressing room. Then I grabbed a glass of sparkling wine from one of the sales associates and chugged half of it.

"Are you okay?" Logan asked.

"Fine."

"You don't seem fine."

My resolve to go with the flow shattered. "Why would I possibly be upset? Because you led me to believe I'd have some say in how I'd look on my wedding day? Because you made me buy a headpiece that looks like something I should've flushed? What could I possibly have to be upset about?"

"You knew what you were signing up for. I lied before. We have to take the veil because the maker donated it. We can get them to make some alterations, but that's it. I'm sorry." He glanced to where Great Hair filmed us, then lowered his voice. "I know it's hideous. If I can come up with anything to make it better, I will."

"Promise?"

"Hey, look at me." He moved around the couch to grasp my hands in his. His blue eyes peered into my soul. "I want this wedding to go well. My ass is on the line here, too, remember? I'm doing this to promote my own show. You're only in this for a few weeks, but I'm trying to get picked up for multiple seasons. If I don't do what the Network says, they'll replace me in a heartbeat."

As he spoke, a knot formed in my stomach. I'd become horribly self-involved, not thinking about why other people were here and what they might have to give up to do the show. I squeezed his hands. "I'm sorry, Logan."

"It's okay. I'm here for you. But I still work for the Network." His eyes twinkled at me. "Can we hug it out?"

"Sure."

Logan tugged on my hands, pulling me into an embrace. His musky scent filled my nose, and I inhaled deeply. My arms went around him. I'd intended this to be a quick pat-on-the-back tight hug, but when I started to pull away, his arms tightened. He drew in a long, deep breath, smelling my hair. He was excellent at seduction. I still didn't know his endgame, but he was doomed to fail.

"I'm sorry, Jen," he whispered in my ear.

"It's okay," I said, pulling back.

One of his hands grazed the side of my breast, sending a jolt through me. With a sharp inhale, I froze. I suspected it wasn't an accident, but it wasn't time to call him out yet. At the same time, I couldn't bring myself to lean in or take this any further. No matter what Justin and I agreed, I didn't want Logan touching me. I pulled away.

Before letting me go, he tilted my chin up to meet his eyes. "Friends again?"

"Of course."

Leaning forward, Logan brushed his lips against my cheek, a hair too close to the corner of my mouth. We were playing a dangerous game, and I didn't know all the rules.

We stared at each other for a long moment. His tongue darted out, moistening his plump, soft-looking lips. The longer I sat in his arms, taking in his nearness, the more confused I got. That was some good cologne. My body screamed for me to move forward, while my brain held me in check. No one had affected me like this since I met Justin.

The thought was like a bucket of cold water, dousing my emotions. Justin. The man I loved. The man I was marrying on national television in a week, who I'd already secretly married. The man I planned to spend the rest of my life with.

Rustling fabric and squeaking wheels broke the last remnants of the spell between us. Behind Logan, the salon owner approached with a rack of bridesmaids' dresses. We shot apart. Part of me wondered what she'd seen, but Great Hair stood in the corner, silently filming, so it didn't matter. At some point, the producers would start asking me questions about my response to my wedding planner. When they did, my fake answers would be ready.

Grateful for the interruption, I went to the rack and made a big show of reviewing each dress. Sure, no one cared about my opinion, but the viewers didn't know that. Logan stood nearby, close enough for the heat of his body to leech into mine, asking my opinions and making comments intended to steer my choices.

This came as no surprise. From the moment I walked onto the set, the wedding had been out of my hands—not that I'd had a choice in whether to come on the show, either. Logan was here, like Connor said, to steer the wedding along and stir things up. The Network had even paid him to increase the drama. I suspected they'd paid him to flirt with me, to feign an attraction, to make me fall for him. What could increase the drama of a reality TV wedding more than the bride announcing at the altar that she was ditching the groom for the wedding planner?

Paranoid? Probably. Outside the realm of possibility? Not after everything I'd been through. Other than Connor, I didn't trust the producers farther than pregnant Birdie could throw them, and Connor was only third in command. He did his best, but he didn't call the shots. Had they not put Justin's job at risk, no power in the universe would have gotten me back on reality

TV. Especially not with the same producers who screwed us over last fall.

Once the owner took the dresses to Rachel and Birdie, I moved away from Logan, making a big show of texting. The messages didn't go to anyone; I just needed a moment alone to compose myself, to think about what almost happened and how I felt about it. Justin would get a full update later. Maybe he could give me some tips on how to tone things down without turning into an ice queen.

Oblivious to my inner turmoil, Logan chatted with the camera crew, his usual easygoing, friendly self. It was almost like he hadn't tried to kiss an engaged woman on national television.

Birdie returned to the room first, wearing a low-cut, strappy peach gown that matched her skin tone perfectly. She looked naked from the waist up. The skirt was somewhat better, a simple floor-length sheath, but I couldn't get over the top half. With her pregnancy boobs, she looked like she belonged in a porno, not my (theoretically) elegant William-and-Kate-inspired wedding.

"No pressure, Jen, but if you pick this, I'm defecting and substituting Ed as bridesmaid," she said.

"I wouldn't blame you." I turned to Logan. "Do I get any say over the choice here?"

He waved one hand. "Pick whatever you want. The Network gets final approval, but I only steered you toward this one to get the reactions."

Relief surged through me. Finally, some part of the wedding would be mine. We could find Birdie and Rachel dresses to make them feel amazing.

"Oh, thank God. I'm taking this crap off and finding something in navy." With a swish of chiffon, Birdie vanished back into the dressing rooms.

I turned to Logan. "Do they have to wear the same dress?"

"I don't care. Same color, complementary colors, same style, complementary styles. As long as it is looks good on camera,

I'll recommend the Network approve it. What are you thinking?"

"Well, Rachel and Sarah have similar body types and coloring. They'll look lovely in the same dress. But Birdie's much shorter and very pregnant. She'll probably be most comfortable in an Empire waist. Did the Network add any other bridesmaids I don't know about? One of Amanda's friends, maybe, or Braden's sister?"

Laughing, Logan glanced at Great Hair, still in the corner capturing every bit of this exchange on video. "Don't give them any ideas."

Before I could respond, Rachel emerged from the dressing room, this time with Birdie in tow.

"Sorry, y'all," she said. "Birdie needed some help getting out of that other contraption. What do you think of these?"

The next dresses were forgettable, and as Birdie and Rachel rotated through the store, the cuts and fabrics all started to blur together. Bright colors, muted colors, strapless, long sleeves, short sleeves, no sleeves, lace, beads, feathers. Feathers? That one went quickly into the "no" pile.

Just as I teetered on the edge of despair, Logan told me there were only about four more dresses in both fitting rooms, and he'd told the owner to save some of the best for last. I eyed him skeptically, but sipped my complimentary drink instead of commenting. If those horrible dresses he put me into were "the best" in his opinion, I had very little faith in his estimate of…well, anything.

When my friends returned, though, I felt bad for not trusting my planner's taste. Rachel wore a simple, floor-length navy-blue gown with a lace inset around her neck and a slit up the side. Birdie wore a strapless emerald green dress with a gathered Empire waist that fell to her knees. They both looked stunning.

"I love you, Jen, but I can't do strapless," Birdie said. "Not unless you want my boobs to pop out. These things are enormous."

She had a point. I turned to the store's owner. "Do you have anything with a cowl neck?" I didn't feel the need to copy Pippa Middleton's white bridesmaid dress exactly, but maybe we could find something similar in another color.

She shook her head with a sad smile. "Not on such short notice. Those dresses are reserved through 2020."

"If I may," Logan said. "Jen, this is going to be *the* wedding of the year. I appreciate that William and Kate had an amazing wedding, but it was years ago. You don't need to copy them. Be this year's trendsetter. Whatever you pick, other brides will be desperate to wear next year. Make the look your own."

"And give your bridesmaids boob control," Birdie added.

He turned to her. "We can add straps to this one if you like it. It's an easy modification."

"A cowl neck would provide boob control. Surely, the Network could help us get one."

"Yeah, but is that what you want? To be a follower?" Logan said.

"I can't wear a cowl neck with an Empire waist," Birdie said. "It would look ridiculous."

"She's right," Rachel said. "And an Empire waist is better for a pregnant belly."

Their words swarmed around me. I wished I had a real wedding planner, someone more interested in my vision than in pushing the Network's agenda or flirting with the bride. But Birdie was right. Empire waist didn't go with cowl neck, and my pregnant friend's needs trumped my weird fixation on copying the royal wedding. Besides, what did it matter? Nothing else about this wedding would resemble that one. I might as well get dresses that made my friends happy.

I started to chew on a thumbnail, but Rachel stopped me with a look. Two blue dresses, once Sarah arrived, and one green. Blue and green, like the ocean. Like everything in the Fishbowl. Like the theme of the show, where Justin and I met. It could be a nice throwback. Or we could go all the way. "Do you have these dresses in turquoise?"

Birdie exhaled, as if she'd been worried I'd pick the peach monstrosity. Rachel glanced into the mirror as if picturing how a blue-green dress would look. But the owner simply nodded and ushered them both into the dressing room.

I sipped my growing-flat sparkling wine while we waited, worried this was all a trick and Rachel would reappear in blue-green body paint or they'd make Birdie dress her stomach up as a glittering disco ball.

When the store owner reappeared to introduce Rachel and Birdie in the new dresses, I sighed in relief. They looked beautiful. The gowns required only minor alterations, and the store owner promised the work could be done by Thursday. Even better, Sarah could try on the dress at her local store in Miami, then call here to reserve her size before flying out.

Finally, something was going right. The wedding was starting to turn around.

CHAPTER 9.5

On the Groom Cam, Tuesday:

The camera opens inside a bakery. Black and white tiles line the floor. Stencils of stars and television sets line the walls. A glass case displays rows of cupcakes, cookies, and brownies.

Justin: My trial's over. Sarah and I are flying out tomorrow. We're at Sweet Reality to put the finishing touches on her gift to us.

Sarah: Well, we're calling it a groom's cake so they'll let us bring it, but it's mostly a gift for Jen. I couldn't believe it when she told me the Network is making her eat vegan cake at her wedding. Not on my watch!

The camera follows Sarah through a swinging door to the kitchen. A sheet cake lays on a metal table near the rear wall.

Sarah: This is Jen's current favorite.

Justin: Yeah, her 'favorite' changes a lot.

Sarah: What can I say? I make good cakes. Anyway, this is a yellow sheet cake with a layer of crushed hazelnuts and chocolate ganache in the middle, with chocolate hazelnut frosting. But come look at the best part.

The camera peers down at the top of the cake. Sarah has printed the scene from Jen and Justin's final moment on *The Fish-*

bowl: Jen and Justin, standing outside on the driveway, sharing their first real kiss. Raindrops sparkle across the surface.

Justin: Did you put glitter on my cake?

Sarah: It's edible glitter. Don't worry. I wanted to go fancier, since you only get one wedding cake.

Justin: Technically, we're getting two.

Sarah shoots a withering look at the camera. *Do you want it to be just one?*

Justin: Sorry. Continue.

Sarah: So, anyway, I wanted multiple tiers, something spectacular, but since I'm carrying this with me on the plane–and it'll have to go through security–that wasn't feasible. But I think Jen will like this.

Justin: Are you kidding? She's going to be blown away. Thank you.

CHAPTER TEN

Jen Reid to Justin Taylor:
Pretending to plan my dream wedding is fun and all, but I miss you.
Justin Taylor to MRS. Reid:
Are you saying that so I won't get mad at you for going cake tasting without me?
Jen Reid to Justin Taylor:
Maaaaaaaaaaaaaybe.
Ok, no. I really do miss you.
Justin Taylor to MRS. Reid:
And you really are going cake tasting without me?
Jen Reid to Justin Taylor:
You get all the cake you want from Sarah.
Justin Taylor to MRS. Reid:
Yes, I can. No sugar-free vegan cake in Sweet Reality!
Jen Reid to Justin Taylor:
:-P Now I don't feel bad. Also, the wedding planner keeps hitting on me, and it's your fault.
Justin Taylor to MRS. Reid:
Sorry. :-(But you can handle him. It's only a couple more days.
Jen Reid to Justin Taylor:

If he tries to kiss me again, I'm going to be very cross with you.
<u>Justin Taylor to MRS. Reid:</u>
Would it make you feel better if I kiss J-dawg when I get out there?
<u>Jen Reid to Justin Taylor:</u>
......
<u>Jen Reid to Justin Taylor:</u>
Depends on how good a kisser Logan is.

On Tuesday morning, I insisted that Logan take us cake tasting. Oh, sure, the Network had already decided on some probiotic kale cake or maybe a tower of cardboard or whatever, but that didn't mean I had to miss out on the most fun part of the process. Even for someone who owned a bakery.

The tasting went better than dress shopping, largely because we got to eat whatever we wanted. Vanilla cake with chocolate frosting; vanilla cake with strawberry filling and whipped cream topping, much like the cupcake Justin hid my engagement ring in; chocolate cake with a caramel center and chocolate caramel candies on top. The cakes were light and airy. I made a mental list of notes to text Sarah when I got back to the house.

Never put a whole strawberry inside the shortcake cupcake.

We need a cupcake with ROLOs.

The bakery even offered to create a maze of cupcakes, much like the hedge maze on the grounds. Only more delicious.

Logan dragged me away from the cashier before I could finish placing an order. Behind me, Great Hair stuffed a suspiciously bulging cardboard box into one of her camera bags. I wondered if she'd be willing to share later.

"This is a wedding, Jen, not a birthday party. There's no room for kitschy cakes at a wedding," Logan said.

"If this were *my* wedding, there would be. A cupcake maze or a puzzle cake sounds perfect for me and Justin."

"I agree," Rachel said. "Don't forget, puzzles brought them together."

"The Network brought them together," Logan said. "And the Network isn't paying for creatively arranged cupcakes or anything sugar-filled. The cake's already been bought."

"#Killjoy," Birdie said.

"I'm not trying to ruin your fun. I let you eat cake all morning. It's time to get back to the house. We've got things to do."

"Like what? You want me to *ooh* and *ahh* over the napkin arrangements?"

Logan smiled lazily and tilted his head at me. "Sure, Jen. I'd love to show you my *napkins*."

My cheeks flamed. How he managed to make even little random things sound dirty, I'd never know. Rachel shot me a questioning look, but now wasn't the time. Instead, I stuffed a final bite of cake into my mouth, a bit too big to allow for talking. It was delicious. I wondered what would happen if I snuck out of the house and called the bakery later, pretending to be Janine. Or maybe Sarah could call for me. I reached for one more bite, but Logan grabbed my hand.

"Seriously, it's time to go. Sorry."

We grumbled, but followed him back to the car. Birdie disappeared up the stairs for a nap as soon as we got back to the house, muttering something that sounded like "#sugarcoma." Rachel followed to change into her swimsuit. For a few minutes, I had the lower level to myself, which made this the perfect time to check my phone.

The Network allowed me to keep it with me in the house, as long as I used the speaker when making calls. But when we went out into the world, my phone stayed behind. Logan and whichever PAs were assigned to me had phones in case of emergency, but they didn't want me to sneak out to make secret calls or something.

Not totally paranoid of them, considering I'd ducked into the maze to call Justin twice since getting here. And they didn't know about all the texts we exchanged from the burner phone stashed under my mattress.

Returning to the kitchen, I pulled my phone out of the drawer where we kept it and turned it on. Seven texts from Justin and three voicemails. What the hell? Was he already in Los Angeles, on his way to see me?

Instead of checking the messages, I tapped his name immediately. He answered on the third ring. "Jen, I'm...sorry."

Those words didn't do anything to quell the growing sense of dread within my stomach. "What's wrong?"

"..."

With a sigh, I moved toward the patio doors to get a better signal. Really, I needed to replace this phone after the wedding. "Justin, the reception is terrible, I can't hear you."

"...texts..."

My phone had four bars, so the problem wasn't me. "Justin, can you walk somewhere with better reception?"

"No...I...ry."

My heart skipped a beat. "What's going on?"

"...arah..."

Sarah?

Oh, no. The thought of something horrible happening to my sister-in-law and best friend left me momentarily unable to speak. With shaking hands, I filled a glass with water. It took two swallows before I could reply. "Sarah? What about Sarah? Is she okay? Is she with you?"

"Not...sister."

His twin wasn't his sister? That didn't make any sense. "Justin, I can't hear you. Where are you?"

"Airport...on."

I fought the urge to chuck my useless phone across the room. "What? Justin, I can't understand anything you're saying. We've got a terrible connection."

The phone went dead. I called him back immediately, but nothing happened. The several voicemails he'd left shed no additional light on anything: a lot of static, a couple of broken airline announcements in the background, crowd noise, and one that sounded like a butt dial from the men's room. Awesome. My concern grew with each uninformative message. All the texts were variations of "Please call me ASAP."

Heart pounding, I dialed Sarah's number. The call went straight to voicemail. She should be on a plane, not at the bakery, but I dialed the landline, anyway. The phone at Sweet Reality rang and rang until the line started buzzing. Since the shop should be open, getting no answer made me even more nervous.

I was still standing in the kitchen, staring out over the pool, when Rachel entered wearing her swimsuit. "You okay? One of the producers said they heard yelling."

"Yes. No. I don't know."

"Well, that clears things right up." She tilted her head at me, eyes full of concern. "What's wrong?"

"I don't know. Justin called, but the reception was all wonky, and it sounded like there was some issue with his sister. I tried to call Sarah, too, but her phone's off. I hope she's okay."

"Hold on a sec. He said there's a problem with Sarah?"

"Yeah."

"When are they supposed to be flying in?" Rachel pulled out her phone and started tapping. "Do you have the flight number?"

"He was supposed to fly out of Florida a few hours ago. When he called, I thought his flight landed early, but he was apologizing and sounding stressed. It doesn't sound like they were on the plane. Should I go to the airport, just in case?"

Rachel kept tapping, a grim look on her face. Then she held her phone out to me. "No, Jen, I don't think you should."

I snatched her phone out of her hand. Then all the wind rushed out of me. She'd pulled up a news site. HURRICANE CARA STRANDS THOUSANDS. Below the headline, a picture showed a Florida airport, absolutely packed with people.

He said Cara, not Sarah.

"I'm sorry, Jen," Rachel said, "but I don't think Justin's flying in tonight. According to this site, he might not be able to get a flight for days."

"What about Atlanta? Can he drive to Atlanta? My family's flying through there."

She tapped a few more times, biting her lip. I found the answer on my phone right when a low murmur told me Rachel saw it, too.

All flights canceled. My entire family stranded.

My heart sank. Just when things finally started to go right, when I started to think the whole wedding might not be a complete disaster, my groom wasn't even coming.

ABOUT AN HOUR LATER, I finally got a text from Justin. He confirmed that he and Sarah were stranded. He also told me his roommate wasn't going to make it as best man, which under the circumstances didn't seem to matter. With no groom, no family other than the bride's mother, and no idea how the wedding would proceed, I didn't care whether the best man showed. I wanted to spend the afternoon sulking, but the show must go on. One of the producers sent me and Rachel out to the pool. I didn't have any better ideas, so I went.

When we got there, Joshua, Logan, and some guy I'd never seen before waited. He was cute, but I didn't know who he was or why he was there. A friend of Joshua? Birdie's eBay date? I approached him and held out one hand. "Hi, I'm Jen."

Logan intervened before he could respond. "This is Koji. He joined the wedding party a couple of hours ago."

I blinked rapidly in response. "He… What? Why? How?"

"The producers got an email that Aaron wasn't going to make it. Justin told you?"

"Yeah. I got the message like five minutes ago."

"Well, lucky for you, we got the message right after lunch. We had time to get Koji here as a stand-in."

The list of men who would be more welcome in my wedding party than a total stranger would almost stretch to the end of the sweeping driveway. Struggling to remain calm, I pasted a smile on my face. "And no one I've met was available? What about Abram?"

"Abe's not coming to the wedding, I'm afraid. He and his family moved to South America to work for Habitat for Humanity."

Darn. Not only would I miss Abram, but not knowing that made me feel like a crappy friend. Nevertheless, I persisted. "What about one of the Fish who already lives in LA? Raj? Mike?"

"Mike doesn't want anything to do with the show after the way he left. Raj got a nose job yesterday, of all the dumb ideas. He'll be at the ceremony, but with a swollen face and two black eyes, he can't do the wedding party. Sorry, but Koji is filling in."

The Network would not get a reaction out of me. Inwardly I sighed, but outwardly I forced the corners of my mouth upward and extended one hand. After all, it wasn't Koji's fault the Network sucked. "It's nice to meet you."

"You, too." My new groomsman grinned, flashing even, white teeth that made me wonder if he and Logan met at the dentist. Koji stood a few inches taller than me, with jet-black hair and friendly brown eyes. He'd look good in a tux. That was literally all I knew about him, other than his name. It would have to be enough. This wasn't my wedding. Not anymore. I didn't even have someone to marry.

On either side of the pool, a long table had been set up. Vases, flowers, potting soil, beads, glitter, and all kinds of other stuff littered the tables. At the front of the pool, three square tables sat side by side, one with a pink tablecloth, one white, one blue. Logan stood between two of the smaller tables holding a microphone.

"We're all having fun getting ready for *Jen & Justin's Big Day*," he said. "But let's not forget, we're first and foremost a reality show. And not any show: our happy couple started their relationship at this house, while filming *The Fishbowl*."

It didn't seem worth mentioning that Justin and I actually met at the audition. When I found out we'd both been cast, I'd been secretly thrilled to see him again.

"*The Fishbowl* was all about puzzles and challenges," Logan said. "So what could be better than putting the two together in a series of wedding-based challenges?"

For the first time since arriving in the house, I started to get excited about the show. The challenges were my favorite part of *The Fishbowl,* and I'd had no idea the producers planned to bring them back for this series. My ears perked up at the thought of having something to focus on and a way to burn off some nervous energy.

Beside me, Birdie looked at her stomach, then back at the tables. "Please tell me this isn't a physical challenge."

"No, Birdie, you're in luck." Logan laughed. "No physical challenges at all, unless we have to do some kind of Duck, Duck, Goose to find a stand-in for Justin."

My stomach twisted at the thought. My husband had plenty of time to show up, so it was a bit soon for stand-in jokes. Still, walking down the aisle to greet no one would be humiliating if he couldn't get a flight. What if the Network twisted everything so it looked like he jilted me? All it would take is a blond actor with a similar build putting on a tux and racing down the driveway, away from the house.

Dozens of cake samples churned in my belly, and I wondered how the show would spin it if I blew chunks on the deck. Talky Ted would have a field day.

Deep breaths. It didn't matter. None of this mattered. Justin and I were already legally bound. Nothing about this week changed our relationship. We couldn't control the weather. It wasn't my husband's fault he was later than expected.

"One of the most important things about a wedding is the decor," Logan said, speaking to the cameras. "I wanted to do this with all of the attendants and Justin, but unfortunately, the weather rained on our parade. Instead of Bride and Groom versus the Attendants, Jen, you'll be paired with Ed. The bridesmaids will form a second team, and Joshua and Koji will be the third."

"What does the winner get?" On *The Fishbowl*, challenge winners earned immunity from elimination, but as far as I knew, we weren't about to start voting people out of my wedding. That could get interesting, but wasn't the way I wanted to start my marriage.

"Members of the winning team will have an edible gift basket delivered to their homes after the show wraps up, courtesy of our sponsors."

At Logan's beckoning, Rachel and Birdie joined him at the front of the pool. They stood behind the table with the pink cloth, while Ed and I moved to a second table, covered by a white cloth. Joshua and Koji waited behind the last table.

Logan said, "Koji, Birdie, Jen, you'll be given a picture of what the final centerpiece is supposed to look like. The three of you will be giving directions to your teammates, explaining how to put the centerpieces together. I'm going to walk away so I can't see.

"After five minutes, you'll each place your centerpiece on this table to my left, in random order. Then I'll review your work. The winner will be the team that comes closest to matching the centerpiece in the picture."

"I'm watching you," Birdie muttered to Joshua. "Cheater."

"Get over it, chickadee. I was playing a role. The new me isn't a cheater. Right?" He winked at Rachel, who blushed. I tried not to puke into the pool.

"Is everybody ready?" Logan asked, ignoring the tension. "Okay, then, directors, take these stools. Here are your pictures. You get sixty seconds to study it."

Obediently, I took the photograph they gave me and sat on a white stool on the other side of the pool. We each got a Bluetooth to speak into. Ed, Rachel, and Joshua got headsets with an earmuff on one end. Those of us giving instructions could hear each other, but the other three would only hear their teammate.

Whether this centerpiece would actually grace the tables at the wedding, I had no idea. But I didn't hate it, which put it miles ahead of most of the wedding arrangements. White and blue flowers formed a base, supporting two glass (plastic?) columns, which led to a larger arrangement of more white and blue flowers. Curly ribbon or something filled the columns. A few flowers floated around the vases on attached strings.

It looked lovely. It also looked like the Network had given us an impossible task. After staring at the thing for a full forty-five seconds, I didn't have the first clue how to tell someone to make it. Hopefully, they had a real florist on standby. The pictures were gorgeous, but I couldn't imagine anything created during this challenge coming close.

It didn't matter. I should've documented this entire experience on Instagram with #MyTackyAssWedding. I might as well enjoy the challenge.

Five minutes flies by when you're trying to walk someone through creating a flower arrangement. Maybe I could've figured this out if given the picture and a list of supplies, but describing it to Ed—when I couldn't even see what he had available to work with—resulted in him asking if I wanted him to attach the blue thingamabob to the white whirlygig or the green whatsit.

We weren't going to win, but at least he had me laughing until tears flowed down my cheeks.

When Logan called time, we went to see the finished products. Three white cardboard screens stood on a short rectangular table, blocking the finished arrangements from view.

"Before we judge the final project, Jen, what did you think of the picture?" Logan asked.

"I love the centerpieces." He made a "go on" gesture with one hand, so I embellished. "They're absolutely breathtaking, Logan! The guests will be blown away. I can't wait to see how my friends have done recreating these masterpieces!"

Behind Logan, Birdie rolled her eyes. Joshua made a gagging motion. Rachel stared at the ground, lips twitching. Okay, maybe I laid it on a little too thick. Whatevs.

"Glad you like them," Logan said. "Now, let's take a look. First up, centerpiece number one."

The first centerpiece looked like a jellyfish. It had the blue and white flowers, same as the original, but that was about it. It didn't have a base, or the columns. Tendrils of what looked like ivy trailed away from the center mass of flowers.

"If I walk closer, will it sting me?" Logan asked.

No one answered, but Joshua hid a snicker behind one hand.

Logan removed the cover from centerpiece number two, which looked much better. Whoever created it managed to do two tiers of flowers in peach and purple. Beads filled the glass columns.

When he removed the third cover, several people chuckled. I stole a glance at Ed, whose lips twitched. The "centerpiece" contained no vase. It also contained no flowers. Instead, someone had written out "Jen and Justin 4-Eva" in glass beads on a turquoise plate. It didn't take me long to guess exactly who that someone was. Ed had many talents, but he wasn't exactly renowned for his arts-and-crafts abilities.

Logan stepped closer, running one hand over the beads. "It appears one team wasn't entirely clear on what the challenge was about. Half a point for creativity, I suppose."

Rachel clapped enthusiastically and whooped. I nudged her with my elbow.

"What?" she whispered. "At least I know I'm not going to come in last."

Logan walked up and down in front of the table, examining each "arrangement" in turn. He tapped one finger against his lips, pretending to be torn. "I don't know, guys. The first one doesn't say 'wedding centerpiece' to me so much as 'fun day at the aquarium'."

Joshua snorted. No one else moved or spoke.

"The second one," Logan said, "looks lovely, but the color of the flowers is all wrong. The original centerpiece is blue and white, but this is peach and purple. It's not even close. I'm not even going to dignify entry three with a response. You guys could have made some effort to create a centerpiece."

"All three of us were giving directions," I told him. "It's not our fault someone didn't listen."

"Maybe not, but that person also doesn't get a win," he said. "Okay, I've made my decision."

On the other side of the table, Ed's eyes twinkled with laughter. The two of us wouldn't be enjoying a basket of fruit shaped like flowers when the show ended. I did appreciate the sentiment of centerpiece three, though. I blew him a kiss, and he winked at me.

"Centerpiece two is the most well-constructed, which isn't saying much. Unfortunately, the flowers are incorrect. It's got some structural issues, but the flowers *are* the right color, and I do love jellyfish, so the winner is—centerpiece one."

Joshua and Koji whooped, and for a moment, I wished the "prize" for winning this challenge had been elimination. Ah, well. At least there was no immunity or right to give a speech at the reception attached. Not that it wouldn't be amusing to listen to someone neither Justin nor I knew wax poetic about our relationship in front of the cameras.

Joshua said, "Really, Birdie? What's up with the peach and purple flowers? I know you're a ginger, but I thought you at least had some grasp of the color wheel. They teach it in kindergarten."

Birdie turned bright red. Before she could respond, Rachel stepped forward. "That was my fault. I dropped the white roses in the pool and had to sub something in at the last minute. By the time I got everything else all set up, there was no time to sort through for the blue flowers. I did the best I could."

"At least you tried," I said. "Not like my teammate."

Ed shrugged. "Whatever. It's not like the loser of these challenges gets eliminated."

"Removing someone from the house wouldn't be the worst thing in the world," I said, eyes on the other two groomsmen. Koji seemed okay, although he hadn't really talked to me. Too bad neither of those things could be said for Joshua.

"Too bad we WON, loser! You couldn't eliminate us, anyway," Joshua said.

"Too bad I'm supposed to celebrate winning with this tool," Koji said. "Takes the sweetness out of our victory."

Ed sidled closer to me, speaking out the side of his mouth. "Too bad you can't swap J-dawg for Justin and get your groom here on your wedding day."

I sighed. "Too bad, indeed."

"Whatevs," Joshua said. "You wouldn't swap me for Justin. Until your precious groom gets here, there's no one to mind when that rich dude drools all over you."

Logan froze where he stood putting away the "centerpieces." Then he turned and strode into the house, pretending he hadn't heard anything. My face grew warm as I watched him walk away. How embarrassing. "Don't be ridiculous."

Rachel lowered her voice and stepped toward me. "Actually, we've all kind of noticed the way Logan flirts with you."

"Even I see it," Koji said. "And I just met him."

"Oh, yeah. He's totally into you," Birdie said. "#Unrequited."

In shock, I looked from one friend to the next. "You can't be serious. This is the guy who's slept with more people than I went to high school with. He's doing it to create drama."

"Even players have feelings," Joshua said.

Ed cleared his throat. I glared at him. "Oh, no. Don't tell me you're on their side, too."

"All I was going to say is, sometimes players sleep around because they haven't found anyone to care about."

I couldn't believe this ambush. It had to be a trick for the cameras. Without getting upset, I needed to set the record straight. "You guys, there's no way. Logan and I are friends. And apparently, he's one of the few people in this house on my side."

They stared, openmouthed, as I turned to follow Logan into the house.

CHAPTER ELEVEN

<u>Confessions from the Chapel, Tuesday evening:</u>

Logan: There's something different about Jen. In LA, everyone's a phony. But she's so real. I like that about her. And she's drawn to me, too. I can feel it.

Rachel: Jen would never cheat on Justin. Not even with someone as hot and delectable as Logan Cassidy. He makes me wish I hadn't brought Joshua.

Koji: This is the weirdest wedding ever, bro. First, there's no groom. Second, I'm in the wedding party, and I don't think the bride knows my name. Third, the wedding planner creeps me out. A couple of years ago, he was in these commercials for a cologne that had pheromones in it. Supposed to make the wearer literally irresistible. I don't think they aired in the States, but I saw them all over Japan when visiting my obaachan. What's that guy doing flirting with the bride?

Jen: I don't believe for a second Logan has feelings for me. He's friendly with everyone. Right?

<u>Dominic Rossellini to Jen Reid:</u>

Hey, Jen, I know you didn't want me to have to go through the pain of watching you marry someone else. But I heard

Justin's stranded in Florida and can't make it to the wedding. I'd be happy to drive down if you need another groom. You know we could make things work.

<u>Dominic Rossellini to Jen Reid:</u>

Jen???????

<u>Jen Reid to DO NOT PICK UP:</u>

Yes, Dominic, that sounds splendid. There's nothing I'd like more than to marry the ex-boyfriend who cheated on me, lied to me, conspired with the Network against me, and had all of America thinking I'm a home-wrecker. Are you high?

<u>Dominic Rossellini to Jen Reid:</u>

I'll give you half of whatever the Network offers me.

<u>Jen Reid to DO NOT PICK UP:</u>

Never text me again. If I see you in Los Angeles, I'm calling the police.

WEDNESDAY MORNING, the producers announced another surprise: as a gift, Patrick had arranged for the wedding party to visit a local escape room. Everyone piled into a bus while Logan stood at the front and explained what was going to happen.

We'd be locked in a room with an actor dressed as a zombie, chained to an armoire. Every five minutes, a few inches of chain would release. We would navigate around the zombie and solve puzzles to escape the room, and we only had an hour. Anyone the zombie touched or tapped "died" and had to wait in the corner. People in the corner could help those still "alive" by talking through puzzles, but they couldn't touch anything or interfere with the zombie.

My pulse quickened as Logan explained. Justin and I loved escape rooms. We'd even been talking about honeymooning in Boston to try out this amazing questing warehouse we'd heard about. That place was like an escape room on steroids. Too bad Justin couldn't be here to do the challenge. Not only was he excellent at solving puzzles, but we worked well together. Much better than I'd work with, say, Joshua. Or Koji, who I'd exchanged approximately eleven words with since he arrived. Nothing personal, but I had no way of knowing he wasn't a Network spy. Still, eight heads were better than two, and putting the entire wedding party together seemed like a great way to help us bond.

When we arrived at our destination, Patrick waited outside. I eyed him warily. Arranging this outing was a nice gesture, but showing up to get a pat on the back made it go down a bit like the time I chugged a glass of vodka, thinking it was water.

He held the door open, hanging back to allow everyone else inside.

"Thanks for doing this," I said. "I didn't expect you to be here."

"I wasn't planning on it, but since Justin's not here, someone needed to fill in."

On the bus, when Logan mentioned eight heads, I'd assumed he was naming the maximum allowed, not our current number. Now, I did a silent head count: Me, Rachel, Birdie, Ed, Joshua, Koji, Logan...and Patrick. I swallowed back a groan. They couldn't have waited for Adam to arrive? Or brought in Mom? She'd helped foster a love of puzzles and games in me and Adam; this type of event was right up her alley.

On the other hand, if she knew Patrick arranged the event, she'd probably refuse to come, anyway. And getting some bonding moments between me and my father would make better TV than hanging out with my mom, as much as I loved her. Guessing Patrick would be around after we escaped, I'd asked the Network to keep Mom busy for the day. Connor arranged for her to go on a tour of the stars' homes with some of the other out-of-town guests.

The cameras rolled, so instead of arguing, I smiled at Patrick and placed a hand on his arm. "I'm glad you stepped up. It means a lot to me to see how much you've changed. What made you think of doing an escape room?"

If he liked escape rooms, maybe we had something in common other than DNA.

"I read an interview with you and Justin last year," he said. "You talked about how much you loved this type of thing."

An odd feeling fluttered within me. He'd seen the interview? He remembered? Maybe I'd misjudged my father. I wondered if fifteen years without his daughter was punishment enough. He seemed to be making a genuine effort.

He continued, "The interview said the two of you were going to do every escape room you could find, so I wanted one here in SoCal. Tonight was the only night the Network would let me arrange it, though. Sorry we couldn't wait until Justin got to LA."

"It's okay," I said, "I appreciate the effort. We'll still have fun."

Inside the building, a man with long black dreadlocks and gleaming white teeth went over the rules: We got one hour, don't hurt the zombie, don't break the furniture, don't climb the furniture, don't get killed by the zombie. He said that last bit so solemnly, I started to get a bit nervous.

Rachel nudged me. "Relax. Zombies aren't real. They're not going to actually kill us."

"Are you sure?" Birdie mumbled on the other side of me. "I wouldn't put anything past the Network after the cruise."

Our host led the group into the square room, started a timer, then retreated into a corner so he could pull "dead" people out of the game. We had about a hundred square feet to work with. Eight adults did not fit comfortably. An armoire dominated the room, hulking against the back wall, intimidating largely because it was the only space in the room big enough to hold a zombie. A glass case took up most of one wall, with three shelves, each secured by a different type of padlock. A bookcase stood opposite the case, with a desk between the two. The desk had no chair; the only other "furniture" in the room was a filing cabinet, also locked.

Every padlock had different requirements to open it: one required four numbers, one asked for shapes, one wanted five letters, one required a key, one was the standard padlock that adorned every locker in my high school. We got to decipher various clues and solve puzzles to figure out how to open each of them.

Justin would have loved this room. Part of me didn't want to do it without him. Surely, we could wait a couple of days and save ourselves from zombies after Justin arrived? But the Network had a full schedule for the week.

With eight puzzle-solvers, a host, a camerawoman, and eventually a zombie, the temperature in the room went up ten degrees. The Network wasn't allowed to air the solutions to any puzzles, but they'd gotten the okay to take some shots of the zombie and the setup. We barely had room to maneuver. Every time I moved, I tripped over Birdie, or Logan's breath whispered down the back of my neck, making me shiver. But we only had an hour, and soon enough, the presence of a zombie would make it impossible to search the far side of the room for clues. So I dove into the challenge.

At my direction, Rachel darted for the far wall, peeking beneath the portraits and lifting a corner of the carpet. Since she was less mobile, Birdie went for a bookcase next to the door and started seeking clues within the pages of each book. I dropped to the ground and crawled under the desk.

Five minutes later, an alarm sounded, jolting us out of our concentration. Logan shrieked and grabbed my arm. The armoire door cracked open, which triggered everyone else to stop and race for the far corner. Everyone except me and Patrick. We stood with our hands on our hips, glaring at them.

"He's not even out yet," Patrick said. "Come on, kids."

I'd been nervous about him joining us, but my father turned out to be a huge help. He kept a level head while people yelled out fragments of clues. He found paper and a pen and started writing things down. When the zombie emerged and grabbed

Joshua's foot, Patrick convinced him to sit quietly in the corner without break-dancing the way he did when eliminated from *The Fishbowl.*

The group worked steadily, with little time to argue. After only ten minutes, we opened one of the padlocks, which gave us the first symbol for removing the final padlock on the main door. Eight of us celebrated as one. As the clock ticked down the seconds toward our win or loss, I became more and more inclined to trust the man who'd fathered me. I hadn't known anything about him, not really. He deserved more of a chance.

With ten minutes left, only Rachel, Patrick, and I remained "alive." The others sat in the far corner, where Birdie deciphered an encoded paragraph we'd found inside one of the books. The underlined letters, theoretically, would give us one of the final clues. Rachel moved marbles around a Chinese checkers set while Patrick and I called out commands hidden on light fixtures on opposite sides of the room–while dodging the zombie and trying not to trip over the chain tethering him to the armoire. Not the easiest task, but the two of us worked well together. Almost as well as me and Justin.

The last marble clicked into place. Rachel yelled out "heart" from her spot near the desk, right before the zombie grabbed her in a bear hug. She moved into the corner, huffing, while I examined my path to the door. Patrick grabbed the desk and shoved it into the middle of the room, creating a buffer between me and certain "death." The zombie moved backward. While its eyes focused on Patrick, I looped a length of chain around the bottom of the armoire, then darted out of the way.

"I've got it!" Birdie said. "The final clue is, '_____ are a girl's best friend.' Diamonds."

"Don't be so materialistic," Joshua said. "Maybe it's brains."

Koji rolled his eyes. "Yeah, bro, some girls like brains. Which doesn't explain why any of them like you."

Materialistic or not, "diamonds" fit the puzzle in a way "brains" did not. Or cupcakes, which were my best friend outside of, you know, actual human beings. The zombie made a half-hearted swipe as I passed where he lay on the floor. Blinking sweat out of my eyes, I lunged for the final padlock and punched the four symbols I'd been given. Nothing happened.

"It's wrong!" I shouted, trying to keep one eye on the clock, one on the zombie, and one on the padlock. Unfortunately, I didn't have three eyes.

"Did you clear it first?" Patrick asked.

"What?"

"Before you put in the code, you have to push the mechanism to the right twice," he said.

Right. The host had explained how to operate the final lock when we walked in. In my excitement, I completely forgot. With shaking hands, I reached for the padlock again, pushing to the right once, then again.

The zombie growled and lurched for me. I leapt back, away from the door. Patrick skirted the desk, racing back for the armoire. I watched, stuck in one spot. Where I stood, the zombie couldn't reach me, but he blocked me from the exit, and the clock ticked steadily down toward zero. Less than a minute left.

Then the zombie grunted and moved backward. He stumbled, falling to his knees.

"I got him!" Patrick yelled.

Out of the corner of my eye, Patrick held the gathered chain, which forced the zombie toward the armoire. It turned and reached for him. Wiping my hands on the sides of my pants, I lunged for the padlock again.

For the second time, I entered the code. Diamond, spade, heart, spade.

The zombie spun around, reaching for me.

The lock clicked open. I yanked it off the door, wrenching the knob with all my strength. The stale, increasingly ripe air in the tiny room whooshed outward. I stumbled through the doorway, jumping up and down as everyone in the room cheered.

Success!

Patrick grabbed me from behind, sweeping me into his arms and lifting me up over his head. I screamed and clapped before turning around and closing him in a massive hug.

It was the sweetest victory I'd experienced in a long time.

AFTER WE DID our wrap-up interviews, Logan insisted that Patrick accompany us back to the Fishbowl to celebrate our victory with drinks and dessert. After all, he set up the event; he deserved to enjoy the spoils.

I sat beside my father on the bus ride back, reliving every moment of the experience. For those few minutes, it felt like we'd never been apart. When we reached the house and everyone else stampeded into the kitchen, he hung back, motioning me into the living room.

"Thanks for letting me come," Patrick said. "I was worried you would ban me."

"I thought about it. But at the end of the day, it wouldn't have been fair." Also, it would have gone completely against the Plan. I needed to go with the flow, even when I didn't want to. Even when flirting with Logan made me uncomfortable. "Besides, if the producers wanted you there, nothing I could've said would make a difference."

"True, but it means a lot. And I appreciate being included in the party."

"Well, you did save me from a zombie. It would've been horribly rude to deny you ice cream after."

He took my hands and led me to the couch. "Sit down, Jen. I want to ask you something.'

The change in his tone and intense look he gave me made me wonder if he needed my spare kidney. Maybe that was why he'd come back after all these years: not for fame or fortune or to make things right, but because he needed an organ only Adam or I could provide.

"I'm so proud of you, Pumpkin," he said. "I know you don't want to hear this, and I know you must hate me, but I feel so grateful every time I look at you."

"I never hated you," I said, surprised that the words felt true. "I hated that you left us."

"I never wanted to leave you. Your mom and I were like oil and vinegar. There was no way to make it work. And the unfortunate reality of life is that sometimes, when couples split, the kids pay the price. I wish that weren't true."

"It doesn't have to be true. Plenty of divorced couples prioritize their kids."

"You're right, and maybe things would've been different if I hadn't been in the slammer. But I'm here now, and I want to make things right."

"Well, taking me on a zombie adventure was a good start. Really, I appreciate it."

"I'm glad." He swallowed and wiped his hands on his pants before catching my gaze. "Now, listen. I know I have no right to ask you this…"

Here it was. He wanted one of my kidneys. That's why he'd come.

"I've been trying real hard to prove myself to you. We had a nice dinner the other night, and today was a blast. The most fun I've had in ages."

"It was a great day," I said. "Thank you again."

"I want to be your father in truth, Jen," he said. "I don't want to be just some guy sitting in the audience when my baby girl gets married. I've missed too much of your life."

With a start, I realized where he was going. I could have stopped him, given an immediate answer, not made him ask the question that hurt his pride. But I wanted to hear him apologize, to weigh the sincerity of his tone. I wished I were watching this moment on TV, so I could pause and walk away and be certain of my feelings before saying something that could damage the fragile truce we were forming. I wanted to call Mom, ask how she felt. But real life didn't give time-outs. Besides, I knew how she felt about my father's reappearance.

When he spoke again, tears glistened in his eyes. "I know you're not property and you certainly don't need to be 'given away,' and I know I don't have any right to ask, but it would mean the world to me if you'd let me walk you down the aisle on Saturday."

Never would I have predicted the gut punch those words carried. My mouth went dry. For fifteen years, I would've done anything in the world to get my father's attention. I'd have walked over hot coals if it meant he'd attend the father-daughter dance so I wouldn't be the only girl who missed out. And now, here he was in front of me, extending the olive branch I'd dreamed of.

My heart pounded. The Network held me over an emotional chasm the size of the Grand Canyon. I didn't know if I could walk next to the father who abandoned me with a smile. I didn't know if I wanted to. But the cameras were on me, and he deserved an answer. The Network obviously wanted me to say yes. They might make me reshoot if I didn't play along. Or perhaps they'd stage another, more touching father-daughter moment tomorrow.

Not knowing what to do, I pictured myself walking into the wedding alone. Then I pictured it again, this time holding on to my father's arm. In my imagination, he looked so dashing in his tux, I could see why Mom fell for him, all those years ago. My heart ached.

To my surprise, my vision blurred. I blinked repeatedly to gain control of myself. I started to speak, but my mouth was dry. Someone handed me a glass of water, which I gulped gratefully before trying again.

"I appreciate how hard it must have been for you to come here this week," I said. "You probably weren't expecting to be welcomed back with open arms, and it takes guts to show up anyway. It means a lot to me. On top of that, you spent a lot of time–"

Raised voices floated through the doorway from the hall, cutting me off.

"Don't be ridiculous!"

Mom. I wondered who she was talking to.

"I'm going in to see my daughter. I don't care what you're filming. Get your hands off me, young man!"

At that, I stood. I didn't know what was going on, but I wasn't about to let them manhandle my mother. My guess was, they didn't want my parents to meet face-to-face without exactly the right contrived moment.

Before I made it across the room, Mom appeared in the doorway. "Jen! There are you. I don't know what's wrong with the producers. They told me not to disturb you."

"You're always welcome in this house, Mom. It's okay."

"I figured you were with the wedding planner." She spotted my father and turned to him, extending one hand. "Hello. I'm Tina Carter. Who are you?"

CHAPTER 11.5

The camera opens on an exterior shot of a bridal boutique.

Justin: No, I'm not looking for a wedding gown. Since we still don't have a flight, Sarah and I are here to try on her dress. She's a bit camera-shy when she's not talking about baked goods, so I told her to meet me here in another ten minutes. I've worked out a surprise.

The camera goes dark. A moment later, racks of white dresses in plastic bags fill the scene. The camera pans to the left, past the dressing room doors, then onto a rainbow of bridesmaid and mother-of-the-bride dresses.

Justin (voice from inside the dressing room): *Ready?*

A woman's voice (off-camera): *Ready!*

The dressing room door opens. Justin stands in a strapless, floor-length white gown with a lace bodice and a wide ribbon around the waist. The bottom of the dress bells out. A glittering belt wraps all the way up his left arm. On his head sits a tiara with a veil. He exits the dressing room, the train of the dress and the long veil flowing out behind him.

A bell rings, out of sight. The camera pans to Sarah, standing in the doorway. She takes one look at Justin and bursts out laughing.

Justin: What's so funny? Am I not a beautiful bride?

Sarah is doubled over, unable to speak. Justin pulls on the sash around his waist, and it comes off. The bottom of the dress falls away, leaving Justin in a lace sheath.

Justin: Look! I'm ready for the reception.

Sarah wipes her eyes. Stop! I'm crying here.

Justin: I don't know what's so funny. Cut your hair, and you're looking at your own wedding day, twin sister. It's the happiest day of your life!

Sarah straightens. Right. My wedding day is something we need to discuss when I haven't met anyone I wanted to date in like a year.

Justin: Two and a half, but who's counting?

Sarah shoots her brother a dirty look. The camera returns to an extreme close-up of Justin. Okay, so I lied about not trying on dresses. But it was worth it for the look on Sarah's face.

The shop's owner greets Sarah in the voice previously heard off-camera. The camera is handed off to someone else before another woman shows Sarah a rack of three teal dresses. She takes all three into the dressing room with a stern look back at the camera. *Don't even try to follow me with that thing.*

A moment later, the dressing room door opens, revealing Sarah in a black trash bag, head and arms sticking out a hole in the top.

Justin: You know, I always said you'd be a knockout even in a garbage bag, but isn't this a bit much?

Sarah sticks out her lower lip. Well, I had the idea before I got here, and I couldn't let you ruin it. Hold on.

A moment later, the door opens again. Sarah wears a shimmering, mermaid-style, floor-length, blue-green gown. *We're all wearing this? Isn't Birdie nine months pregnant?*

Justin: Eight. She's wearing something else. Same color, I think.

Sarah: Great! If we're all in different styles, I'm going to dye my trash bag. She sticks her tongue out at the camera.

Justin: Ladies and gentlemen, I'd like to apologize for my sister.

Sarah: Don't blame me. You're the one who wanted to become a reality star.

Justin's voice, still off-camera, softens. *Best decision I ever made.*

Sarah smiles. *I think so, too. But I'm still glad I didn't go with you.* She moves toward the camera, arms outstretched. The scene is lost behind a mass of curly blond hair. *I'm so happy for you and Jen!*

CHAPTER TWELVE

<u>Confessions from the Chapel, Wednesday:</u>

Jen: I feel so stupid. I can't believe I fell for the Network's tricks. Of course he's not my father. My father would never care enough to show up for my wedding. Excuse me.

Tina: This is what you people do for a living? How do you sleep at night? This is it for me and the reality TV stuff. I'll be back for my daughter's wedding. And I won't have anything to say to you then, either.

"Patrick": What do you want me to say? GOTCHA! I was doing good, am I right? She loved how helpful I was in the escape room. The Network gave me all the answers before we went in. It's too bad her mom showed up and ruined our touching moment. Tina's a knockout, but what awful timing.

My MOTHER'S words punched me in the stomach. "Who are you?" echoed throughout the room until those words were the only thing that existed. I stared at the man I'd thought to be my father until the second my mother failed to recognize him.

"Close your mouth, dear," Mom said. "You're catching flies."

The man beside me turned bright red. He started to say something, but I found my voice and cut him off.

"Mom. This man came to the house as part of the show, to 'give me away'." I struggled to keep my voice steady. I should've known something like this would happen. The Network always had another trick. The moment Patrick walked in the door, I suspected something was up. But I wanted so badly to believe my father was back in my life, I'd ignored my instincts.

"Why on earth would he do that?"

"I'm Jen's father," he said.

Mom laughed. "No, you're not."

"'Course I am."

"I'm pretty sure I'd remember having sex with you," Mom said. "Jen, I don't know who this man is, but he's not your father."

"I gathered." To Not-Patrick, I said, "Who the fuck are you? Actually, on second thought, I don't care. It doesn't matter."

"Jan, wait, let me explain," he said. "Oh, shit. Jen. Sorry. *Jen*, let me explain."

"No. No. No. Nononono."

Spinning around, I stormed out of the living room, not sure where to go. All I knew was that I needed to get out of there. I raced through the kitchen, pausing to snatch my phone out of its drawer before bolting through the back doors onto the patio. My friends sat there, but I couldn't talk to them yet.

When Birdie saw my face, she broke off speaking to Rachel, who spun around. Both of them took a step toward me, but I held up my hand in a "stop" sign without breaking my stride. Neither of them could make me feel better.

I needed Justin. I didn't even slow down when I reached the maze, ducking under the yellow tape blocking the entrance and heading straight for the center. Almost two years after the last time I'd been here, I didn't expect to remember all the twists and turns, but it didn't matter. I needed to get away. If I didn't come out, someone would find me. My legs ached by the time I found a bench and flopped onto it.

The Network couldn't be trusted. That wasn't a secret. Leanna, Janine, and the higher-ups only cared about ratings and drama. That wasn't a secret, either. But I couldn't believe they'd hire a stranger to pretend to be my estranged father. To show up, apologize for everything, make amends, and then what? What were they going to do, anyway? Have my alcoholic "father" get drunk and ruin the reception? Puke on me before the ceremony? Arrange a face-to-face meeting with my mother to blow up at the worst possible moment?

Despair filled me. I didn't know how many more of these surprises I could handle on my own. The Plan required me and Justin to roll with the punches, to do what we needed to do, but when we made the Plan, we expected to stand together as a team. Half my team remained in Florida while I dealt with all the crap by myself. We stood stronger together, and the Network's emotional manipulation might break me without my partner by my side.

When I pulled out my phone, my arm shook with rage. I was so furious I didn't even realize I'd started crying until teardrops splashed onto the screen. Justin's phone went straight to voice mail. I sent him a 911 text, then let the device drop out of my hand onto the grass. Not knowing what else to do, I lowered my head into my hands and sobbed.

Why did any of this surprise me? The Network brought both my ex-boyfriend and his ex-wife on a cruise ship with me for a week. They stranded me in a foreign country with Dominic. One of the producers stole a video I'd taken of Ariana with Dominic and broadcast it on the upper decks to humiliate her. Obviously, hiring an actor to play my estranged father wasn't beneath them.

Stupid me, I'd thought Connor was on my side. I'd thought having my best friend's partner as a senior member of the production staff might make a difference. But here I was, back on their turf, letting them play with my emotions. Would I never learn?

The sun cast long shadows through the maze by the time anyone found me. Rustling leaves and crackling twigs signaled someone's approach. Ed appeared first, hands spread wide, looking more serious than I'd seen him in ages. "I come in peace."

"Tell me you didn't know about this." If one of my best friends had been in on the Network's plot, nothing in my world made any sense. I'd hop the next flight east and worry about getting sued later.

"I had no idea," he said.

"What about your other half?"

Ed gestured, and a white T-shirt waved at the end of the row of hedges. A moment later, Connor poked his head into view, looking sheepish. "I told them not to do it."

"You knew?"

"And you didn't tell me?" Ed said, pain cracking his voice.

"I didn't know, exactly," he said. "It was clear something was up, but I didn't know what bombshell they planned to drop. Even though I have a confidentiality agreement, too, I guess Janine and Leanna didn't trust me with something this big. Which sucks. If anyone finds out they think I'm in cahoots with the talent, I'll never get a job in this town again."

"That doesn't sound so bad," I muttered under my breath.

"Maybe not for you," Connor said, "but this is my *life*. This is what I've always wanted. I've dreamed about this since I was five years old. Not this show, per se, but television. I need to pay my dues to get the type of show where I can make a difference. They're already watching me because of Ed. Soon, the closest I'll be able to get to TV is answering phones at the PBS telethon."

"So you're willing to sell out your friends for your job?"

"Of course not," he insisted. "They didn't tell me."

Nibbling on one thumbnail, I considered his words. If he knew and didn't tell me, I didn't see any way we could continue being friends. The Network's betrayal went way beyond the reality show antics I'd come to expect. But he seemed sincere.

I let out a heavy sigh. "What did you know?"

"I tried to find your father to bring him in. But we never made contact. When that guy showed up, I figured they'd used the Network's resources to track him down. I didn't know what your dad looked like."

After everything I'd been through, his words sparked nothing in me. Of course they hadn't found my real father. And he probably wouldn't have come, even if they had. That was why I hadn't been happy to see Fake Patrick when he showed up. I should've trusted my instincts.

"I want to believe you."

"Would it help if I told you what I found out after you stormed out?"

"Maybe," I said. "Tell me, and then I'll decide."

"They were going to detain your mother to keep her away from the ceremony. Flat tire, I think. Then the actor playing your father was going to get drunk before the ceremony and cause a scene walking you down the aisle. A fight maybe, step on your dress and 'accidentally' rip it off, or maybe trip and push you into the pool."

"He can't do that," I said. "There's no way to make it as dramatic as when I fell off the balcony of the *Queen Kelly* last year."

Ed sat beside me. "Glad to see you've still got your sense of humor."

"I can't afford to lose it. The producers are determined to get to me. I refuse to let them."

"Not all the producers," Connor said. This time, I gave a small smile to let him know I believed him. "Why don't we go talk to your mom?"

I followed him down the row to a fork in the maze. I started to turn left, toward the front, when he called me back.

"That's a dead end," I said.

"No it's not," Ed said, winking at me. "It's a secret exit."

They had to be messing with me, but I followed, waiting to see the rest of the joke. To my surprise, when we got to the corner nearest the house, Connor reached into the maze and tugged. The hedge in front of us swung outward.

"Ed, how did you know about this?" I asked.

"During *The Fishbowl*, Connor and I met here in the middle of the night. There weren't any cameras in that part of the maze. You can open it from the other side, but it's harder to find the trigger. Inside, it's next to this discolored branch." He pointed.

I couldn't believe my eyes. Eight weeks in the house two summers ago, and I hadn't the slightest idea.

After we left the maze, the three of us followed the yard around to the pool, where my mom sat at an umbrella-covered table, sipping an iced tea.

She stood when she saw me and came over for a hug. Connor and Ed turned toward the kitchen, giving us some privacy.

"You showed up at the perfect moment. How did you know?"

"One of the PAs came to my hotel and asked me to come back to the house with her. Vera something."

"Vera?" The name meant nothing to me. "They all told me they weren't allowed to give out names. How do you know it was a PA?"

"She followed us around Tiffany. Tall, black, excellent hair?"

"Oh. Great Hair?"

"Great, excellent. Whatever. Her name is Vera." Mom sighed and shook her head. "Honestly, what were the producers thinking would happen? Did they think I wouldn't recognize my ex-husband because we divorced so long ago? It's not like I haven't seen or talked to him since the judge entered the decree."

I raised my eyebrows at her. "You've seen him?"

"Of course I have. Every year when he dragged me back to court to try to get his child support reduced, I saw him for fifteen minutes in the courtroom."

I sighed. "I didn't know. Sorry."

"Don't you be sorry," she said. "It's my job to protect my children from these things. When the Network asked me for your father's address and phone number, of course I refused to give them anything. But…"

"But what?"

She took a sudden interest in her perfectly manicured pink fingernails. "Nothing. Never mind."

"Mother." My voice took on the same tone she used when she found seven-year-old me removing stitches from Adam's knee to see how they worked. "Do you know where my father is?"

"Do you want him here?"

"No."

"Then why does it matter?"

She had a point, and yet, it did matter. "Because you led me to believe he walked out and severed all ties and no one has heard from him since. Because the actor hired by the Network told me you ordered him to stay away from me and Adam, and I'm suddenly wondering if there's a nugget of truth to that. Because you never talked about what happened between the two of you."

"Nothing *happened*," she said. "Sometimes two people grow apart. We married pretty young, you know—we were both in our twenties."

A lump grew in my throat. "I'm twenty-seven. Justin's twenty-eight."

"Oh, sure, but you know yourself. You and Justin have been together almost two years. You're living with his sister, and the two of you own a business together. You see each other every day. You're cemented into the Taylor family. We didn't have any of that. We had a whirlwind romance that gave us two kids before we managed to catch our collective breath, and when the dust settled, we realized we didn't like each other very much."

I'd never heard this version of my parents' marriage. When they divorced, Mom was so sad, I didn't ask about it. And I hadn't let myself think about him much since. It never occurred to me that it took two people to end their marriage.

"That sucks." Realizing your parents are real people also sucks, but I didn't say so.

"It's fine. I got over our failed marriage when you were a child. Filing the paperwork came as a relief. What hurt most was the way he disappeared on you and your brother after we split. He didn't realize ending the marriage didn't have to end his relationship with you two. But I let go of all that years ago. So should you."

"But you know where he is?"

"Yeah, I do. Do you want him here?"

I thought about it for a long time. "No. I really don't."

"If you change your mind, I'll call him. You can have his info any time."

Curiosity gripped me. "Has he changed?"

"I don't know. Maybe it's time to reach out to him, either way. Then at least you'd get some closure." She nodded toward the patio. Logan stood with his hands in his pockets, looking at the ground. "It looks like the Network needs you."

I sighed as she stood. "Fine, I'll see what they want. Thanks, Mom."

"No problem. Remember, this show is one week of your lives. Your marriage is forever."

Her words sent a pang into my heart. It killed me that she didn't know we were married already. I'd have to find a way to tell her, off camera, before Saturday, especially if Justin didn't make it. But I didn't want her to see I was bothered, so I forced a smile. "Thanks, Mom."

She walked away. Not willing to give an inch to the Network, I gazed at the table until a shadow fell across it.

"Is this seat taken?" Logan asked.

"Who's asking?" I said. "For a representative of the Network, the seat is most definitely taken."

"What about for Logan, the devastatingly handsome, incredibly charming guy who made it his primary goal to keep you happy until the wedding?"

"I guess Logan can sit." Finally, I met his eyes. "Did you plan this?"

"The fake dad? Oh, hell no. I throw awesome parties. Cake toppers and favors and vows and stuff. I don't create faux drama. That's the Network."

"Why are you helping me? Why do the show at all? Hell, why are you even doing your *own* show? Wasn't being De-Virginizer of the Stars working for you?"

He winced. "That was never me."

"Don't tell me. It was your wacky identical twin cousin?" He snorted, and I continued. "Don't get me wrong. I don't care who you sleep with. But your show seemed like a total one-eighty from the Logan Cassidy plastered across the Internet every day when I was in college."

"That was the point," he said. "We needed to turn my image around. I mean, most of that stuff you saw in the tabloids was garbage. I didn't have a threesome with two eighteen-year-olds. I saw some guy at the bar slip something into their drinks. I followed them, punched him out, and took them home. The paparazzi saw me leaving the cabin with a girl on each arm, but no one bothered to get the full story."

His words made me pause. That story seemed more in sync with the person I'd come to know than what I'd read online. And I knew better than most how the media liked to distort stories to make them more sensational. Facts had no place in "news" anymore. At the same time, he'd been faking an attraction to me all week. Unless Rachel and Joshua and Koji were right. Hell, I didn't know what to believe anymore.

"That was great of you. But then why did you enter rehab?"

"Because I *was* completely stoned when it happened. And pretty much every day before that. Just because I didn't do one specific terrible thing doesn't mean I didn't need help."

"True. Why didn't you tell anyone the truth about the girls?"

"Because it didn't matter." He shrugged. "People read the flashy headlines, not the tiny retractions. For the record, I also didn't seduce the princess of some foreign country I can't even remember."

I chuckled at the memory of that rumor. "Genovia."

"See? I don't even know where that is."

"It's the made-up country from *The Princess Diaries*." I smiled at him. "Some of us knew it wasn't true."

He shook his head. "The world has gotten so weird. Anyway, yeah, I partied a bit in school. Who didn't? I drank a lot, did drugs, slept around. I'm not proud of it, but I'm not ashamed, either. It's part of who I am."

"Then why the makeover?"

"Two things. One, my mom freaked when she saw the headlines. She believed me when I told her what happened, but insisted I improve my image."

I thought about how my mom would react to a headline about me having sex with two teenagers. Even legal teenagers. "Fair enough. Two?"

"When I got out of school, I realized I didn't want to go straight into the hotel business. I wanted to make something of myself first, see if I could be more than just the rich kid who caused trouble. I like weddings. And some day, this will all help me with events in our hotels. Win, win, win, you know?"

The patio door slid open, and Rachel stuck her head out, mouthing an "OK?" over Logan's shoulder. Birdie peeked out below her, and Ed's head appeared above Rachel's. I nodded and flashed a thumbs-up at them. Logan gave me a quizzical look, but didn't turn around. My friends vanished from the doorway, but a second later, the door opened all the way, and the three of them passed by on their way to the pool.

The warm water seemed inviting, stress-free. No fake dads or body paint lurked beneath the waves.

"I get it," I said. "Thanks, Logan. If the Network doesn't need me right now, I'm going to join my friends."

He reached across the table as I stood, his thumb rubbing the back of my hand. His blue eyes filled with sincerity. "You've got a friend here, too, you know. Whenever you need one. I'll do anything I can to help make this wedding go smoothly."

At least someone in the house was on my side. Maybe.

CHAPTER THIRTEEN

Madison Green to Jen Reid:

We're flying out tonight! Can't wait to see you!

Jen Reid to Madison Green:

Me, too! Is your flight okay? Half the wedding party is stranded due to Hurricane Cara.

Madison Green to Jen Reid:

I got a direct from JFK to LAX. Should be fine. Storm is way south.

Jen Reid to Madison Green:

Great! Can't wait to see your beautiful baby.

Madison Green to Jen Reid:

We'll see. I got 45 minutes of sleep last night. He might not make it to LA.

Jen Reid to Madison Green:

Please do not get arrested on the way to my wedding. Talky Ted would have a field day.

Madison Green to Jen Reid:

I'll do my best. For you, of course.

. . .

THE NEXT MORNING AFTER BREAKFAST, Logan took me around the grounds, pointing out his vision for the ceremony. It all sounded lovely, if exactly the same as when he last explained it. At least I felt calmer about the disaster this wedding was turning into after getting outside and walking around for a while.

Our tour ended on the patio beside the pool. I waited while he told me again about rose petals on the pool and fairy lights spelling out "Jen & Justin 4-Eva." At least they weren't dyeing the pool water red as a testament to our love or something.

"Everything sounds wonderful," I said, trying to mean it. "Thank you for all the work you put into this."

"I've got a confession to make," he said. "I didn't just bring you out here so we could walk around the grounds."

"Oh, no? You didn't want the joy of listening to me rant about the evilness of the Network and how annoying Joshua is for the past forty-five minutes?"

He laughed, not the horrible forced sound he used on-air, but the real laugh saved for more private moments. I liked it. "Not that you aren't delightful company, but no. There's something else we need to talk about."

"Please tell me there isn't more bad news about my cake." My plan to call and order a real cake had been foiled by the simple fact that the Network had my purse—and all my credit cards—until filming wrapped up. I'd never managed to reach Sarah.

"I'm going to assume you consider 'it's still going to be all natural' to be terrible news."

"Yup," I said. "What's wrong now?"

"I wouldn't necessarily say *wrong*," Logan said, "But I've got your vows here, and I don't think you're going to like them."

"What do you mean, I won't like them? Did I imagine you helping me write vows the other day? Justin's working on his, too."

"Yeah, I gave those to Janine, and she sent me back with this.

She said your vows didn't have enough 'wow factor,' and they wanted something people would remember."

"Wow factor? She said my vows needed *wow factor*? Is she high? Wedding vows should come from the heart."

Cartoon smoke must have been emerging from my ears, because Logan stepped away, stuffing the pages into his back pocket. "It's no big deal. I can give them to you later."

"Don't you dare."

"No, it's fine. I'm sorry. You're having a rough week. Let's go do something fun."

Hands out, I approached. He stepped backward again, onto the cement edge of the pool. "Give me the pages, Logan. If it's as bad as you say, we'll do shots after."

"Actually, I lied," he said smoothly, sidestepping me. "They're wonderful. I'm sure you've always wanted to tell Justin that your love is as vast as the ocean, and that you pray you never have to make him walk the plank."

I stopped dead. "It doesn't say that."

"Of course it doesn't. Who would think because you got engaged on a cruise ship, you wanted vows full of nautical references? My personal favorite part is where Justin talks about embarking on life's journey with you, praying for smooth waters."

His eyes twinkled, but he met my gaze squarely. Logan was highly amused at the train wreck…er, shipwreck…someone had made of my vows. But he wasn't lying. Not about this.

"We're not going to say those things," I said. "But you have to let me see it."

"If you're not going to say them, what does it matter?"

"Because I want to know what they're going to dub over my actual vows when the show airs."

Laughing, I put my arms out, and again he moved away. This was getting ridiculous. I lunged forward, grabbing Logan by the wrist and pulling him toward me, harder than I meant to. Our bodies collided, and the firmness pressing against my stomach made my eyes widen. I looked up, prepared to demand the vows again, but impact of his body against mine knocked the words out of me.

Instead of speaking, I reached my arms around Logan's back, pulling him even closer. His pupils dilated. I pressed my boobs into him, watching his gaze drop to the top of my sundress. Logan's hands found my hips.

"You're not laughing anymore," he said.

"Suddenly, things don't seem very funny."

My hands moved down his back, tracing the firm muscles beneath his too-tight T-shirt. I slipped one hand into the pocket of his jeans, cupping his ass firmly with my right hand. As Logan dipped his head down toward my lips, my questing fingers found their prize in his other back pocket. Triumphantly, I pulled the vows out of Logan's pocket and shoved away from him.

My sudden movement threw him off balance. Logan stepped backward, his foot slipping into the open air above the pool. As he fell, his long fingers closed around my wrist. The two of us flew through the toward into the deep end. With my last coherent thought before we hit the surface, I tossed the papers behind me, hoping they landed on the deck so I could still read them.

WE LANDED WITH A SPLASH. Cold water enveloped us. Chlorinated water filled my still-open mouth. My hair swarmed around me, blinding me with a mass of extensions. I put my hands out, wanting to put some distance between me and Logan before pushing for the surface. My palm came into contact with something firm, yet soft. It was only after the object began to grow and harden that I realized what I'd inadvertently grabbed.

Snatching my hand away like I'd been burned, I planted my feet against the bottom of the eight-foot-deep pool, and stretched for the sunlight above me. One good kick, and I was out in the air again, coughing and sputtering. Despite the coolness of the water, my face burned when I emerged, gasping for breath.

I didn't want to see Logan's face when he broke the surface. Instead, I swam for the stairs in the shallow end.

On the other side of the pool, I gasped for breath, willing my racing heart to slow. So Logan had almost kissed me. It didn't mean anything. I'd only gotten close to him to steal the vows. Vows he knew I'd tackle him to get if necessary. This was the guy who was famous for being a player. He'd probably perfected those moves in kindergarten. Standing a little too close, flirting a little too much.

The memory of those pages made me turn to scan the water, but I didn't like what I saw. Not the papers, Logan. His head broke the surface, gasping, then went back under. His arms flailed. Uh-oh. I didn't know he couldn't swim. He'd sat on the sidelines when we were splashing around, but I'd figured he had better things to do than join us.

"Hold on, Logan!" I yelled. "I'm coming for you."

With a lunge, I pushed off the side of the pool, my arms and legs slicing through the water. Seconds later, I reached his side.

"It's okay, Logan. I've got you."

One of his flailing arms hit me in the eye, sending my head under the water. I tried to grab him, but he was moving around too much. His left hand tangled in my hair with a force that brought tears to my eyes. This would never work.

Usually, when someone is hysterical, they say the answer is to slap them. However, the water slowed my movement, so instead of a slap, I found myself cupping Logan's face, the brush of his stubble sending tingles up my arm.

His wide eyes met mine beneath the surface, and the flailing stopped. A shiver went through me. Even though it was June, it was still morning, and this water chilled me to the bone. We needed to get out of here.

"It's okay," I mouthed. "I've got you."

Logan was bigger than me, more muscular, heavier, and his clothes weighed him down. I tugged at him, managing to break the surface and gasp some air before he dragged me back down. This wasn't working.

When I was in college, they made everyone on the diving team take a lifeguarding course, but it had been years. I reached for his belt, pulling at the leather so I could tow him to the deck. Once the belt came free, Logan's pants dropped, revealing very tight purple boxer briefs I never needed to see. My eyes went to his crotch involuntarily, and my hand burned as if the earlier contact branded me. He kicked out of his shoes, letting the pants float away.

Without the weight of his heavy shoes, we shot to the surface. I egg-beatered my legs, placing the leather belt into Logan's hand while maintaining a safe distance. We couldn't afford for him to keep pulling me under.

"Hold this. Lie on your back."

He didn't respond. I rolled him over, but his eyes were shut. Oh, no. Here I was distracted by the bulge in his pants, and my friend was drowning. What the hell was wrong with me?

With not a second to lose, I grabbed the collar of his shirt and towed Logan to the shallow end. I pulled him up the steps, resting his head on the top. His eyes were still shut. I slapped him lightly.

"Logan? Logan? Can you hear me?"

No response.

Tilting his head to the side, I opened his mouth. Water dribbled out. He wasn't moving. Groping for his wrist, I found a pulse. But when I moved my head closer to his, I couldn't hear any breathing. Couldn't feel air against my cheek.

With a deep breath, I plugged his nose with my left hand, and pressed my mouth to his.

Logan moaned, a deep rumble in his throat. His strong arms came around me, pulling my body flush against his, and his lips moved beneath me. Before I could react, his tongue darted into my mouth, circling mine. This was not the response of a drowning man. I started to pull away, but Logan rolled, landing firmly on top of me, his crotch rubbing between my legs.

Oh, hell. Technically, this was part of the Plan, but when Justin and I made the Plan, I'd never expected to feel so awkward. Logan's lips mashed against my teeth until I could barely breathe. His tongue helicoptered around mine. He had the most enormous tongue in the world. Maybe he was in the Guinness World Records book for it. In stark contrast to his usual pleasant, musky scent, the stench of chlorine filled my nostrils.

Kissing him back wasn't even an option. I couldn't move my head. There wasn't room in my mouth for both our tongues. His teeth scraped mine. Not knowing what else to do, I whimpered. I tangled my hands into his hair, tugging slightly. When he pulled back enough for me to get a breath, I let out a breathy sigh.

"Oh, Justin…"

He jerked his head back, allowing glorious oxygen to rush into my lungs. "What did you say?"

One hand went to my mouth. "What the hell are you doing?"

"What the hell are you doing, kissing me and using some other guy's name?"

I suppressed a giggle at his outrage. "What are you doing, kissing me like that at all? I'm about to marry that other guy!"

"Sweetheart, I hate to break it to you, but you kissed me."

"That's called mouth-to-mouth," I said. "I thought you were dying."

He smiled, a slow, sensual movement that reminded me of his entire body still pressed against mine. "Well, I'm glad to see you'll miss me when I'm gone."

Rolling my eyes, I shoved at him. "Get off me. I was trying to save your life."

Even knowing it was okay, even knowing I could kiss Logan

if I wanted for the show, it felt wrong. I wasn't positive his feelings for me were pretend. He wasn't some random guy. Logan was a friend. If his flirtation was more than an act for the cameras, taking advantage made me a horrible person.

He raised himself up on his arms, allowing me to slither out from under him, pulling myself out of the pool. "I've never been a lifeguard, but I didn't think mouth-to-mouth involved tongues and full-body contact."

"That was all you, *bro*." I said. "Next time I'll let you drown."

Ugh. Justin seriously owed me for this. The last thing I wanted to do when I came on the show was argue over who initiated the worst kiss of my life.

The papers that started this whole mess sat beside the pool. Water covered most of the deck, but I still wanted to see what vows the Network wrote for me. Ignoring Logan, I swept the pages up with one hand and turned toward the house.

"You keep telling yourself that."

The words brought me to a halt. I spun around. "What are you talking about?"

"We've had a connection since day one." Logan pulled himself out of the pool slowly, shedding water as he went. I tried not to notice the way his sodden shirt plastered itself to his muscular frame. The bulge in his drenched boxers. "Before we went into the water, you put your arms around me. You looked deep into my eyes, and I know you felt the same thing I did."

"I was trying to get the damn pages you were hiding behind your back," I said, waving them in the air.

That sensual smile never left his face. He kept walking toward me, a tiger stalking his prey. I was suddenly very aware of the way my very cold nipples pressed against my wet sundress. When Logan stood only a step away, he spoke again. This time his voice was low, like a caress. "You wanted to kiss me. I saw it in your eyes."

"You're imagining things. I'm in love with Justin."

"Justin's not here."

"I still love him!"

"Maybe, but you *want* me," he said. "And you know I want you. You felt it in the pool."

I couldn't move. Couldn't speak. He stepped closer again. His pupils obliterated the blue of his eyes.

The producers must be giddy, watching us. I swallowed, letting the air stretch and thicken between us.

"I'm getting married in less than a week," I finally said.

"Maybe. Or maybe within the next week, you'll be lying with me, our limbs tangled, breathing hard." His lips nearly touched my ear. "We've gotten to know each other very well the last few days, and I think I'm falling in love with you, Jen."

A shiver went through me. I wanted to push him away, but couldn't. This wasn't part of the Plan. My whole body shook, whether with rage or the cold, I didn't know. This needed to stop, immediately.

Logan continued to speak, his voice moving along my jaw. "In a second, I'm going to kiss you again. You're going to kiss me back. And you're not going to be able to blame it on the vows, or the pool, or anything other than how badly you want me."

Justin and I talked about this. I could kiss him again. It would boost the ratings. It wasn't cheating. It probably would be only the second-worst kiss of my life, if I were expecting it. But I didn't want to kiss him. Not even when it wasn't real.

Joshua's words by the pool the other day came rushing back to me. The words Ed and Rachel and even Koji all seemed to agree with: Did Logan have feelings for me? I assumed he was putting on an act for the show, but if he were sincere, playing with him wasn't an option. I couldn't allow myself to take that step as long as it might mean something to him. No matter how strongly I suspected he felt nothing, playing with Logan's emotions wasn't fair to him, to me, or to Justin.

That thought finally broke through my stupor, bringing me back to reality. As Logan's lips descended toward mine, I put one hand over his mouth. My voice shook. "No. You're wrong. You may be an expert at seduction, but this isn't going to happen."

Before he could change my mind, I turned and bolted for the house.

CHAPTER FOURTEEN

Jen Reid to Justin Taylor:

Grossest. Kiss. EVER. Thank you for never trying to choke me to death with your tongue.

Justin Taylor to MRS. Reid:

You're welcome? Or I'm sorry?

Jen Reid to Justin Taylor:

You should be. I guess it's a small price to pay for your ongoing employment.

Justin Taylor to MRS. Reid:

You're the best. I promise to kiss whoever you want when I get there.

Jen Reid to Justin Taylor:

Don't tempt me. Anyway, Rach and J-dawg and Koji seem to think Logan has real feelings for me. I can't do this anymore. I'll go with the flow, but no more flirting. Definitely no more kisses.

Justin Taylor to MRS. Reid:

Fair enough.

Justin Taylor to MRS. Reid:

Who's Koji?

. . .

My dress fitting went smoothly, thankfully. The Network still seemed to be planning to let me wear a dress I loved, it fit, and the alterations were no big deal. Sponsors sent a variety of shoes to the shop, I found a pair I liked, and they were the perfect height with the hem. The seamstress promised to deliver dress, shoes, and accessories to the Fishbowl the following afternoon.

After lunch, all the members of the wedding party who'd made it to Los Angeles went out to the pool area, where floodlights blazed in the daylight. Five podiums had been set up, like on *Jeopardy!* Affixed to the front of each was one of the color-coded fish we'd used during *The Fishbowl*, each with a different person's name on it.

No one had mentioned the kiss yet, and for a moment, I worried this was a setup where they'd confront me with it. But that didn't seem quite dramatic enough.

Logan stood in front of the podiums. "The original plan for this afternoon was to put Jen and Justin through a *Newlywed*-style game to see which of them knows the other better."

"I do," I said automatically.

"I'm sure you do, Jen," Logan said, with his cheesy TV-host wink. "But you admit the game's a wee bit less fair if your spouse isn't here to play along?"

I nodded, and he continued. "Anyway, so we had to mix it up a bit. There are no teams for this challenge. It's every person for himself," Logan said. "We've got five contestants, competing to answer the question: Who Knows Jen *and* Justin the Best?"

Rachel and Ed exchanged fake glares.

"Oh, it is *on* like Donkey Kong!" Rachel said.

"Whatever," Ed said. "Who's her best friend?"

"Um…Sarah is," Rachel shot back. "Which you'd know, if you knew her best."

Rachel was right. Had Sarah made it in time to participate in this game, she'd have blown everyone else away. They would have needed to give her a disadvantage. One person answering all the questions correctly makes for boring TV.

Logan cleared his throat. "Funny you should mention that. Since Sarah couldn't be here today, and *The Newlywed Game* is off the table, she emailed me a list of questions."

Rachel smirked at Ed. Birdie put one hand on her stomach, looking a little queasy, but assured us she was fine. Joshua had gone pale. Koji pulled out his phone and started tapping. He could have been looking up some random facts or texting a friend to meet him for drinks later.

"You've each got a buzzer, thanks to our sponsor, Cheap-O Buzzers 'R Us," Logan said. "I'm going to ask a question. You'll hit your buzzer. Whoever buzzes in first gets to answer. Jen will tell you if you're right or wrong. Five points per right answer. If you're wrong, it's negative three points, and someone else gets to buzz in. The winner gets to join Jen at the spa on Saturday morning for side-by-side massages."

Birdie rubbed her lower back and grinned. "Oh, step back everyone. That prize is mine! #PregnancySucks."

"Any questions? Okay, take your places!"

Everyone moved behind their podiums, and I went to stand by Logan, not knowing where else to go. "Try not to give anything away, okay? Unless I ask you for a hint."

"No problem," I said. "They'll be fine."

The questions started off easy enough: What does Justin do for a living, what's the name of my bakery, what's Justin's sister's name? The key to winning seemed to lie in buzzing-in first. Joshua, Rachel, and Ed answered questions easily, while Birdie shook her buzzer and scowled at it. Koji never touched his buzzer, but at least he put his phone down.

After about half a dozen warm-up questions, the questions moved from preliminaries into specific events from the shows.

"How many stories did Jen fall from the deck of the *Boaty McBoatface*?" Logan asked. "J-dawg, you lit up first."

"Ugh. My buzzer isn't working," Birdie said.

Logan shrugged. "Well, they're called Cheap-O Buzzers, not Awesomely Working Buzzers. Keep clicking."

She glared at him, but he ignored her. "J-dawg?"

"Trick question, Logan," he answered smoothly. "Jen didn't fall from the *Boaty McBoatface*, a small yacht that carried her from Jamaica to the Cayman Islands. She fell from the cruise ship, called the *Queen Kelly*."

My jaw dropped. I shouldn't have been surprised he watched the show, since Rachel was on it, but why would he pay attention to the parts with me and Justin? He winked at me. "Not just a pretty face, am I?"

I didn't answer.

Ed muttered "kiss-ass" under his breath.

"That is correct, J-dawg. Next question: How many stories did Jen fall from the *Queen Kelly*?" As he said the ship's name, Logan met Joshua's eyes, adding emphasis.

Rachel buzzed in first. "Ten! Our room was on the tenth floor."

"I'm sorry, Rachel, but that is not correct." Logan told her. "J-dawg, you were second to buzz in."

"It was the *eighth* deck, Logan," he said smugly. "Jen fell from the balcony of Ariana's suite, God rest her soul. And that was eight stories above the water."

Logan turned to me. "Is that right?"

"That is correct! A fall from any higher probably would've seriously injured me, but I was lucky that my high school training as a diver paid off."

"And we're all glad it did," Logan said smoothly, with all the sincerity of the guy in the Geico commercials. "Let's take a look."

A screen behind Logan flared to life, giving a bird's-eye view of the deck. The ship lurching one way, me going the other. Ariana fell off the balcony, into the ship, and I flew through the air, dropping into the open ocean. I'd never seen this footage.

We figured the fall would be an excellent end-of-episode cliffhanger, so I made Sarah watch for me and tell me when to turn off the recording. A good thing, too, because now I spotted what looked like a shark fin, off to the side of the screen. The creature must have passed only a few feet from me. I'd been scared enough when I fell; if I'd seen the fin while in the water, I'd have pooped my pants.

"Six points for form!" Logan's voice intruded on my thoughts. "Did that feel as terrifying as it looked?"

"It was mostly a blur," I said. "I only had a few seconds to think about how to break my fall. I needed to protect my head and neck. Once I was in the water, the shock of the cold water and the impact kept me from panicking."

"Well, that certainly does look chilling," Logan said. Ed snickered at the pun; Rachel rolled her eyes. "Question 12: where did Jen get her famed 'secret' cookie recipe?"

And so it went. Logan asked questions, with video clips from the shows punctuating the answers. My friends tried to buzz in first, but Joshua beat them left and right. He boasted that all the time spent playing video games must've paid off. I started to get creeped out about how much this guy knew about me. Not just Joshua: all of America.

Finally, *finally*, Ed managed to buzz in first. He let out a whoop, then said, "Jen and Justin's first kiss was about two hundred feet from where we're standing, at the end of the driveway."

The memory of the kiss, as always, brought a smile to my face. But then Joshua's voice intruded. "Nope!"

"What are you talking about? We've all seen that kiss a thousand times. It was plastered on every tabloid in America for weeks."

"It's on the wall of my bakery." Every day, at least one customer commented on it.

"And that was your *second* kiss," Joshua said. "Your first kiss took place about ten feet away, right before Jen chucked her fish into the pool and accepted the offer to leave. I was sitting right there, bro."

Birdie tilted her head at me. "Really? You never mentioned that."

That first kiss hadn't made it into the final cut of the show. It didn't fit the narrative the show wanted to portray. "It was a peck. Not a real kiss."

"Not a real kiss? Well, let's see for ourselves," Logan said. "Thankfully, I have the tape right here. This is previously unseen footage from the vault."

The video screen behind Logan lit up again, showing the very patio where we stood. Joshua and Rachel were in the hot tub. Justin and I sat on two lawn chairs, each holding a glass of wine. A bottle sat on the ground nearby. My heart sang at the sight of him. We'd been apart too long. Making this show was fun and all, but it would be so much better if Justin were here with me. Especially since the show was supposed to be about us getting married. I couldn't even think about what happened if the groom didn't manage to arrive in time for the wedding.

"Holy shit," Justin said on the screen, pointing over my shoulder.

I watched myself spin around, see the offer. "Fifty thousand dollars."

"That's an incredible offer, Jen," Justin said.

"I know."

"Take it."

I paused, nibbling my lower lip and shifting back and forth.

My face was flushed, and I wondered how much I'd had to drink. It hadn't seemed like much at the time, but a nearly empty bottle of wine sat on the deck beside me.

"I have to take it."

"I know."

Thunder crashed, and raindrops splattered the camera. I bit my lip.

"Goodbye, Justin."

Then I leaned over and planted a quick kiss on his soft lips. I stood, grabbed my fish, and tossed it into the pool.

The screen went dark, and Joshua put his arms over his head, letting out a bellow. "You. Are. OWNED. J-dawg 4-Eva!"

Ed shot me a sheepish look. I shrugged and raised my hands. Joshua won fair and square. Meaning I got to start my wedding day with the last person in the house I ever wanted to be alone with. Even Koji would have been preferable, and I didn't know him at all. But there was nothing I could do about it.

———

AFTER THE GAME ENDED, I tried calling Justin half a dozen times, but my calls went straight to voice mail. Hopefully that meant he'd managed to get a flight out of Miami. Weird neither he nor Sarah texted me, but maybe there wasn't time. I called her, too, but she didn't answer, either. Not knowing what else to do, I called Mrs. Taylor. My in-laws were the only people I knew in Florida who still had a landline.

"Jen!" She sounded breezy, unconcerned. "How's the show going?"

"Well, not great," I admitted. "Have you heard from Justin or Sarah? I can't get ahold of either of them."

"Oh, they're fine, dear. All the flights were canceled, but he's at the airport trying to get another one. Justin asked me to call you, but I figured I'd wait until after my soaps. No need to worry."

I exhaled slowly, trying not to let frustration mingle with my relief. Justin must not have heard the alert sounds for my latest texts in the bustle of the airport. And they couldn't know their mom would decide calling me was less important than watching her soaps. They were doing their best. "Thank you so much. And what about you and Greg?"

"We were planning to fly out Friday evening. I'm sure our flights will be fine. Can't wait to see you, dear. Oh, the commercial break is over! Talk to you Friday." She hung up.

I shot Justin and Sarah a quick text, then went to see what everyone else was doing. Logan was thankfully nowhere to be seen. Rachel and Joshua hung out by the pool, so I gave them a wide berth. Inside the kitchen, I found Ed preparing enchiladas.

I poured us each a glass of wine and settled onto a stool at the bar to catch him up on what happened.

He laughed and shook his head. "I tell you, Jen, you have the best problems."

"Come on, Ed, this is really bad."

"I know, I'm sorry. But Justin will get here soon enough."

I tipped my wineglass at him. "I'll drink to that."

After dinner, I went back outside. Logan hadn't reappeared, but I needed to figure out what to do when he showed his face. I walked and walked for what felt like hours, calling and texting Justin over and over until frustration and exhaustion overwhelmed me. Since the first day on *The Fishbowl*, we'd never spent so much time apart. All I wanted was to hear Justin's voice, see his face, and know everything was going to be okay. My ex-boyfriend Dominic "traveled" a lot, and I'd missed him, but I never ached for him. Not like this.

My wandering feet brought me to the hedge maze. I ran one hand along it, letting the feel of the brush against my hand soothe me. With a big sigh, I stopped and leaned back against the wall. Above me, the sun peered down from a gorgeous, cloudless blue sky. Just another perfect California summer evening with zero humidity.

"Jen."

Behind me, someone said my name. Before I could see who it was, a hand snaked out of the hedge and locked around my wrist. Then I was pulled into the darkness of the maze, and a hand wrapped around my mouth.

This was like an episode of *UnREAL*. The Network was having me kidnapped, less than forty-eight hours before my wedding.

CHAPTER FIFTEEN

Rachel: We're all going out tonight to blow off some steam. Some of us are going a little stir-crazy from being cooped up all week. I'm looking forward to it.

J-dawg: Wooooooooooooooooooooooooooooooooooooooooo!   I'm gonna get LIT! Marijuana's legal in California, bro! This is gonna be EPIC!

Rachel: Yeah…like I said. Some people need to get out.

Ed: I've got my dancing shoes on! We are ready to party. As soon as we find Jen.

*Birdie: Man, this little guy's active today. *pats belly* I hope my little Guppy here sleeps through the ceremony. *to her stomach* You can be America's next reality star when you're older, kid.*

I STRUGGLED against the arms holding me, but they grew tighter. Screaming did no good with the hand clapped over my mouth, so I licked it. Had the assailant been my older brother, that would have made him back off in a hurry.

"Gross!" Joshua. Of course. I struggled harder, but the guy had arms of steel.

"Hey, Jen, calm down." The second voice belonged to Ed.

Instantly, I relaxed. He wouldn't let anyone hurt me, no matter what stupid idea Joshua or the Network concocted.

A blindfold slipped over my eyes, and someone slid a gag between my teeth. I tried to bite, but Ed laughed. "Stop. You know I like that."

Hands pulled my arms in front of me and tied them with some kind of cloth. I tugged my hands apart, but nothing happened. Silently, I cursed Rachel for teaching Ed how to do knots during our season on *The Fishbowl*. She had to be the 4-H hog-tying champion and not the top cookie seller?

"Come with us," Joshua said.

They didn't leave me much choice, so I moved one foot in front of the other. Neither of them spoke. A rough hand gripped my left shoulder, a gentler one on my right elbow. The clean, artificial pine-fresh scent that filled the maze gave way to freshly mowed lawn aroma. They walked me up a hill, so we must've been heading toward the front of the house.

I considered dropping to the ground and refusing to move until I got an explanation, but didn't want to risk Joshua tossing me over his shoulder like a sack of flour. Ed probably wouldn't stop him.

Something crunched beneath my foot. The texture told me we'd stepped onto the gravel covering the driveway. The stench of exhaust hit my nose. An engine growled: not a car, but something larger. The Network was taking me on a field trip somewhere.

We came to a halt. Whatever sat in front of the house exhaled a loud puff of air, and then air-conditioning hit my face. A bus. We were getting on a bus.

"Step up," Ed said gently, leading me into the interior. "Turn this way."

Someone lifted the blindfold, and I blinked rapidly to clear my vision.

"Surprise!" a chorus of people yelled.

We were on a bus, like I thought, but one completely unlike any public transit I'd ever seen. The entire interior was dark, but blue and green neon lights outlined the windows and tracked along the ceiling. Instead of a dozen or more rows of seats separated by an aisle, a long bench ran under blacked-out windows. These were no ordinary bus benches, either. The seat covers waved in a pattern up and down the walls of the bus, creating a sea of black leather.

The back half of the bus held what appeared to be a fully stocked wet bar. My friends were already there: Rachel and Birdie stood near the bar, chatting with Mom. Koji chatted with Logan as they tossed back shots.

"Surprise? Where are we?"

Joshua said, "Welcome to your bachelorette party!"

"My party's on a bus?"

"The bus *is* the party on the way to the party! Isn't this epic?" He squeezed past me and Ed to sit next to Rachel. Her smile faltered when he leaned over to kiss her cheek.

As Ed led me to a seat, he explained. "Originally, this was a joint bachelor/ette party. We were taking you both to a club in downtown LA. The Network packed the place with wedding guests."

An entire evening of fun outside the Fishbowl sounded fantastic. Some of the tension fell away from my shoulders when I settled into my seat. "Did you hire a stripper?"

"Come on," he said. "How well do you know me?"

"Well enough to think I should've brought some dollar bills."

He winked. "Smart. But you can't wear yoga pants and a tank top. I hung an outfit for you in the bathroom at the back of the bus."

"There's a bathroom on the bus?"

"Of course there is. It's a traveling bar. Bathroom required. Now go change, so we can leave."

After seeing what the Network had chosen for me to wear thus far, I felt a little like I was walking to my own funeral as I headed toward the back of the bus. When I closed the bathroom door and spotted the outfit, a sigh of relief escaped me. A little black dress, taken from the clothes brought from home, just in case; fishnet stockings I'd never seen before; and a pair of sky-high red heels, also mine. No bra, but that probably wasn't an accident.

Quickly I changed, ran my fingers through my hair, pinched my cheeks to make them pinker, and rubbed my lips together. The blindfold had smudged my existing eye makeup, but with a little tissue and water, it looked good enough.

On my way back to the party, I grabbed a drink—something called a Fishbowl, naturally, a blue-and-green beverage in a globe-shaped glass that thankfully had a lid. Then I settled into a seat between Birdie and my mom. My mom passed me her compact, a travel-sized tube of mascara and a lipstick. I'd thought I looked okay before, but less than a minute later, I felt like a million bucks.

Everyone else got settled, and the bus started down the driveway. Despite my concern that we'd get "pulled over" and boarded by a stripper dressed as a police officer en route to our destination, the trip was uneventful. Before I knew it, we poured out onto the sidewalk in front of a building the news touted as "the current Los Angeles hot spot." It must've cost the Network a fortune to book the place for even a few hours.

Inside the dark club, writhing bodies filled a large dance floor to the left, gyrating to the beat played by a band on a stage against the far wall. People with video cameras swarmed around, filming the party. On the right, pub tables lined the walls. Waitstaff circulated with trays carrying food and more alcoholic beverages.

My stomach let out a howl at the sight of the sliders being passed around the room, reminding me I hadn't eaten in hours. Grabbing Birdie by the wrist so I wouldn't lose her in the crush, I pushed through the crowd toward one of the tables. Every few steps, someone stopped us to congratulate me on the wedding.

Madison was there and Danielle. I even thought I spotted Braden dancing across the room. Attending what should've been your own bachelor party seemed weird to me, but I supposed free booze was free booze.

Since it was too loud to talk, Birdie smiled at me gratefully once we reached our destination. A moment later, Mom settled onto the third stool and motioned for a server.

We ate brie and apple-stuffed puff pastries, tiny steak quesadillas, and the smallest tomato bisque portions I'd ever seen. Everything tasted delicious. All around me, people sipped the same blue-and-green beverage they'd offered on the bus. Not caring what was in it, I grabbed another. I was on my third drink, seventh tiny appetizer plate, when the music stopped. Bright lights flooded the room.

Logan's voice blared through the speakers on the walls. "Jen? Jennifer Reid, where are you?"

I waved my arms. "Here!"

"Don't just sit there. Come on down!"

The crowd parted, revealing Ed and Logan on the stage where the band sat when I arrived. Each of them held a microphone. An empty stool in the middle of the stage gave me the sneaking suspicion I was about to find myself the center of attention, right when I'd started to enjoy blending into the background.

Birdie and I exchanged glances, and she pushed my drink toward me. I tossed back the rest, and another magically appeared on the table beside me.

"You're an excellent friend," I said to her.

She winked at me. "Figured you could drink my share tonight."

With no idea what the Network had planned, I grabbed the new glass like a lifeline before heading for the stage.

Logan's gaze met mine as I strode through the crowd with my head high, trying not to show how confused I was. When I reached the stage, two muscular bouncers lifted me up without spilling my drink.

"Please have a seat." Logan gestured toward the stool.

"What's going on?" I asked.

"You'll see."

Behind me, a screen lowered into place. A moment later, Justin's face filled the screen. "Hey, beautiful."

A wave of longing hit me at the sight of him. "Hi! Where are you?" Please say you're nearby. Or that you'll be here soon. I miss you so much.

"Nowhere near Los Angeles, I'm afraid. But the Network was kind enough to set up this call so I could attend our bachelor-slash-ette party."

"Jen, Justin, welcome to your roast!" Logan announced.

The audience roared, pulling my attention away from the screen. Now that the lights were on, I realized most of the people in the crowd had been on my TV at one time or another. The Network had pulled out all the stops, inviting all the reality show royalty in the area. The only *Fishbowl* costar not present, other than Justin and Ariana, was Abram, who was building houses for the poor with his kids in South America. I couldn't exactly fault him for not flying back. Maria, the beauty queen from Texas, waved when I caught her eye. With a grin, I waved back.

Behind her, I spotted the *Real Housewives* star Chloe had mistaken my mom for when we were in Beverly Hills. I made a mental note to introduce them later. Then again, Evelyn wasn't known for her sense of humor. She might not appreciate the story as much as I'd enjoy telling it.

I wished I could ask if he were still sitting at the airport. What he was doing to get here. "Thanks for coming. I can't wait to see you."

Before he could reply, Logan spoke into the microphone. "All week, we've been holding mini-competitions for the bridal party. Trivia challenges, centerpiece-making challenges, etcetera. Jen knew about all of those events and even participated in the centerpiece-making. What she doesn't know is that we assigned points for each competition based on how well people did. Yes, even the zombie escape room."

A pang hit me at the reminder of my "father" and the event he'd supposedly planned. My smile faltered. On the screen, Justin's eyes flashed, but he didn't say anything. We'd talked the day before about what happened, me hiding in the maze, Justin shouting over road noise in his car on the way to visit his parents. It hadn't been a long conversation, but he definitely conveyed his opinion of the Network's tactics. If he'd been on site, I'd almost have felt sorry for the producers.

A scan of the audience revealed no sign of fake Patrick, so that was something. If he appeared at my bachelorette party, after everything, I might give up and head home.

Logan continued, "They weren't fighting for things like spa days; they were actually competing for the opportunity to roast Jen and Justin!"

The audience laughed, and I suddenly understood why Joshua wanted to win these contests so badly. He hadn't tried nearly so hard on *The Fishbowl*, preferring to cheat rather than put forth any effort. He couldn't cheat at Jen and Justin trivia, though.

Confirming my fears, Logan said, "Up first, the winner of two attendant challenges, and receiving an impressive twenty points overall this week, from the first season of *The Fishbowl*, Joshua 'J-dawg' Adams! Come on up, J-dawg!"

Justin and I exchanged a look. My smile froze. I could feel the words his green eyes bored into me. *Just go with it. Smile, laugh, go with it.* That was the deal we made, and I could do it. Especially if I was drunk enough. I took a big gulp of my fruity beverage. On the screen, Justin blew me a kiss, then raised a flask to his lips.

The movement took my attention off his face, and I wondered where my husband was calling from. The background definitely didn't come from either of our apartments. He didn't appear to be sitting at the airport, either, although the Network could have set him up with a private room in one of the lounges. Why wasn't he on his way to Los Angeles? Would he be picking up a flight in the morning? Before I could ask, Joshua bounded onto the stage, arms raised above his head in a V-for-Victory.

"Whaddup, losers? I told you the J-dawg was ready to play!"

The audience responded so enthusiastically, I wondered if there was an "applause" sign lit up behind my head. Or maybe they were all really, really drunk. I took another sip from my glass. Mmmm, boozy goodness.

"I'd take it easy on the alcohol if I were you, Jen. You don't want to wind up puking all over Justin's feet at the wedding. Oh, wait. That wasn't you."

I laughed at the reminder of the night we almost kissed for the first time. Almost, because Justin drank too much and wound up throwing up on my toes. On screen, my husband's face reddened, but he laughed and raised his glass in a toast.

Joshua said, "Anyway, I had the pleasure of being present for Jen and Justin's first kiss. He told her to go away, she grabbed him by the face. I guess that's one way to get a guy to notice you. Kudos, Jen!"

The audience laughed, and I chuckled good naturedly while raising my glass toward Joshua. If that was the best he could do, I'd have no problem handling this roast.

The producers must have warned him about how I felt about body-shaming, because he didn't call a single person fat during his entire two-minute spiel. Instead, he focused on my now-famous burnt chocolate-chip cookies from my audition video, the time I choked on Justin's engagement ring (which Rachel must have told him), and the time I got stuck with my ex in Jamaica. Nothing I couldn't handle. At least half his jokes had been told in different forms on late-night talk shows, blogs, or Twitter. Some of them by Ed.

As Joshua spoke, I focused on Justin instead. My eyes never

left his. When he mouthed "I love you," the crowd *awwed*. Joshua stopped mid-sentence, tilted his head at Justin, then shook his head at me. "Really, guys? Save it for the honeymoon. If you can even figure out how to get hitched while in different states. Did anyone explain to you how this marriage thing was supposed to work? Or did Justin figure getting stranded was a great way to back out without looking like the bad guy?"

His words rolled past me like water off a duck's back. Surely, the Network had some plan to get Justin here or he wouldn't seem so relaxed.

In the crowd, Skye and Mike, also from my season of *The Fishbowl*, laughed so hard they held on to each other for support. Raj stood nearby, snuggling with a guy I didn't recognize. They'd all probably be at the wedding. Even though I wouldn't have invited Skye or Mike, I didn't care. As long as Justin made it in time and everyone had fun, nothing else mattered.

When Joshua finally said thank you and exited, Ed appeared in his place. He hesitated at the edge of the stage. He looked nervously at the ground, then beamed up at Justin. He turned to the crowd and shrugged, looking confused. As he moved toward center stage, Ed gnawed one thumbnail and smoothed imaginary hair back out of his face in such a perfect impression of me, I almost fell off my stool laughing.

"Hi, I'm Jen," Ed said, his voice unnaturally high. "I really, really like Justin, but I don't want to tell him, and I don't know if he likes me. What do I do? It's so hard being thin and pretty and incredibly smart!"

The audience laughed. Justin let out a wolf whistle, which made everyone laugh harder.

When Ed finished his routine, he whipped a hat out of his pocket and put it on his head sideways. "And what's a roast if you can't poke a little fun at everyone! Yo yo yo, 'sup! The J-dawg is here y'all, and it's gonna be tiiiiiiiight."

By the time he left the stage, tears streamed down my face. I could hardly breathe. Next up was Rachel, who curtsied and addressed the audience. "Good evening, y'all. I'm afraid I'm not the funny one in this cast, and I'm not good at making fun of my friends, so I thought I'd share some of my dad's favorite jokes. What does a thesaurus eat for breakfast?"

The audience went quiet. Someone yelled out, "People?"

"No, not a dinosaur, a thesaurus!" Rachel said. "Anyone? Okay, y'all—it's a synonym roll!"

A good-natured groan went through the crowd, punctuated by a few chuckles. Rachel blushed prettily. "Hey, I said they were Daddy's favorite jokes, not the funniest ones."

She told a few more jokes, all with the same corny humor, than thanked everyone for listening. On her way off the stage, Rachel handed off the microphone to someone I hadn't expected to see here: Braden, from *The Marrying Kind*. That had been him in the crowd. Oddly.

He took a bow, nearly falling, and introduced himself to the audience. "You know, this was supposed to be my show. I should've been getting ready to marry Amanda. This should be our party, our roast."

His words slurred. I shifted uneasily on my stool, wondering how much he'd had to drink and where he was going with this.

The crowd stared back at him. You could've heard a pin drop. At the back of the room, Logan looked stricken. He started toward the stage, but got caught in a throng of girls in pastel minidresses. Whether they were admirers or plants by the Network intended to stop him from pulling Braden offstage, it would take time to get through them. I hesitated, wondering if I should jump up and take the microphone.

Sure, at a roast, the center of attention isn't supposed to participate, but things could go bad fast if no one intervened. Desperately, I sought Ed in the audience, but couldn't find him or Connor anywhere.

Braden pulled some index cards from his pocket, then turned to face the screen. His speech slurred. "Justin, my man! Kudos at stirring up a hurricane to avoid the ol' ball and chain. If I'd thought of that, maybe we wouldn't be here. It would just be my faithless bride sitting there on the stool while I talked about how much I loved her like some dumb-ass sucker."

No one laughed. He looked at the audience, then dropped to the stage, the cards fluttering around him. "What am I even doing here, man? What's wrong with me? Why doesn't anyone love me?"

Justin tilted his head almost imperceptibly at Braden, and I nodded. Enough was enough. I stood and walked toward the poor guy, now sitting on the floor.

He turned toward me, scooting toward the far edge of the stage. "Oh, no. You took my show. You don't get to take my moment in the spotlight."

If he moved any further backward, he'd fall off the stage into the crowd. I froze, not sure if I should go back to my stool, walk away, or try to get to him before he hurt himself.

Before I made a decision, Ed rushed the stage, Rachel steps behind him. She put an arm around Braden's shoulders, helped him stand, and coaxed him toward the exit, while Ed picked up the microphone from where it had rolled.

"Let's all hear it for Braden from *The Marrying Kind*, everyone! Thanks for the lovely roast. May you one day find as much happiness as Jen and Justin, whether on-screen or off."

"And thank you for making our big day so special," Justin said from his spot on the wall. "We literally wouldn't be where we are without you. At least, Jen wouldn't. I would probably be in Florida, either way."

From the side of the stage, Braden yell-sobbed, "Don't do it, man! Marriage will ruin you. Look what love did to me."

"We all appreciate your perspective, Braden," Ed said into the microphone, "but I'm pretty sure our bride and groom are still planning to get married on Saturday. Personally, I can't wait. Thank you everyone for coming out tonight.

"Let's hear it for Jen and Justin!"

CHAPTER SIXTEEN

<u>Jen in the Chapel, Friday morning:</u>

The bachelorette party was amazing! I've always known Ed's super funny, but I loved the chance to see him on stage. I just wish Justin could have been sitting beside me. We could've roasted each other.

This morning's supposed to be pretty low key, I think. Logan said something about working on decorations? I'm not sure. Mostly, I need to call Justin to see if he got a flight yet, make sure Sarah's dress is being delivered, check in with the guests stranded in Atlanta, and see if we need to push the ceremony back a few days.

What do you mean, do I mind postponing the wedding? I can't get married without a groom. It sucks, but it is what it is.

FRIDAY MORNING AFTER BREAKFAST, Janine strode into the kitchen where I sat with Birdie, Rachel, and Ed. I immediately sat up straighter, not just because of the way she commanded a room, but because I'd barely seen her since my arrival. All key information thus far had been conveyed to me through Connor and Logan. The fact that she was in the house, looking for me, meant something was up.

With any luck, Janine came to tell me how they planned to

get Justin to LA before Saturday. A private jet owned by the Network perhaps, a helicopter, or maybe they could get him a ticket out of another airport not far from Miami. Or maybe they had some news on the rest of my family.

Before I could ask what she wanted, Janine said, "You need to go get your marriage license after you're done. One of the PAs will drive you over."

As she spoke, my slowly filling balloon of hope deflated with a whoosh. Then I mentally shook myself. Of course she wasn't here with good news. She wasn't even here with a logical request.

"I can't go get a marriage license today. Justin's still in Florida. We'll go when he gets here. Unless you have some way of helping him arrive sooner? Did he get a flight yet?"

"No, I'm afraid we can't control the weather or TSA," Janine said. "He's been on standby all week, but there's nothing we can do at this point. The courthouse isn't open on Saturday, so it's today or nothing. As far as I know, Justin's not even on a plane yet, so I'm afraid you'll have to go without him. You're going early, in case there's a line."

"But Justin's still in Florida," I repeated. "He might not even get here by tomorrow. We both have to go get the license, right? I'm not going to stand in line all day for nothing. What does it matter? He'll fly in tonight or tomorrow, we'll do a public ceremony, you'll film it, and it'll be beautiful. Reality TV fans all over the world will tune in. Who cares if we don't have a marriage license? Justin and I can fix that when we get home."

Or, we could do nothing, since we're already legally married, I silently added.

With a glance at each other, Rachel, Ed and Birdie sidled toward the door leading outside. I let them go. If things exploded, they didn't need to get caught in the crossfire.

Janine frowned at me. "I'm afraid that's not how it works. If word gets out that there was no marriage license, people will think the marriage was a sham thrown together for ratings. Then they'll think your whole relationship was nothing but a show-mance. They'll realize how much of these shows is manufactured for entertainment value, and they'll stop watching."

"No one is going to care whether Justin and I got a marriage license before or after the wedding. If it comes up, we'll show the one from Florida."

"You think that'll settle it? How long did people insist President Obama wasn't really born in the United States?"

"That's a little different, isn't it? Justin and I aren't running for president."

She waved her hand. "Look, I don't have time to argue. You're going to City Hall, and you're getting a marriage license. Logan will go with you."

"Does he have an ID that says he's Justin Taylor?"

"He doesn't need one. He has an ID that says he's Logan Cassidy."

She couldn't be suggesting what it sounded like she might be suggesting. "I don't understand."

"We can't wait for Justin to get here," Janine said. "The show needs more drama. Thus far, other than you whining about the cake and your mom's dress freak-out, it's pretty boring. That kiss was hot, but it didn't go far enough. You marrying Logan instead of Justin? That's drama."

My jaw hit the floor. Needing time to think, I sipped my orange juice. "That's ridiculous. I'm not marrying Logan."

"You are if we say you are. You signed a contract, remember?"

"There's no way the contract says I have to marry a total stranger." Would that even be legal? For the thousandth time, I cursed Hurricane Cara for keeping Justin away. Not only would this nonsense not be happening, but he knew how to debate the fine points of a contract. I couldn't believe the Plan had backfired so horribly. "Even if it said that, it can't be legal."

"You signed a contract for nonessential services. The terms are binding. And one of the terms says you give the Network final say over all wedding decisions." Janine folded her arms across her chest and tossed her head. "And as a representative of the Network, I say you need to go to City Hall and get a marriage license. Marry Ed for all I care. But you owe me a reality TV wedding."

Remember the Plan. The stupid, useless Plan. The Plan that very well might be the reason I was in this predicament in the first place. But it was all I had to hold on to until I got to Justin.

"I'm happy to have a reality TV wedding," I snapped at her. "You owe me the man I agreed to marry. You need to get Justin here, *now.* Doesn't the Network own a plane? A helicopter? Why aren't you doing more to get him here?"

Watching Janine's face as I spoke, I suddenly understood. The Network didn't care if Justin got here before the wedding. They wanted the drama and the ratings. They wanted the viewers to see me have a meltdown when I found out he wasn't coming. They wanted to make me look like the type of heartless woman who would plan a wedding to one man and marry another. They probably celebrated when Hurricane Cara hit the coast of Florida.

Her words only confirmed my thoughts. "Getting Justin here is not our number-one priority anymore. The show must go on."

My heart pounded, but I couldn't lose control now. I wouldn't give Janine the satisfaction. Even though I wanted to claw her eyes out, I forced myself to take slow, deep breaths. What would Justin say about this? I imagined him standing beside me, holding my hand. Talking to the producers for me. Immediately, my frantic heartbeat calmed.

"From the look on your face, I'd say you don't think marrying Logan is such a terrible idea," Janine said.

"I'm thinking about Justin," I snapped.

This was the most ridiculous thing I'd ever heard. Throughout this week, I'd been fairly easygoing. I tried on a thousand hideous dresses. After my initial protests, I didn't complain when Koji, a total stranger to both of us, joined the wedding party. They wanted Joshua, the single most obnoxious person I knew, to be a groomsman? Fine. When they told me my estranged father had arrived, I went out of my way to give him a chance he didn't deserve. Only after it turned out that he'd been a planted actor did I throw him out. Still, I let them invite whoever they wanted (except the aforementioned actor). I worked on stupid-looking floral arrangements, I stuffed dozens of goodie bags with useless crap that cost more than my annual food budget.

They picked the location, the cake, the flowers, the place settings. I didn't point out that plate chargers were the biggest waste of money I'd ever heard of—and I still didn't know what a plate charger was. (It did not have a USB port, I checked.) I sat on stage and let my least favorite person insult me in front of a cheering crowd. No matter what stupid ideas the Network came up with, I let it go. But even a good sport has a limit. They hit mine. This wasn't going to happen.

The Network was *not* picking my groom, on top of everything else.

"Nope. Nuh-uh. No way," I said. "When Justin gets here, I'll marry him. If that's not on Saturday, we'll push it back. We'll do a symbolic, ceremonial wedding, with or without a license. Or we move the whole thing until Tuesday, and he should be here by then. But I am not going to marry Logan, or Ed, or Connor, or Joshua, or Koji. I will not marry *anyone* other than Justin, and that's final."

"Yes, you will," Janine said. "You signed a contract. If you bail now, you and Justin owe the Network three hundred and fifty thousand dollars."

CHAPTER SEVENTEEN

Confessions from the Chapel, Friday morning:

Jen: No no no no no. What the hell are the producers thinking? I can't marry Logan! I know Justin and I said we'd roll with the punches, but this is off-the-charts wrong. No way, no how.

I don't have any idea where we'll get three hundred fifty thousand dollars. I don't know what I'm going to do. I'm trying to reach Justin. There's got to be a loophole. Some kind of out for acts of God. It's not our fault Justin's not here. I get that the show must go on, but this is Hollywood! Why can't they just push everything back a few days? They don't even have to film the interim—we can pretend Justin arrived in the nick of time.

Ed: Logan's totally hot. Jen could do worse. And he's rich, right?

Rachel: Don't help, Ed.

On the Groom Cam, Friday:

I'm doing my best to get there. All the airports are still closed, even in Georgia. This hurricane caused a lot of destruction. But I'm not about to let Jen marry someone else.

• • •

Janine's words hung in the air between us. All I could do was stare, mouth agape.

She uncrossed her arms and stood up straight, tossing her hair back over one shoulder. "Are we done here? Because I've got a show to produce."

Finally, I found my voice. "No, we're not done yet. What are you talking about?"

"Did you read the contract before you signed it?"

"Justin went over it with me. He didn't mention anything about a three hundred-fifty-thousand-dollar penalty for canceling."

"It's not a penalty. It's a liquidated damages clause," she said, like that cleared anything up. She might as well have called it a purple alligator. "By signing the contract, you agreed to provide the Network with a reality star wedding for our viewers. You and Justin each signed a separate contract, right? Neither agreement is contingent upon the other appearing for the final episode."

"What are you saying?"

"I'm saying, you agreed to let the Network throw you a wedding, at which you would get married. Justin isn't in breach for not being here, because it's an act of God. There's nothing we can do about him. But you still have to get married, which means we can use a substitute. The series airs in a few weeks, and we can't wait."

"Okay, so throw in someone who looks like Justin for filming additional scenes. You can do that, right?" That was the clause in the original contract for *The Fishbowl*, and the Network never used it. When I read the agreement for this show, I'd seen something similar. But it never occurred to me that we'd need someone to stand in for Justin during the actual ceremony.

"We can add a substitute for any purpose."

"Okay, so find some blond guy about Justin's height with hair like his, and we'll fake the wedding. Why do I need a marriage license?"

"Because you owe the public a real wedding, not a show-mance. Remember?"

My heart sank. We were going in circles, and Janine hadn't budged an inch. I couldn't marry Logan even if I wanted to. *I was already married to Justin!* Bigamy statutes didn't have any sort of reality TV loophole, as far as I knew.

Janine said, "Look, I know you hate me, but I'm just doing my job. I was doing my job in Jamaica, and I'm doing it now."

"The fact that you're okay with a job ruining people's lives doesn't make me like you any better."

She laughed, a hollow sound. "Girl, we made you! You are a household name because of us. Your bakery is a success because of the Network, and the shows you've done. Don't stand there playing the victim."

If looks could kill, I'd have skipped out the front door and hailed a taxi to the airport while Janine collapsed on the kitchen floor. As it was, no matter how hard I glared, her head refused to explode. Stupid Janine, never accommodating anyone.

"I didn't complain about anything. When people ask what reality TV is like, I don't tell them the truth. It's all, 'Oh, Carson, being on a reality show was the most amazing experience!' But you're talking about my life here. Until death do us part, remember? Some people take those vows seriously."

"If you took the vows that seriously, you shouldn't have agreed to exchange them on reality television."

White, hot fury blinded me. I couldn't think, couldn't form any words. And yet, my arm jerked, and suddenly Janine was blinking orange juice out of her eyes. I let the now-empty cup clatter onto the table to stop me from throwing it at her.

"If you want to throw drinks, do it on camera," Janine said. "Again, I'm doing my job."

God, was I sick of employers who made unreasonable demands on their employees. "If you're about to tell me you'll get fired if I don't marry a stranger, we're done here. Get fired, I don't care. You've done your best to ruin my life since the day we met. I'm not going out of my way to help you."

"It's not about you, Jen. Honestly, I like you."

"Whatever. A, I don't believe you, and B, the feeling is definitely not mutual."

"I don't like being the bad guy! It's my *job*."

"It's my *life*."

"You signed your life away," Janine said. "That's what we're talking about. If you don't comply with the contract you signed, you're going to owe the Network a lot of money."

"What if Justin arrives before Saturday? Can we get a marriage license on Monday when City Hall opens again and have the wedding then?"

"Only if you want to pay the increased production costs," she said. "We have a week's worth of footage of you getting ready to get married, you and Logan talking and getting to know each other, you and Logan flirting, you and Logan kissing. There's almost no footage of you and Justin. What we have now fits this new narrative. If you marry Justin, we need to redo half the series."

She probably wasn't seriously offering to let us pay the difference, but her words got me thinking. Considering Justin would get fired if we didn't finish the show, paying the Network to ensure that the show went on—and that I wasn't forced to jilt him on national television—wasn't the worst idea. Maybe we could get Justin's company to pay it.

I asked her to estimate the amount, but when she stated a number, I gasped. She had to be inflating it to scare me. But she pursed her lips, tilted her head to one side, and dared me with her eyes to argue. She might have looked scarier if she didn't have orange juice dripping down her toned arms onto the floor.

With a sigh, I broke eye contact. This conversation wasn't getting me anywhere. I needed to talk to Justin about our contract, then Connor. If anyone could get the producers to see sense, it was one of their own. Failing that, I needed to have a long conversation with Logan. If he refused to marry me, maybe Janine would see reason. Surely they wouldn't tie us up and carry us both down the aisle for ratings. What would they call the show? *Married at Gunpoint*? *Married by the Network*?

"Can we go to Vegas and get married when Justin gets here? People get married last-minute in Vegas all the time."

She shrugged. "Sure. You pay to transport the entire wedding party and all five hundred guests to Nevada, we'll talk."

The Network had me over a barrel, and Janine knew it.

"Give me a copy of the contract," I snapped.

Wordlessly, she held it out. I skimmed it, but without a lawyer to explain, all I accomplished was delaying the argument.

"Let me talk to Justin," I said.

I needed to make sure we wouldn't have to pay if I didn't marry *someone*. Also, I needed to figure out if bigamy was still illegal in California and what the penalties were. But I didn't say any of that to her. Now wasn't the time.

"You and Logan leave for City Hall in half an hour," she said. "Talk fast."

A BRIEF CONVERSATION with Justin confirmed most of what Janine told me. The damages clause was valid if three hundred fifty thousand was a reasonable estimate of how much the Network would lose by canceling our show at the last minute—and in reality, that was probably low. Without their cap as a limit on damages, we might have found ourselves owing even more.

"Why didn't Braden and Amanda have to pay?" I asked.

"We don't know that they didn't, but they probably offered us up as a substitute. Which means we can get out of paying if you can convince Rachel to take one for the team and marry J-dawg tomorrow."

I snorted. "I'll work on it. Unless she's an extremely talented actress, it's fair to say that whatever she was feeling has run its course."

"That's highly unfortunate for us. Good for Rach, though. I'm glad she came to her senses."

"Back to the fake wedding," I said. "Does the fact that we're already married make any difference?"

"Well, if necessary, you'll refuse to sign the marriage certificate after the ceremony. They can't hold your hand and make you do it. But let's not get to that point. We'll keep working on a better solution. Especially because it's perjury to go to City Hall and swear an oath that there are no lawful impediments to getting married."

This kept getting better and better. "I'm not going to jail for the Network."

"You won't have to. We'll figure it out."

"Does the fact that you can't make it to the wedding come into play at all?"

"It might," he said. "If they sue us, you could raise impossibility as a defense. We could even tell the judge that we're already married and that it would therefore be illegal for you to marry someone else."

My ears perked up. If we had a defense to a lawsuit, I had no problem throwing a fit on national television. Sure, they'd edit it to make me look bad, but so? Refusing to marry Logan couldn't possibly make me look worse than actually marrying him. "I like that. What's the downside?"

"If we don't get married on the show, the Network pulls their business from my law firm, and I get fired."

My hopes crashed. Our light at the end of the tunnel turned into an oncoming train. I'd completely forgotten about our little "incentive" to coming on the show in the first place.

"Uuuuuuggggggggggggggggggghhhhhhhhh. This sucks!"

"Exactly. Also, the contract has a clause that says, if there's an issue, we agree to be sued in Los Angeles. We'd have to fly out for the duration of the trial."

"...leaving Sarah on her own to manage the bakery without me, again. I am the worst business partner ever. She should fire me."

Justin sighed into the phone. "You're a great partner, but this is a mess we need to untangle. I'll work on it. Meanwhile, play along."

"You want me to go get a license to marry someone else? Should I cross my fingers behind my back while saying 'I do'?"

"Can you move to Plan B?" he asked, referencing one of the things we talked about when this all started, a million years ago.

"Yeah, I think we have to," I said. "Let me talk to—"

Janine and Connor appeared in the doorway, and I shut my mouth in a hurry. Connor couldn't help me at the moment, and I didn't want him to get fired for trying. Janine motioned toward the driveway with one hand. Time to go. I had about twenty minutes in the car to talk Logan out of this farce and figure out how to execute Plan B before I found myself committing an involuntary felony. Awesome.

I told Justin I'd call him later, overdid the I love you's solely to annoy my audience, then stalked past Janine without looking at her, so close I almost touched her. She smelled like oranges, which made me smirk.

"Get Ed," I said to Connor out the side of my mouth. If anyone could make this horrible trip remotely enjoyable, it was him. I'd need the moral support.

Logan waited in the backseat of the limo when I slid in. A blinking red light told me cameras already filmed our every move. He started to talk before I finished buckling my seat belt. "I had nothing to do with this, it wasn't my idea, and I don't want to marry you."

"Great! Then let's get out of the car."

"I'm afraid it's not that easy," he said. "I have a contract, too."

"So the Network can blackmail both of us into getting married?" I thought about telling Logan the truth, that I was already married, but ever since our kiss by the pool, I wasn't sure he supported me and Justin as much as I wanted to believe.

He shrugged. "We agreed to it."

"I'm sorry, Logan, but I never agreed to marry *you*. I agreed to marry Justin, and only Justin. I'm going to find a solution."

"Like what?"

The front door of the car slammed shut. A moment later, the rear door flung open, and Ed poked his head in. He looked from me to Logan and back. "Is this a private wake, or can anyone join in?"

"Who invited him?" Logan asked.

"I did. Just keeping my options open," I lied.

Gnawing on my thumbnail, I stared out the tinted window as the car pulled away from the Fishbowl. Everything looked darker, just the way I felt. I didn't care if I ever saw the stupid fishbowl-shaped glass house ever again. Maybe I should run out the back door of City Hall, request a ride-share on my phone, and head to the nearest airport.

No one spoke as the car traveled down the driveway, turning onto the street. The famous Los Angeles traffic was nowhere to be seen. Just when I wanted to waste three hours traveling less than five miles, the car wove through the streets as if a siren blared on the front.

For most of the drive, I considered our options. Logan was pretty well connected. He didn't want to marry me, either. His family had a lot of money. His family also had lawyers and notaries and anything a person could need. Maybe the best solution here wouldn't take a lot of time or cost a lot of money.

"Do you know any good artists?" I asked.

"My ex-girlfriend used to paint. We're still pretty friendly. Why, you want an engagement portrait?"

"Shut up," I said. "Can she do a fake marriage license?"

CHAPTER EIGHTEEN

Adam Reid to Jen Reid:

Hey, I'm so sorry to do this, but we're going to miss the wedding. It could be days before they get us a flight out of Atlanta. We're renting a car and driving home.

Jen Reid to Adam-Banana:

:-(We'll miss you.

Adam Reid to Jen Reid:

Congratulations, little sister. Give Justin a fist bump for me when you see him.

Jen Reid to Justin Taylor:

This is a nightmare. I need you here.

Justin Taylor to MRS. Reid:

I'm doing everything I can. Remember the Plan. I love you. Please don't marry Logan.

Jen Reid to Justin Taylor:

Get here, and I won't. :-P

Jen Reid to Justin Taylor:

Okay, I won't, either way. But don't tell the Network. I'm playing along. Stupid Plan.

. . .

AFTER LOGAN CALLED HIS EX, we got out of the car. I stood on the sidewalk, taking long, slow, deep breaths. It couldn't be more obvious that I didn't want to go in. Countless criminals had been sentenced here, countless couples had obtained marriage licenses. How many of those "happy" couples were being blackmailed? How many others secretly committed a felony by being there?

"It'll be okay," Logan said. "Let's go inside and get this over with."

I nodded. Standing on the sidewalk all morning would only give me a sunburn.

Connor filmed the two of us walking into the LAX Courthouse where the County Register/Recorder's Office was housed. Ed trailed behind, carrying a spare battery and light for the camera. On the way in, he tripped, knocking the camera out of Connor's hand and sending it skittering across the floor. When we retrieved it, the lens was cracked.

"I'm such a klutz!" Ed said with a dramatic sigh. "Now there won't be any footage of you two getting your marriage license."

"Save the theatrics for the confessional," I said. "No one can hear you."

"Oh, right. Sorry."

Logan glanced at the floor, then back at Ed. "I can't believe a little girl tripped you with her skateboard."

Connor chuckled, shook his head. I normally didn't advocate for destruction of property, but we needed to explain to the Network why there was no footage of me and Logan obtaining a wedding license I had no intention of getting. Besides, I'd pay for the camera out of the per diem from the show.

"I'm going to see if I can make this work," he said. "Ed, come help? You two, don't get a license until I get back."

"No worries," I said.

The line at City Hall was oddly long for a weekday. Logan's ex, who worked nearby, dropped in to chat about the wedding while we waited. She seemed nice enough. After about half an hour, Ed and Connor returned with coffee for everyone. Ed cracked jokes about adding Logan's ex to the wedding party since Sarah couldn't make it, while I daydreamed about gagging him. Three hours passed before we emerged, fake documents in hand.

On the way back, Logan reviewed my remaining schedule. If I weren't being forced to marry a virtual stranger, everything should be smooth sailing: The rehearsal dinner would be that night, then a car would take me, Rachel, and Birdie to a hotel. In the morning, I had a "romantic" massage with Joshua, which no one knew I'd already given to Rachel. I'd relax alone in my hotel room, thanks.

After hair and makeup at the hotel, a horse-drawn carriage would bring me back to the Fishbowl with my bridesmaids.

"Are they sea horses?" Ed asked.

Logan gave him an odd look. "Uh, no, bro. Regular horses."

He swore up and down that no body paint would be involved at any stage of preparations. The actual wedding would be at one o'clock in the afternoon, followed by dancing and partying basically until everyone collapsed from exhaustion. A car would take me and Justin to the airport at eight to catch a flight, leaving the reception to continue without us. I still didn't know where we were going on our honeymoon, but it didn't matter anymore. Everything sounded lovely—other than the vegan cake—if only I had the right groom.

When Logan finished outlining the day, I tilted my head back and closed my eyes, sensing the beginnings of a tension headache. I hadn't told anyone about the pact Justin and I made, about the prenuptial agreement allowing a bit of kissing if neces-sary, about the fact that we were already married, or about the kiss near the pool. Silly me, I'd expected to have Justin here as an ally, so there was no need to bring anyone else in on our secret. But it was time to have a long talk with Ed after we got back to the Fishbowl. He knew I'd rather die than marry Logan, but not the rest of it.

Hiding my phone in the shadow between my leg and the wall of the car, I sent a text. *We need to talk. Meet me in the maze ten minutes after we get back?*

His phone beeped. A moment later, Ed caught my eye and nodded, not bothering to send a reply. Fixated on his own phone, Logan ignored us.

The minute the car pulled into the driveway, I found Janine and gave her the fake marriage certificate, my heart pounding. It looked like the pictures of California marriage certificates I'd found on Google, but what if she somehow knew it was fake?

I needn't have worried. She barely glanced at the paper before shoving it toward one of the PAs and sending Logan on a mission to find attendant gifts for my bridesmaids. Rachel and Birdie were at the pool with Joshua and Koji. I should join them, spend some time with the whole wedding party. Learn Koji's last name. How sad was it that I didn't even know one of my groomsmen at all? And that my groom didn't know him, either?

Justin's roommate and I weren't exactly besties, but at least if Aaron had shown up, I'd know who he was. And his last name.

But this wasn't my wedding, not really. It belonged to the Network. I was only here to play the role of besieged bride, struggling against the stress of planning a massive wedding that I was barely involved in.

I slipped out the front door, around the side of the house, and down to the maze without anyone paying any attention to me. In the center of the maze, I found Ed tapping away on his phone. "Are you about to tell me something I'm going to have to keep a secret from Connor?"

"No," I said. "But you can't tell anyone else. Not even Birdie or Rachel."

Quickly, I filled him in on everything that happened from the moment Connor called me the previous Wednesday. I couldn't believe it had been less than ten days. He listened without injecting any jokes, which told me he understood the severity of the situation. He didn't stop his mouth from dropping open, but he didn't interrupt.

When I finished, he let out a low whistle. "Wow."

"Yup."

"I don't even know what to say. Is Logan a good kisser?"

"Horrible. It was super awkward."

"Oh, right, sure," he said. "Don't let me live vicariously."

"I'm sure Connor is a better kisser. He'd have to be."

"He's got many skills." Ed grinned at me. "At least now I understand why you were so chill about letting J-dawg back in. Oh, and hey, congratulations!"

We snuck out the secret maze exit and started back to the house. Halfway there, Logan jogged over to meet us.

"What's wrong? Is there a problem with the gifts?"

"I'm not going to get gifts. The gifts were bought weeks ago. I know you wanted me out of the way."

"Oh. Then why didn't you leave?" I didn't realize how rude the words sounded until they were out of my mouth, but after the week I'd had…whatever. I couldn't even.

"Jen, we need to talk," he said, breathing hard.

"No, we don't," I said.

Ed glanced from Logan to me and back again. "Guys, I'm heading up to the house to start dinner. I'll let you talk alone."

When he vanished over the hill leading back to the house, Logan said, "C'mon, Jen. Are you really going to marry Justin?"

"Of course I am. I love Justin. I'd marry him a dozen times." Well, at least twice, anyway. In the same month, if necessary. "You don't want to marry me, anyway."

"I lied," he said. My stomach lurched at his words. "You can't tell me that kiss didn't mean anything."

"It means I thought you were drowning," I said. "Any lifeguard or teenage babysitter would've done the same thing."

"Come on, Jen, it was more than that and you know it."

I turned away, and he grabbed my arm. He pulled me against

his chest, and I put my hands between us. He smelled good, but I didn't want him touching me. "Stop. You are being creepy."

Surprised, he released me.

I shoved against his chest, putting space between us. "You told me how you felt. Okay, fine. You have a right to do that. I told you how I feel. You need to respect my wishes. You don't have a right to argue until I change my mind. I'm in love with Justin, and I'm going to marry him."

"Actually, you're going to marry me."

"Don't be ridiculous. I played along and got a fake marriage license, but I'm not going to stand on national television and vow to love, honor, and obey you." I hadn't actually agreed to obey Justin, either, but that was beside the point. "It wouldn't even be legal."

Logan's grin widened, making him look like a wolf. "Yes, it would. That's not a fake marriage certificate."

"What the hell are you talking about?"

"My ex-girlfriend's not an artist. That girl wasn't even an ex. One of my dad's friends has a daughter who works at the clerk's office. She snuck a real certificate out and brought it to me. That's who you met."

"That's not funny, Logan."

"I'm not joking." He stepped closer, and I moved away. "Saturday night, you and I are getting married. And if you refuse, the Network will sue you, and there's not a damn thing your precious Justin can do to stop it from three thousand miles away."

CHAPTER NINETEEN

More confessions from the Chapel, Friday:

Jen: *Seriously, I should've seen that coming. I thought Logan was my friend. I should've known he was working for the Network the whole time.*

Logan: *Of course I'm working for the Network! Jen knew that—I told her up front I'm a paid wedding planner. She knows I have another series with them. It's not my fault that she never asked for the full extent of my duties. And it doesn't matter. Jen's going to marry me, and then my show gets renewed. Who knows? Maybe we'll do a joint series: Jen and Logan: Love at First 'Action'.*

Birdie: *Man, I miss all the good stuff. I hate having to nap like fourteen times a day.*

J-dawg: *Bro, this is EPIC! I'm so peanut butter and jelly right now that I never thought of something like this. I am handing over my crown. Logan is by far the best reality show villain I've ever seen. Double fist bump!*

Birdie: *His crown? His joker mask, more like it.*

• • •

HAVING ALREADY DROPPED HIS BOMBSHELL, Logan smiled sweetly at me. My hand itched to slap that smug look off his face. I stared at him in horror, with no idea what to say.

None of this would've happened if Justin had gotten on the plane with me in Miami. If we'd flown out here together. If we'd had more notice before we needed to start filming, so he could get the days off rather than having to wrap up a trial. If Amanda and Braden had gone through with their wedding. Why did they get to call things off when we didn't?

Silently, I cursed the lawyers who wrote that contract, the producers, Justin's boss, Logan, me, and my husband. We knew better. Of course we knew better. Reality TV thrives on drama. If the participants don't create enough of it, the show makes bad things happen. At that point, I wouldn't have put it past them to have created a hurricane so Justin couldn't fly out of Florida. We were lucky they didn't wait for his plane to take flight and shoot it down over the Gulf of Mexico to make things more interesting. They could have added an entire survivalist slant to the show. Dropped us off in the Las Vegas desert with nothing but a compass and called it *Will They Survive Until the Wedding*?

I didn't trust myself to speak, but I needed to get away from Logan before I broke down completely. I moved around him, intending to race for the front door once I had an open path. He stopped me before I made it three steps, placing a hand on my arm that almost made me trip over my own feet. Just what I needed: to face-plant on national television after everything. Especially when I'd so carefully avoided walking into the glass walls all week.

"What are you doing?" I shook my arm free, but stopped walking. "In case you missed the clue of me walking away, I'm not in the mood to chat."

"C'mon, Jen. We need to talk. We can do it here, or we can do it inside, in front of everyone."

Rolling my eyes, I gestured vaguely around the grounds. "This whole thing is being filmed. There's nowhere we can talk privately, even if I wanted to." No way would I tell him about the privacy inside the maze.

"You know what I mean. Rachel and Birdie and J-dawg and Koji don't need to see this until it airs."

He'd said the magic words. The only thing I wanted less than to have this conversation was to do it with Joshua's commentary. I crossed my arms. "Fine. You talk. I'll stand here."

He stepped closer, lowering his voice. "I'm sorry that you're pissed. I did what needed to be done for the show."

His body hulked over mine, which didn't improve my attitude toward him. There was no need for him to intimidate me with his muscles, even if he intended to keep the people in the house from overhearing. Stepping backward, I put a hand between us, forcing him to keep his distance.

"For my show, or yours? Why do you even want to marry me? You could have any one of a thousand women. Hell, you *have* had a thousand women."

"Closer to two. But my past doesn't matter. I'm trying to repair my image. We could make it work," he said. "A simple, pretty lie for the cameras. A quiet divorce later. Or not, if things go well. We've got this great chemistry. You might like being married to me. It's like an arranged marriage."

"It's nothing like an arranged marriage. We know each other, and at the moment, I intensely dislike you. I'm in love with Justin." Not to mention that the two of us were already legally married. "And there's nothing between us. You're a stand-in until Justin gets here. Even if I went ahead with the wedding, which I won't, you'd be a substitute for what I really want. That's not fair to either of us."

"That hurts. I thought we were friends."

"So did I, until you tricked me. Now we're not friends. We're not anything."

"Is that what you're telling yourself?" His voice was husky, thick. "Come on, you know we've got a connection. We've got this heat."

"That energy you're feeling between us? It's called anger. I'm so pissed right now, you have no idea," I said, speaking through clenched teeth. "I don't want to be with you. I don't want to be your friend. Stop turning this into something it's not. There is nothing between us, and there never can be."

"Dump Justin."

My fingernails dug into my palms, and I forced myself to breathe deeply. "It's not about Justin. It's about you. I don't want you. Period."

"You can't mean that."

He grabbed my waist and yanked me against him. Before I could stop him, he pressed his lips against mine. His mouth was hard, his body unyielding. Fury made me gasp, and his tongue wormed its way between my lips.

Without a thought, I clamped my teeth together. I stomped my foot down on his instep. Logan jerked. I released his tongue, shoved him backward, then stepped forward and slapped him across the face as hard as I could.

"I said, NO, Logan. Leave me alone."

THE PRODUCERS HUSTLED Logan into the medical van that always waited by the side of the driveway to check him for injuries. I told them to check his head while they were at it. If he thought this was the way to win me over, they should look for bumps.

Connor assured me that Logan was only pursuing me to boost the ratings, but they'd tell him to tone it down. Between the unwanted kiss and the forged marriage license, I was angry enough to walk out and tell them to forget the whole thing. Unfortunately, Justin and I had made promises: not just to the Network, but to each other.

At the end of the show, my husband would have his dream job. We wouldn't have to worry about money as much. As long as the Network told Logan to back off, I wouldn't walk away.

Especially not without talking to Justin. This wasn't my decision to make. The show was his, too, even though he hadn't appeared on it yet.

When Connor produced a new, second waiver for me to sign, I gave him a withering look. He flushed and put it away. "I'll, uh, tell them I couldn't find you."

Then I bolted for the house to do a video call with Justin. No maze this time. This call wouldn't be private. The viewers needed to see what was going on, needed to hear our fury. If the Network could be convinced to air any of it.

As I replayed the day's activities, a variety of emotions washed across his face. By the time I got to the end, his face was red, moving toward purple.

"I'm going to kick Logan's ass."

"Make sure you get it on camera. I'd hate for you to get arrested without it boosting our ratings," I said dryly. He wouldn't really hit Logan, and we both knew it. But seeing how offended he was on my behalf eased some of my frustration.

"You're not upset?"

"I am, but I took care of it. He'll think twice before kissing another woman who said no. Hopefully, so will the viewers."

"I hope you're right. I know you can fight your own battles." He paused, listening to something in the background. "The good news is, this is television gold! Sarah's already making notes for The Logan cupcake."

"Lovely. When do you get a flight?"

He shrugged, a gesture that made me have to stop and take a yoga breath to calm down. Didn't he care at all? "The winds have started to die down, and some planes are taking off, but Sarah and I are on standby. I promised her the first seat we got."

"Don't you dare," I said.

At the same moment, Sarah's voice sounded from off-camera. "Don't be an asshole."

"Sorry," he said. "That wasn't funny."

"Not even a little bit. Doesn't the Network have a plane?" I asked.

"They do. I talked to Janine, but it's still too windy for small planes to take off."

"And you believed her?"

"What choice do I have? The Network is powerful, and shady as fuck, but they don't run air traffic control. I'll get a flight when I get a flight."

Awesome. On top of everything else, my fiancé seemed unconcerned about missing our wedding and found the idea of me being forced to marry someone else hilarious. It was all too much. His attitude made me want to scream, but I couldn't give the Network what they wanted. No screaming, no drama.

"If it's not in the next four hours or so, don't bother. There's no point in you showing up after the Network makes me marry Logan." I hissed the words at him.

"Jen—"

"I have to go."

Turning my phone off, I shoved it in a drawer and went outside. This was all too much. The Network wasn't going to get the satisfaction of making me cry, not this time, but my blood boiled. I needed to get away from the house, from the cameras, until I got myself under control. And I needed my friends.

Outside, the buzz of activity in the backyard stopped me in my tracks. Crew milled around, setting up chairs. A giant white tent stretched as far as I could see. Through the flap, at least two dozen tables were already set up. Logan stood at the center, overseeing everything. He apparently hadn't had an attack of conscience in the past fifteen minutes and decided to call things off.

From a table by the pool, Rachel beckoned me over. "This place looks amazing. Have you been inside the tent yet?"

"No, but I peeked. Not in the mood to deal with Logan."

"Did you see the card box?" Birdie asked.

I grinned at her. "A giant fishbowl? Yeah. Whatever. I gave up trying to have any input on this party days ago."

"A wise choice."

"I'm just glad I talked them out of having people throw fish food when Justin and I leave for our honeymoon."

"Yuck." Rachel wrinkled her nose. "Have they told you yet where you're going?"

"Nope. But I'm not worried."

Not because I trusted the Network. Because nowhere they could send us would possibly be worse than the week I'd experienced on the Network's dime. Anywhere with Justin would be a massive improvement.

Well, it would've been a week ago. I didn't even know if I wanted to go on vacation with the Justin who didn't care at all about missing our wedding. The wedding we were only doing so he could keep his job. Maybe I should take Ed or Rachel, instead. Birdie couldn't fly right now.

My suitcase contained mostly skirts, shorts, tank tops, and sandals, three swimsuits, a couple of light sweaters. The clothes should be appropriate anywhere we went in the Northern Hemisphere. Which probably meant they'd booked us on a cruise to Antarctica, but I'd worry about that tomorrow. For all I knew, the Network was planning to send me on a "romantic" getaway with Logan. Or so they thought.

No way would I board a plane with that man, not after everything. They'd have to carry me bound and gagged.

But I couldn't worry about that yet. One thing at a time, and I still needed to survive the rehearsal dinner. Then, after I refused to marry Logan in front of the cameras, the Network might send me back to Florida with nothing but the expectation of a summons. All dreams of a honeymoon seemed as far away as a trip to Mars. Which would be an awesome surprise, if it wasn't impossible.

Connor approached to give me the rundown on the ceremony.

"I'm not rehearsing marrying anyone other than Justin," I said.

"Then address Logan as Justin when you practice. I don't care."

The words made me flinch. "I thought you were my friend. Thanks a lot."

When he spoke again, his voice was low, softer. "Come on, Jen. You and I both know you're not going to marry Logan tomorrow, even if the Network held a gun to your head. So let's go out there and put on a show for the viewers. If the show gets good ratings, the Network might be less inclined to sue, whether you get married or not."

I sighed. Connor was only doing his job, after all, and none of this fiasco was his fault. Also, sticking to the Plan meant playing along with whatever ridiculousness got thrown at me. Until the actual wedding, of course.

"I guess you're right. And it's not like I have anything better to do this evening."

"Thanks for playing along."

He quickly reviewed what was about to happen: Stand at the back, the music will play, walk slowly, blah blah blah. Ed agreed to escort me. Without Sarah, we didn't have even numbers for the bridal party, anyway, and it was too late to find a substitute.

And by "too late," I meant, "Logan's sister was way too short to wear Sarah's dress without it dragging on the ground, unless she used stilts."

At least I wouldn't have to worry that I'd start crying; my journey down the aisle promised to be the funniest walk any bride ever experienced.

The production assistants ushered all of us to where the ceremony would be held. The milling staff had vanished. Now, rows of white seats faced an archway decorated with…algae? Lovely.

Until seeing the seats, I hadn't really thought about how many people would be attending this thing. Logan referred to our wedding as the TV event of the century, but when he talked about me being the new trendsetter, I'd figured he was just sucking up to the Network. To my surprise, they had gone all out. There were about twenty-five rows of seats, ten chairs extending on each side of the aisle.

"How many people were invited?" I whispered to Ed.

"About five hundred, I think." He shrugged. "Plus a bunch of seat fillers."

"Like at the Oscars?"

"Yeah. The Network spent a lot of money on this thing. They want it to look good."

"Wow." This wedding wasn't about me. It was about all the people who worked so hard to put on a good show for the television audience. The production assistants and camerapeople and staffers who put in a ton of hours for low pay. A pang hit me. I hadn't thought of all the non-decision makers who would be affected if I stormed out before the wedding.

Logan stood at the end of the aisle, waiting for me. He caught my eyes and smiled. Glaring, I made a cutting gesture with my finger across my throat. I may have to play along with this farce for another day, but I wasn't about to pretend to enjoy it. Even when the cameras pointed at me.

Janine stood next to Logan, waiting to issue cues. For this rehearsal, Joshua would be filling in for the minister, after he walked in with Rachel. Whatever. It wasn't worth arguing anymore. At the very least, we'd get some good outtakes from this Dumpster fire.

When Rachel and Joshua were halfway to the front, Janine signaled Birdie and Koji.

From six attendants to four. Only the bridesmaids were as originally planned, and even then, I was missing one. If Sarah and Justin managed to fly in at the last minute, we'd have five. With Ed escorting me, the numbers would be off. Which meant we needed another last-minute replacement. Or I'd have to walk alone, which I no longer wanted.

Janine signaled again, and Ed and I started toward her, using that ridiculously slow wedding walk. It was harder than it looked. "You got a brother nearby?"

"Older brother, yeah. Lives in Palm Springs."

"Does he own a tux?"

"He can afford to rent a tux. Why?"

"Once Sarah arrives, we're short a groomsman. My brother can't get a flight to Los Angeles because of the hurricane backlog, so he and his girlfriend are renting a car and driving home. How do you feel about a last-minute substitution?"

"I feel like that's that second-best idea you've ever had," Ed said.

I smiled at my mother when we passed. She thought Logan was only filling in for Justin during the rehearsal. Since I didn't have the slightest intention of actually marrying Logan, there was no reason to upset her. Especially since she would give the Network the drama they so desperately wanted, which I refused to provide. Screw them. Mom caught my eye and mouthed "I love you" at me. I mouthed the words back.

When Ed and I reached the front, he leaned over and kissed my cheek before we turned to Fake Minister Joshua. I forced myself not to let my smile falter when our eyes met.

"Hey, hey, hey!" he said. "J-dawg is in the house! Let's get this show on the road."

Do not roll your eyes, do not roll your eyes, I told myself. This was only a rehearsal. What did it matter if our fake minister was an asshole?

Birdie gasped. Rachel shrieked my name.

"Whoa!" Joshua said. "Birdie just pissed herself. W-T-F, you ho?"

Rachel's voice cut through the cacophony. "No, you idiot. Her water broke. Birdie's going into labor."

CHAPTER TWENTY

<u>Confessions from the Chapel, Friday evening:</u>

*J-dawg: That's *beep* sick, man! I mean, all this crap just came rushin' out of her. I'm so grossed out right now.*

Rachel: It's not gross, it's nature. I grew up on a farm. I've helped deliver countless animals—one while en route to prom. I've got this.

Birdie: No offense. I totally understand that you've got a show to make. But I'm a little busy. Could we maybe do this interview after I get to the hospital? Or tomorrow? Tomorrow would be great.

Jen: Awesome. Perfect timing! I would much rather go to the hospital to help Birdie give birth than 'rehearse' marrying Logan. But, hey, is there any news about Justin?

A FLURRY of activity followed the announcement that Birdie had gone into labor. The Network called an ambulance. Rachel put her arm around Birdie, holding her hand and coaching her through the breathing. The two of them started walking, and I ran into the house to grab the bag she left packed in case she needed it.

Over my mom's strenuous objection, I insisted on riding to the hospital in the ambulance. I didn't need to "rehearse" the wedding. What was there to know? Walk down the aisle, answer questions when asked, nod, say "I do." I'd seen at least two hundred romantic comedies with weddings in them, so I was all set. And I had already learned to say my vows to the groom, not the officiant.

Mom followed me around to the front of the house where Rachel and Birdie waited. Rachel pulled out her phone and opened the stopwatch app.

"Girls, help me out," Mom said. "Babies can take a long time. What if she misses the wedding? Jen, you have to stay here."

"You can't miss your own wedding," I said. "I'll be back. And if I'm late, it won't even matter. This is Los Angeles. Nothing ever starts on time. My groom isn't in the state yet. Not that it matters. The Network can probably find a stand-in."

"They found one for Justin," Birdie pointed out. "Why not marry two completely random people?"

I shot her a look. That comment was a bit too close to the reality I didn't want Mom to hear yet.

Mom persisted. "You'll be exhausted. You'll have bags under your eyes."

"I have a professional makeup team and soft camera filters. I'll be fine."

Rachel said, "You're a bride. All brides are beautiful."

Logan rounded the corner. He took Mom's arm and turned her back toward the house. "Why don't you stand in for Jen while we go over the rest of the arrangements? That way, you can fill her in tomorrow on anything she needs to know."

"Told you they'd get a stand-in." Birdie chuckled. "Jen, I can't wait to see Logan marry your mother tomorrow."

If Mom heard her, she gave no indication. When Logan steered her back around the corner of the house, I prayed he remembered that I'd kick him in the balls if he told her about the Network's change of plans before tomorrow. He thought I wanted to tell her myself at the right moment to fuel the drama. Logan didn't know me at all.

The paramedics bundled Birdie onto a stretcher and put her into the ambulance. Rachel hopped into the back of the truck behind the stretcher and held a hand back to me to help me in.

"Remind me not to vacation with you anymore, Birdie," Rachel said, her tone light. "This is the second time you've left this house in an ambulance."

"Hey, if I hadn't gotten injured and had to leave the show, you might not have won!"

Rachel raised her eyebrows and met Birdie's eyes. I tried to swallow a giggle, but it escaped into the air.

Birdie broke their staring contest when another contraction hit her. "Okay, fine, I would've been out soon, anyway."

"Do you want me to call anyone for you?" I asked. "Your partner? Your parents?"

"I already called Shannon. My parents?" Her laugh turned into a groan, a weird, unnatural sound. "Don't call until it's over. They won't be able to get a flight out of Nashville with all the people still stranded from the storm, and my mom will text all three of us constantly until morning."

"She doesn't have my number," Rachel said.

"Or mine."

"Oh, she won't let that stop her," Birdie said. "Trust me. Call after the baby's born."

"What about Shannon?" I asked.

The contractions were coming faster. A paramedic moved around her, checking vital signs and doing other medical-looking stuff. If only I'd spent my time watching *Grey's Anatomy* instead of reality shows, I might've had some idea what they were doing. Probably not, though.

"I'll call," Rachel said. "Maybe she can catch a flight out."

"No need." Birdie spoke through gritted teeth. "I already texted her. She's staying at a hotel nearby. She'll meet us at the hospital. You two can catch a cab back to the Fishbowl when we get there."

"That'll be about five minutes," the paramedic said.

My phone beeped with a text from Justin. Ed told me about Birdie. Everything OK? How's she doing?

We're almost to the hospital, I replied. Will text an update later. You figure out how to GET HERE ASAP.

The ambulance turned into a parking lot and screeched to a halt before a massive white building. Rachel and I trailed the paramedics out of the ambulance, through the automatic glass doors, and down the halls. In the waiting room, a tall, dark-haired woman jumped to her feet as we entered. For a heartbeat, as her hair swished to obscure her face, I thought I saw Ariana. Then, she smoothed her hair back, and I recognized Shannon from Birdie's social media pages. Her flawless skin was a couple of shades darker than Ariana's. She had high cheekbones and big brown eyes, stretched wide with a mixture of concern and excitement.

"How are you, bae?" She rushed toward us, and Birdie reached out her arms. One of the paramedics stepped between them, and Shannon frowned at him. "It's okay. I'm also the mother."

"She's with me." Birdie gasped out the words, her face red.

The paramedic stepped aside, and Shannon moved closer. She grasped one of Birdie's hands in both of hers, then leaned forward and kissed her forehead.

"Told you so," she said.

"Shut up. You're doing this next time."

"With pleasure." She straightened and turned back to me and Rachel. The doctors started to wheel Birdie down the hall, and the three of us followed. "As you may have guessed, I'm Shannon. It's nice to meet you both."

Rachel introduced us quickly as we walked down the hall.

"You're the one getting married tomorrow?" Shannon asked me. "Are you allowed to be here?"

I shrugged. "This is where I want to be. I've spent all week doing the Network's bidding. I'm not leaving until the baby's born or they drag me out."

"I'll keep that in mind," Birdie said.

"If you can keep the baby in until around four o'clock tomorrow afternoon, it would help me out," I joked.

Birdie flashed a thumbs-up as she disappeared through another doorway. Shannon and the doctors went with her, but Rachel and I sat down to wait. I didn't have any intention of returning to the fake rehearsal. Although I'd been kidding, I wouldn't care if we wound up staying through the ceremony. Not when it would take a miracle for Justin to show up.

As nurses went in and out, muffled voices reached our ears. There wasn't anything for us to do until the baby was born, so I logged onto the hospital's Wi-Fi to send Justin and Ed updates.

Rachel glanced up and down the hall. "Did we just escape the Fishbowl without any production people? How did that happen?"

"I'm sure they're here somewhere. Probably followed in another car. I bet Janine is standing at the admissions desk now, trying to get permission to come in with cameras."

"So, we've got like five minutes to talk while they find the waiver Birdie would have needed to sign?"

"Something like that. Why?"

"What's up with Logan? You're not really going to marry him, right?"

After a glance up and down the hall, I told her everything: The agreement between me and Justin. The real wedding that already took place. Justin's job, the contract, the Network's threats. How I considered Logan a friend and confidant before he got a marriage license without telling me. By the time I finished, her brown eyes resembled saucers.

"Physically, he's attractive. You're not blind; I can't deny that," I said. "He smells amazing. But I never would've flirted with him without Justin's permission. Not even for the cameras."

"OMG, hold on a sec." She pulled out her phone and started swiping frantically.

"What are you looking for?"

"Something J-dawg said. The two of them were riding over to the house one day, and they were talking about all the ladies Logan used to get, back in the day—he's such a tool."

"Which one?"

She glared at me for a second before her face relaxed into a smile. "I was talking about Logan. Anyway, J-dawg asked him how he did it. What he did to convince all those women to sleep with him."

"Being good looking and charming isn't enough?"

"Nope. Hold on." She stopped swiping and turned her phone toward me. "Look at this."

The phone showed an image of a small, glass vial full of an amber liquid. Above it, I had to read the name and description three times.

"He wears pheromones?"

"Yup. I thought it was just locker room exaggeration, but it makes sense now. That's why he always stands so close to you, and why you felt a pull toward him. It's not physical, it's chemical."

A flood of relief hit me. "That also explains why I didn't find him remotely attractive when we fell into the pool. The pheromones washed away."

"So what happens tomorrow?"

I shrugged. "Want to marry Joshua?"

She giggled. "Oh, hell no. I mean, honestly, he is a different person away from the cameras. He's sweet, he's sensitive. He's… amazing in bed."

Her revelation didn't surprise me in the slightest. The air between them had crackled since day one on *The Fishbowl*. They accidentally locked themselves into one of the changing rooms together the first night. I wouldn't have been surprised to hear they'd snuck off onto the grounds during the show, either before Joshua's elimination or after he came back. But I'd never asked, and Rachel was usually pretty private about that stuff.

"But?" I prompted her.

"It's all physical," she said. "I thought I'd develop deeper feelings for him over time. But when we're in public, it's like hanging out with my obnoxious younger brother. I'm ending things for good after the wedding."

"If you want to end things on camera, you be my guest," I said. "That's just what this wedding needs—a break-up halfway through the vows."

"Think I'll pass," she said. "Although I probably would've gone for Logan if he'd been genuine."

"It's just as well that Joshua was here and you never spent much time with him. The last thing we'd need is you actually falling for Logan while he was pretending to fall for me."

"Truth."

The doors at the end of the hall swung open, and Vera appeared, camera already held to her eye. Rachel squeezed my hand, signaling that we'd finish our conversation later. Before going into the delivery room, she recorded quick interviews with both of us.

Less than a minute after the door closed behind her, it opened again. Vera backed through the door, still holding the camera to her eye. Once she cleared the threshold, Shannon appeared, inches in front of her, backing her farther into the hallway.

"Nope nope nope," Shannon said. "I don't care what Birdie signed. You're not doing this. Sue us."

The door slammed shut, and Vera wheeled around to face me and Rachel. We sat stone-faced, not knowing what to say or do. She dropped her bag on the seat beside us, then set the camera on top. "Guess I'll go get some coffee. You guys want anything from the cafeteria?"

We shook our heads, and the doors swung shut behind her. Rachel and I sat in silence, eyes glued to our phones, as if in unspoken agreement not to start any other conversation we didn't want the Network to overhear. I wouldn't put it past the Network to leave a recorder taping inside Vera's bag.

The clock ticked onward, and nothing happened. No one went through the doors. The heart monitor beeped softly. Vera didn't return. After a while, I laid on the bench, using my arms as a pillow. Rachel moved the camera bag to the floor, and did the same. It had been a long and emotional week. Almost as soon as I found a comfortable arrangement, I was out.

Sometime later, the creaking of hinges woke me. The clock on the wall told me it was nearly three o'clock in the morning. A nurse peeked out the door. "Shannon wanted me to tell you it's almost time. Mama's struggling a bit, but both of them should be just fine soon enough."

Rachel started to ask a question, but the nurse shook her head. "I've got to get back in there. Sorry."

In my half-awake state, I couldn't quite manage to form words, so I smiled a thank you. She nodded as if she understood. Rachel put her head back down on the bench and was snoring softly within seconds. Vera sat farther down the hall by the doors, sipping coffee. When our eyes met, she lifted a second cup from beside her and held it toward me.

Although a tiny voice reminded me of the breast milk/pot brownies fiasco from *Real Ocean*, Vera hadn't been involved in that. Besides, my eyes were already drooping again, and she was the one who got Mom when things started to go well with Fake Patrick. The coffee beckoned. I got up, leaned against the wall beside her and accepted the cup gratefully.

"I'm glad we got some time alone," Vera said.

"Me, too, actually. Thank you so much for bringing my mom to the house earlier this week. When I think about what would've happened if I'd spent the rest of the week making amends with that actor…" I shuddered.

"Officially, I have no idea what you're talking about." She winked at me. "But you're welcome. I couldn't watch you grow closer, knowing it was all a farce."

"Did the Network forget to remove your soul when you signed up?"

"Hey, we're not all bad. You seem cozy enough with Connor, and he's one of us."

"True. Sorry."

"That's not what I wanted to talk to you about, though. I've been hoping to get you alone for days," she said. "The Network is not looking out for your best interests. They don't care about you and Justin."

"Tell me something I don't know. Leanna is forcing me to marry a stranger tomorrow." I sipped my coffee, wondering what worse thing the Network could have planned.

"It's not Leanna. It's Janine. She's trying to take over, get her own show."

"But Leanna's in charge, right? I don't trust either of them."

"Technically, but Janine's been pushing her out. She didn't know about Logan, and Janine told her they found your real dad. That girl's a snake."

After the way I'd been treated, it was tough to dredge up any sympathy for any of the producers. But if what Vera was saying was true, maybe Leanna was more like the cool, friendly PA I'd first met than the cutthroat bitch she now seemed. Or maybe this was a trap. "As far as I'm concerned, they're in this together. They're both snakes."

"Then why did you agree to do the show with them?"

With a glance at the camera sitting beside her, I filled her in on Leanna's conversation with Justin's boss. Even if the camera were on, which I doubted, the Network would never air me talking about how they blackmailed people into doing their shows.

Vera held one hand over her mouth until I finished. "That's ridiculous. I'm sorry."

"It's fine. It's almost over." I sipped my coffee again.

"True, but there's still something you gotta know."

Not that I wanted to look a gift horse in the mouth, but it seemed odd that one of the production assistants would just happen to decide to bare her soul to me. There had to be a catch.

This must be some kind of trick, like Logan helping me get a "fake" marriage license that turned out to be real. "Why should I trust you?"

"I'm quitting," she said. "This isn't why I moved to Hollywood. I wanted to make documentaries, deconstruct systemic racism, create movies that changed the world. Not follow some reality diva around—no offense—while the Network manipulated her into ruining her relationship and running away with some trust-fund asshole."

"I would never run away with Logan. I don't know what the Network thinks is going to happen tomorrow, but that's not it."

"They're brainwashing you," she said.

My body went completely still. The Network had done a lot, but invading my mind? No way. "You mean the pheromone-cologne Logan's wearing? That's not strong enough to get me to throw everything away for him."

"No, listen. Janine made subliminal messages to play while you sleep. 'Logan is so smart, Logan is so good-looking, Logan is going to make some lucky woman very happy...' Hella messed-up stuff like that. Pumped into the show's speaker system, hidden beneath a layer of background music."

"No. No way."

"Yes way. Listen." She pulled out her phone and tapped away.

A few seconds later, music poured out of the speakers, filling the room. The same pop-y, fun type of music they played every night before I went to sleep. She tapped the screen, and the music faded. She turned the volume up, and a whispering voice repeated her words.

Chills went down my back. I stared at the phone, hands over my mouth, as the words kept playing. Bile rose in my throat, and I leaned my head back against the wall. "Please turn that off."

"No problem. Just needed you to hear it."

"Have they been playing that all along? Is that why..." *Is that why Logan and I kissed? Is that why he's been affecting me? Because the Network pumped fake emotions into my head and he's wearing pheromones?* There was no way to end that sentence out loud, but Vera saw the conflict in my eyes and answered me, anyway.

"That's probably why you've been drawn to Logan," she said. "But I don't think it's been all week. They started when Justin's flight got canceled. I'm not sure. It was Janine's idea. Maybe the original plan was for you to jilt Justin for Logan, maybe not. But you needed to know."

"Why didn't you tell me earlier?"

"I just found out. While I was in the cafeteria, I got a text from Janine, asking me to play the music while we sat here waiting. Hell, no, I won't."

"Thank you," I said. The words seemed woefully inadequate. "Really. *Thank you.* You have no idea how much this means to me. You could lose your job for telling me."

"Doesn't matter," she said. "Like I said, I'm out. I didn't sign up for this shit."

"Still. If there's ever anything I can do to return the favor, please let me know."

"Just…be true to yourself. Don't let the fame go to your head. There's more to life than reality TV."

A lot more to life, like Justin. Like Sweet Reality. Like Sarah and Rachel and Birdie and all my other friends and family.

"Anyway, I'm outta here," she said. "I'm not going to intrude on a woman giving birth. Janine wanted me to sneak shots of the actual labor, but eff that. I walked in so I could say I tried, but that's it. I don't care what Birdie signed before coming on the show; some things are private. Someone else can interview her and Shannon in the morning. Have a good one."

I thanked her again, and she stood, stretching.

Vera's coffee cup swished into the trash can by the door, and a moment later, she was gone. I remained leaning against the wall, not moving, staring at the still-swinging door. The coffee cup grew heavy in my hand, and I let myself flop down in the spot Vera vacated on the bench lining the wall.

The Network brainwashed me. If Birdie hadn't gone into labor, I'd be sleeping right now in a fancy hotel they arranged, dreaming of Logan with no idea about the garbage they pumped into my head. Was a few nights enough? Would their plan have worked? What if I'd gone on camera and promised to love, honor, and obey Logan because of the Network's interference? If I'd signed the marriage license, they would have made me commit a felony. For ratings.

It didn't matter that no one knew Justin and I were already married. Messing with my mind, with my emotions, with my free will, was wrong. Right then and there, I made a decision.

Tomorrow morning, I'd go back to the house. But I wasn't going to play along anymore. I was going to walk down that aisle, turn around, face the cameras, and flat-out refuse to cooperate. Even if Justin showed up, no way in hell we'd marry on TV now. Then I was going home, to be with my husband, who would never, ever be Logan Cassidy, no matter what anyone said or did.

Behind the door, Birdie screamed, jolting me out of my revenge fantasy and reminding me that something much more important than a fake wedding was happening about fifteen feet away.

Rachel bolted upright on the bench, eyes wide. "What happened? Is she okay?"

"I don't know. The nurse said not much longer about half an hour ago." My voice trembled. Through all the contractions on the way here, Birdie plastered a smile on her face. When she fell and broke her ankle, she didn't scream like that.

Another moan sounded from beyond the wall.

I started toward the door, but Rachel pulled me back down. "There's nothing you can do in there. You'd just be in the way."

Birdie's voice trailed off through the doors. More muffled voices. I couldn't make out any of the words. Overhead, someone said, "Code ninety-nine. OB. Room three. Code ninety-nine. OB. Room three."

"I don't suppose 'Code ninety-nine' means 'the baby is here'?" Rachel asked.

The doors at the end of the hall swung open. Nurses came rushing through, wheeling a cart behind them. They spoke in such a rush, I couldn't make out complete sentences. *Crashed. Mother. Baby.* My blood pounded in my ears.

They opened the door to Birdie's room and pushed the cart inside. I took a step forward, but one of the nurses turned to me. "Authorized personnel only. Sorry."

The door swung shut. I still couldn't hear Birdie's voice. Or a baby.

"No, Rach, I don't think 'Code ninety-nine' is good at all."

CHAPTER TWENTY-ONE

<u>Confessions from the Chapel, Friday night:</u>

Tina: I hope Jen knows what she's doing. You never get a second chance to get your wedding pictures done. What if she has bags under her eyes? This is horrible timing on her friend's part.

Logan: I'm not worried at all. She'll be back. How long can it possibly take to have a baby?

<u>Hospital Cam, two hours earlier:</u>

*Shannon: Get that *beep*camera out of my *beep* face, or I'll break both of you. Out, out, out. Now.*

MY HEART SKIPPED a beat as the significance of what we'd seen crashed down around me. Rachel and I clasped hands, unable to speak. A tear trickled down the side of her face. I couldn't breathe. I forced myself not to look at her. Any more tears, and I'd lose it, too.

Birdie had to be okay. She was young and healthy, and the baby had been fine earlier. They had to be okay. I sent up a thousand silent prayers to whatever deities I could think of that mother and baby would pull through whatever went wrong.

Only the ticking clock on the wall filled the silence. I couldn't speak, couldn't move. Maybe if I remained perfectly still, every-thing would be all right. Stupid, but all I could do was hope.

An eternity passed before the door swung open. Shannon's head poked through the crack. "False alarm. Someone pushed the wrong button. They say it happens all the time. Everything's okay. We have a baby! She's fucking gorgeous, just like her mom."

The entire hallway whooshed with the sigh Rachel and I uttered at those words. Finally, I remembered how to breathe. My heartbeat returned to normal.

We jumped up to hug Shannon, but she'd already disap-peared back into the room. Instead, Rachel and I embraced each other. Tears flowed down my face. If we'd lost Birdie or the baby because she'd traveled to LA for my stupid faux wedding, I never would have forgiven myself.

Half an hour later, an exhausted Shannon stumbled past on her way to the cafeteria and said one of us could go in to see Birdie.

"I didn't get you a wedding gift," Rachel said. "You go first. And congratulations?"

"If I have to marry Logan, I want a real gift," I said. "Like arsenic or karate lessons to keep him away."

Inside the room, a sweaty, smiley Birdie gazed lovingly at a tiny, blanket-wrapped bundle in her arms. I peeked at the little red face poking out. Long lashes lay across her checks as the baby slept. She had a few wispy red hairs. Shannon was right: completely gorgeous.

"Hey," I said. "Thanks for getting me out of an awkward moment back there. Way to keep me from rehearsing to marry a stranger."

"I'm such a good friend."

"The best." I crept toward the bed, afraid I'd break her, or the baby, if I got too close. "Can I hug you?"

"You better. What are you doing here, anyway? Aren't you supposed to be starring in a TV show or something?"

I grinned at her. "I'm headed back to get my beauty rest in a few minutes, *Mom*. But I figured, since you're bailing on my wedding last minute, the least you can do is let me be one of the first to meet your little bundle of joy."

"Right. I broke my water weeks early because I was afraid the Network would make me wear that peach monstrosity after all. #TrueFriend."

Instead of answering, I leaned down and hugged her. Birdie cradled the baby in her arms. She didn't stir when I put my arms around them.

"She's the most beautiful baby I've ever seen," I said. "What's her name?"

"What else? Star."

RACHEL and I stumbled blearily back into the Fishbowl a few minutes past four-thirty in the morning, both of us refusing to leave the hospital until we were positive everything would be okay. I didn't know what hotel they'd originally planned for us to stay at, and I didn't care. After a hospital bench, my regular bed would be a marshmallow.

The wedding started at one o'clock, and my stylist should arrive around eleven to start my hair and makeup. More time than I usually needed, but this was no ordinary day. It wasn't even an ordinary wedding. But at least I was going to look freaking fantastic. After having such short hair since the cruise, I looked forward to the simple pleasure of someone else brushing and styling my extensions for me.

Snaking my bra down my arms and letting it drop to the floor, I crawled into bed, not even bothering to undress. Tears of exhaustion trickled down my face. Exhaustion, or misery? I missed Justin.

All I wanted was for the two of us to get in a car and drive far, far away from the Fishbowl, never looking back. If he were here, he'd feel the same way. But Justin was *still* stuck in Florida, where wind and rain still pummeled the coast, even after the storm moved north. Only a miracle would get him here on time, and I'd used up all my ability to hope for one.

With a heavy sigh, I buried my face in my pillow and choked back a sob. Jen and Justin's Royalty-Inspired Dream Wedding had turned out to be a complete and utter nightmare.

WHEN I WOKE a couple of hours later, my eyes were grainy. My mouth tasted like a dirty sock. But my mind was racing, and I couldn't sleep. After tossing and turning for what seemed like an hour, I washed my face, brushed my teeth, and went out to get some air, still in last night's clothes.

Right before the entrance to the maze, moving shadows stopped me dead in my tracks. Apparently, I wasn't the only one sneaking into the hedges for a bit of privacy. Flattening myself against the wall, I inched toward the entrance, wondering who I'd find and what they were doing out here. Rachel had been sleeping when I left our room, not surprisingly, and I'd heard snores from the guys' room but not bothered to investigate.

Someone coughed, and I froze. A man. Then he cleared his throat, and I recognized the sound. My heart soared.

Justin. Thank God he'd finally made it. All my frustration over the past few days evaporated at realizing he'd gotten here after all. Picking up my pace, I turned the corner into the maze and ran right into him. "Whoa, there."

His arms came up to steady us, and his scent enveloped me. I looked up, losing myself in the emerald of his eyes. Our lips met in a heated rush. My hands roamed up and down his back, wanting to assure myself this was really happening. Tears of relief came to my eyes. Finally, everything would be okay.

When the kiss ended, Justin kissed me softly a second time,

then crushed me against his chest. I settled into his arms, savoring the feel after a few days apart that felt like an eternity.

He spoke again, so quietly he barely breathed his words against my ear. "No one knows I'm here. Don't say my name. We need to move deeper into the maze so no one can overhear us. Okay?"

I nodded, but moved onto my toes to give him one more kiss. I wasn't quite ready to let go of him yet, as if he might vanish the second we lost contact. When our lips met, he moved his hands to my hips and lifted me against him, turning and carrying both of us into the maze. My senses sang. By the time he broke the kiss, both of us were panting.

"Did you miss me?" he asked, his eyes twinkling.

"You have no idea," I said. "And I'll fill you in, but not yet. Let's go closer to the center."

He set me down slowly, my body sliding down the length of his. My pulse quickened at the close contact. Every synapse in my body fired.

As quickly as I dared, I took his hand and tiptoed deep into the maze where no one could overhear us. A few minutes later, I stopped. "This should be okay. What's going on? How are you even here?"

"Later," he said, cupping my face with one hand and brushing his thumb against my lips. I shivered. "There's plenty of time to catch up later. Right now, I need you."

His words sent a thrill through me. I leaned into him, reveling in the feel of his lean, firm body against mine. My hips brushed against his groin, sending a jolt of electricity through me. His hands moved up and down my back.

"You have no idea how much I've missed you."

"I think I do," he said. "Are there cameras in here?"

I shook my head. "We shouldn't even be here. The whole maze is off-limits until the big event. But we can talk without anyone hearing us."

"No." His mouth hovered centimeters above mine. I ached to

close the gap. We had so much to say to each other, but it had been a horrible week. "Right now, I don't want to talk at all."

"Me, neither," I said.

My hands sank into his hair, playing with the blond tendrils at the nape of his neck. His hands found my hips as my lips found his.

We kissed again and again, our bodies doing the talking for us. And as Justin lifted me against him, I knew that, no matter what else the Network threw our way, now that he was here, we'd be able to handle it. Together.

AFTER WE PUT ourselves back together, Justin pulled me toward him, and I leaned my head against his shoulder. "It's so good to see you. I didn't think you were going to make it."

"You know I couldn't let you become a bigamist."

"As if. But thanks. How did you get a flight?"

"I didn't," he said. "I drove."

"You drove from Florida to California? Overnight?" That... wasn't even possible.

"No, I rented a car when they still didn't have a flight for us on Wednesday afternoon. Sarah helped. It only took about forty hours."

"So, you drove through a hurricane for me? And crossed thousands of miles in three days?" My heart grew even more at the thought that he'd been so desperate to get to me, he hadn't waited for a flight. After all the stress of the past week, happy tears prickled the back of my eyes.

"Yeah, I did. Surprise!" He flashed his dimples at me before leaning down for another kiss. "Sarah's here, too, at the hotel. I've been awake for the better part of three days, so we need a plan before I pass out. Do we tell them I'm here? Do we let the drama build? Do we have Connor sneak us away to get a marriage license right now?"

"We don't need a marriage license."

"No one else knows that."

"Right. But the courthouse is unfortunately not open on Saturdays." I chewed on one thumbnail. "Which is fine. There's no way I'd go through with a wedding for the Network after all the stunts they pulled this week. They seriously think I'm going to marry Logan for their ratings."

"You don't have to marry Logan. I'm not letting the show turn you into a felon."

As we walked toward the front of the maze, clasped hands swinging, I filled him in on everything that happened since we last talked.

"Are you okay?" I asked.

"Yeah." He ran one hand through his hair. "It's stupid, the whole thing was my idea. I shouldn't be upset about you kissing Logan."

"I never would have let it go on so long if I didn't think it was okay," I said quickly. "You know I don't want to kiss anyone else."

"It's not that," he said. "I'm not mad at you. I'm mad at my stupid company for making all this shit happen in the first place. Maybe I should have just quit. No job is worth what the Network has put you through."

"Maybe not, but at this point, I've already been through it. If you quit your job, it's all for nothing," I said. "Besides, it's only one week out of our lives. Then you'll have job security and we can move on."

"I wish I believed that. What happens when the Network wants us to do some other harebrained show? What if the next one is *Justin's Big Affair* or *Reality Divorce*? Are we allowed to say no? Or will my boss threaten to fire me again if I reject the next show?"

With a sigh, I stopped, leaning my head back against the hedge. In my haste to save Justin's job and my excitement at the "free" wedding, I hadn't thought ahead to the greater ramifications of what we were doing. "Good point. So what do we do?"

Justin cut me off with two fingers against my mouth. He pursed his lips in the universal "shh" gesture, cocked his head to the left, and pointed behind me. I took a deep breath, forcing my pounding heart to slow, and moved my ear against the hedge.

Footsteps. They echoed down the other side of the maze hedge, between us and the entrance. If whoever was walking around made a couple of right turns, they'd find us unless we moved.

A giggle reached my ears, then a low sigh. A man and a woman. Justin tilted his head at me quizzically. He didn't recognize the voices, but I knew one of them well. And I'd heard the other within the past week.

With my right hand, I made an L sign. Logan.

"Not here. Someone might hear us. I plan to make you scream," the female voice said. Janine. At least she wasn't lying when she said she didn't want me to marry Logan.

He chuckled, still on the other side of the maze. They'd stopped walking, only a couple of feet away, but separated by the greenery. I didn't dare move for fear they'd discover us.

Logan said, "What if we let them hear us? Let the cameras pick up our voices? How's your Jen impression?"

"What are you saying?" Her voice came out breathier, as if Logan's hands were roaming while he talked to her.

"Nothing at all." He raised his voice. "Oh, my God, Jennifer, that feels amazing."

My blood boiled. That bastard. To think I'd considered him a friend.

On the other side of the maze, Janine chuckled. "Mmmm. Oh, you're so evil. I love it."

"I hope you're a screamer," he said. Lips smacked together. "Think about the drama. The ratings. Oh, the viewers are going to love it. Audio footage of two people in the maze…"

A zipper opened. My face grew warm. I couldn't believe we were hearing this.

"Oh, Logan," Janine said. "Oh, God. Think of the ratings. Yes! Ratings. Yes!"

Pain jolted me out of my fury when I clenched my fists so hard, my fingernails drew blood. We needed to get out of there. Logan and Janine had me in an even worse position than they thought: if anyone saw me leaving the maze, the world would never believe they'd staged this encounter.

Justin's eyes met mine. He looked as disturbed as I felt. We were trapped in the maze, inches from two people having sex, one of them pretending to be me, the other very clearly not Justin. I pulled out my phone and mouthed "silent" to Justin, who nodded and pulled out his own phone. Then I sent him a text.

SO MUCH FOR NOT TELLING PEOPLE YOU'RE HERE. WE NEED TO GET TO THE HOUSE, EITHER SO EVERYONE KNOWS I AM NOT IN THE MAZE, OR SO THEY THINK I'M HAVING SEX WITH YOU.

His reply came instantly. ;-)

SHH! NOT NOW.

Behind us, the sounds were getting louder. Turned out, Logan *was* a screamer. Justin blew me a kiss before sending the next text. *IS THERE ANOTHER WAY OUT?*

GENIUS. MY HUSBAND WAS A GENIUS. I'D NEARLY FORGOTTEN. YES! THERE'S A HEDGE THAT SWINGS OPEN, IN THE FAR CORNER. FOR MAINTENANCE.

We pocketed our phones and crept through the maze toward the secret exit Connor had shown me. Their cries of "drama" and "ratings" followed us. I didn't breathe until we swung that portion of the wall outward, revealing the backyard where we'd once played three-legged Pin the Tail on the Donkey. We headed for the house, not even bothering to close the wall. Let people know I'd been there. Let Logan and Janine wonder and sweat. Not my problem.

"I guess this means I'm not going back to the hotel," Justin said.

I was about to agree when a thought hit me. "What if we just go with it?"

"What do you mean?"

"I mean, this show was never about us. It's not *our* wedding, not really. We knew that. That's why we got married before leaving Florida."

"True…"

"So what if we just go along with their scheme? I go back to the house, alone, pull Rachel aside, and tell her I had sex with Logan? Then I go into the confessional and act all torn up about cheating on you?"

Justin burst out laughing, then quickly put a hand over his mouth. "Oh, man, I'd love to see the look on Logan's face when he finds out. Especially if you swear up and down that you had sex with him."

"I could even moan a little, 'Oh, yes, the drama. Oh, drama!'"

Justin wiped tears of laughter from his eyes before replying. "You could call me and make a tearful confession."

It was so, so tempting to mess with Logan that way. Part of me loved the idea of beating the Network at their own game. But my more practical side tapped me on the shoulder and whispered something in my ear that sounded suspiciously like "ramifications."

"We can't do it," I said. "Although it would be hilarious for us, the rest of the viewers wouldn't be in on the joke. Remember all those memes calling me a home-wrecker during *The Fishbowl*? Now that America has embraced us as a couple, they'll turn on me if they think I cheated."

"Right." He sighed. "That would be rough. The tweets and the hate mail. I'd start getting offers to 'make me feel better'. Media hounding us at home again."

"I could handle most of that," I said. "It goes with the territory. The problem is the bakery. Sweet Reality's business would tank. One of the reasons they come in is to see pictures of us."

"Also, we've got a signing scheduled after the honeymoon. Not a lot of people will want our autographs if they watched you marry Logan."

"Nope. And don't even think about inviting Logan to the signing. It's a funny thought, but keeping up the charade would get exhausting, fast. Especially if he tried to choke me with his tongue again."

"Yeah."

I heaved an exaggerated sigh. "Guess I better keep you as my only husband. However will I manage?"

"You're pretty resourceful. You'll find a way." Justin pulled me against him for a kiss. His lips lingered on mine for a long moment. "I like it when you call me your husband."

"My husband."

"Talk like that and we're going to have to go back into the maze." His lips blazed a trail to my earlobe, and I wished I could just abandon the show entirely and follow him back to his hotel room. "I missed you, my wife."

"I missed you, too."

"The good news is, we'll be sleeping under the same roof starting tonight. Where are we going for the honeymoon?"

"No idea. As long as I'm with you, I don't care." I popped onto my toes for one more fleeting kiss. "I refuse to go on a honeymoon with Logan."

"You're not getting any argument from me," Justin said. "So, what do we do now?"

"How did you get here?"

"I parked in front of the house behind this one and walked through the backyard. Why? You planning a great escape?"

"Oh, that would be wonderful," I said. "I'd love to see Leanna's face when it's time for the wedding to start, and I'm not there."

"It's tempting."

"But I don't want to get sued."

"Agreed," Justin said.

"I could do with a mini-escape, though."

"What are you talking about?"

"Well, Logan's in the maze right now, having loud sex and pretending it's with me. I need an alibi. So, let's go back to the hospital. You can meet Star, and I'll get Birdie to swear up and down I was there. We just need Rach to say she came back to the house alone last night."

Justin took my hand and led me out through the rear of the property. At first, I kept checking over my shoulder, but once the hedge maze faded into the distance, I let myself relax and enjoy being with him.

"I'm so glad you're here," I said. "It means a lot that you drove three thousand miles so I wouldn't illegally marry someone else."

"No problem. Someone had to be here to stop you from pretending to make the greatest mistake of your life."

CHAPTER TWENTY-TWO

<u>Confessions from the Chapel, Saturday morning:</u>

Jen: I'm getting married today! Birdie and Star are healthy and happy. Everything is awesome. I'm so excited, I don't even know what questions you're asking me.

Rachel: Joshua's sworn to be on his best behavior through the wedding. But I can't promise he won't try to do a speech, or that it won't be in rhyme.

J-dawg: Admit it, you guys want one poem, right? A'ight. Weddings are whack. I can't wait to get back. This show has been thrillin', but everyone else is always illin'. The J-dawg knows when he's being dissed, so I'm headin' to the bar to get pissed. Peace out.

Ed: So, I had this idea for modifying my tux to make it just a little more me. No offense to J&J, but basic black is pretty boring. Well, modifying isn't the best word. I got a new, more awesome tux. I'm sure Jen will love it

A couple of hours later, Justin and I returned to the house and made a beeline for the maze. The people setting up for the ceremony weren't looking at us, and the last thing they expected was the real groom to be wandering around with a baseball cap pulled down over his forehead, avoiding eye contact, hours before the ceremony.

"This looks great," Justin said. "We would have had a beautiful wedding, if everything hadn't gotten screwed up."

"It is what it is," I said. "We knew everything could go wrong. If you hadn't missed that flight, the Network would have done something else to ruin it for us."

"True. Good times."

"The things we do for money. Or to not become destitute."

"Everything's going to be okay," Justin said.

"I know. We just need to avoid the crew until we get to the maze. Connor's expecting both of us in a few minutes. It's time for you to do your first official interview about how you got here and how you feel about me marrying Logan."

"That's awesome." He raised his voice and spoke slowly in a fairly accurate impression of our head producer. "'Justin, how do you feel about your bride, the woman you love, marrying someone else because we're all a bunch of douchenozzles here at the Network?'"

I giggled.

He continued in his own voice. "Well, of course, Leanna, nothing makes me happier than seeing my bride about to falsely swear to love, honor, and obey some total stranger. Except you guys must all be high, because you had to know there's no freaking way she'd go through with it. Of course I would stop her, if she wasn't planning to stop it herself."

"That's why they pumped in the subliminal messages. Don't forget to mention those."

He sighed, shaking his head. "These people are so fucked up."

"That pretty much sums it up."

"So what are you going to say in the interview?"

"Well, they don't know Vera told me the truth, so I'm going to talk about how sorry I am you couldn't be here, how close

Logan and I have gotten this week, and that I'm sure everything will work out for the best."

"Sounds good," he said. "When they ask me about Logan, I'll mention how hard Ariana's death hit me, and how I jumped the gun by proposing when I found out how sick she was. You know, I took her advice to live in the moment to heart, and maybe I made a mistake? Then I'll talk about how you and Logan seem like a great couple. How does that sound?"

"Almost too convincing. They didn't brainwash you, too, did they?" I gave him the hairy eyeball for a moment before breaking into a smile.

The maze loomed ahead of us. Justin grabbed my hand and ducked into the shadows, planting a kiss on the tip of my nose.

"You and Logan are the dumbest, least sense-making couple I've ever seen."

"That's not entirely true," I said. "You and J-dawg would make less sense."

He shuddered. "Don't give them any ideas. I have much better taste than that."

I pulled his head down to claim his lips. Our time in the maze had only made me crave his touch more. He pulled me close, hands settling on my waist. A thrill went through me. We didn't have much time before people would start looking for me, and the rest of the day could go horribly, so I savored these stolen moments. By the time Justin broke the kiss, I wanted to drag him back into the shadows.

He asked, "Still think I'm brainwashed?"

"Not even a little bit."

"Do you want me to say something else in my interview?"

"It might make more sense if you talk about us. After all, at some point, we're going to tell the world we actually got married, right?"

He shrugged. "Are we? I don't care what the rest of the world thinks."

"Depends. On what happens today, and on the response we

get after the show airs. It might be necessary if Talky Ted starts hounding us."

"So we give him an exclusive."

I choked and stopped. "Him? The guy who plastered the Internet with pictures of Dominic kissing me in Jamaica? Who wrote an article a couple of weeks ago suggesting that we were getting married in a hurry because I'm pregnant or that we broke up in Florida and that's why I left? Or both?"

"You've got to admit, he's a master at producing clickbait. You've almost got to admire the guy," he said. "Besides, I think there's something going on between him and Sarah."

My jaw dropped. "What? You've been holding out on me this whole time?"

"When was I going to tell you? While we were in the maze?" Begrudgingly, I admitted that he had a point, and he continued, "He called her for a comment when you landed in LA, and she told him to fuck off. I guess he likes that in a woman, because he came in to the bakery. They started talking. Not about you, just chatting. While we were stranded in the airport, she spent a lot of time texting, and she finally admitted last night she's talking to him."

"I can't believe it." I groaned. "Your sister, my best friend and business partner, has a thing for the tabloid guy? Are you sure he's not using her for a story?"

"Doubt it. While we were in the car, I heard her say that we'd opened a secret passage to the magical land of Narnia and wouldn't be back in the States until we destroyed the seventh Horcrux. If he didn't like her, he wouldn't still be speaking to her."

"Let's hope for her sake, that's true."

In the entire time I'd known Sarah, she'd never dated anyone. No big drama in her past. She didn't enjoy casual dating, had zero interest in hookups, and was happy that way. She told me once that she's demisexual–she needed to get to know a guy before she felt physical attraction to him.

Before I could pry for more information, Connor and Ed arrived. I did my interview first, hamming it up like Justin and I planned. Then I waited with Ed while my husband gave his interview.

He shifted, looking back and forth between me and the maze before he spoke. "Hey, Jen, are you guys totally, one hundred percent sure about this?"

"Yeah. I've never been more sure of anything in my life," I said.

"The two of you make a wonderful pair, you know."

"Thanks. I think so, too."

"I keep thinking back to when you first met. It was so clear to me, to everyone, that he was into you, but you couldn't see it."

My face grew warm at the memory of those days. I didn't miss the uncertainty at all. "What can I say? I was on the rebound."

He pulled me close, resting his chin on the top of my head. "I'm glad you two finally got it together."

"I never thanked you for your help with that."

"Don't be ridiculous," he said. "I gave my interview back at the house, and I spent half of it bawling like a baby. I'm hoping to dominate the previews before *Big Day* airs. All thanks to you."

"I feel confident Connor can make that happen."

As Justin and Connor exited the maze, Ed planted a kiss on my cheek instead of answering.

"Watch it, Silva," Justin said. "No one else is allowed to try to steal my bride today."

"She's all yours, bro."

Justin and I said our goodbyes, and he went back to the hotel so he could nap before appearing at the right moment. I took a deep breath and reentered the house from the front with Ed. The door slammed behind us, announcing our arrival. Seconds later, the flurry of activity started.

Ed vanished, presumably to get dressed in his room. The producers whisked me away to the second floor, where curtains separated the smaller sitting room from the rest of the house. First, then they herded me into the shower, thankfully allowing me to go in unattended. They did, however, give me strict instructions not to wash my hair. Apparently, updos worked better that way. Then, a bevy of stylists descended on me. They plucked, tweezed, buffed, and shined every inch of my body. When they finished, a familiar face peeked through the curtains.

"Angela!" I hadn't seen the stylist since my audition for *The Fishbowl* when she gave me the best makeup and hair I'd ever had. I'd wished I could take her home as my personal stylist. "How have you been?"

She hugged me enthusiastically. "Jen! I was rooting for you all the way during that season. I'm so happy to see you and Justin here. You're getting married!"

"Thank you!" As she styled my hair, I filled her on everything that happened during the week. The longer I spoke, the deeper the lines in her forehead grew. By the time I got to the Network's decree that I marry Logan, she'd stopped working and simply sat, hands over her mouth, shaking her head back and forth.

"Och, what a mess," Angela said. "Television, huh? What are you going to do?"

As much as I liked the stylist, I barely knew her, and she worked for the Network. I couldn't tell her the Plan. I didn't even tell her Justin had arrived in Los Angeles.

Instead, I picked up a mirror to inspect her handiwork on my face, craning my neck from side to side. She'd pulled my hair into a mass of curls gathered at the nape of my neck. Tendrils escaped on either side, framing my face. "I'm going to…tell you how great my hair looks?"

"Of course it looks great. Your tone is practically an insult." She smiled, taking the bite out of her words. "Now stop talking so I can do your makeup."

With Angela chattering away, time flew. Before I knew what was happening, Rachel arrived, looking stunning as always, to zip me into my dress. She'd found a white headband with a bow on one side to hold back her cropped hair. The turquoise dress fit perfectly, skimming the ground above the tips of white high-heeled sandals.

"Do you want to make a run for it?" she asked.

"Nah," I said. "Justin landed in Los Angeles this morning. When he appears at the wedding after I walk down the aisle, they won't stop him. Not in front of everyone."

She grinned at me. "I can't wait to see their faces."

I traced the outline of the garment bag, smiling at the memory of the way the dress inside hugged my curves. A hint of cleavage, even with my Wonderbra, but nothing over-the-top. The elegant lace bodice. So simple, so beautiful. The dress represented everything I wanted for my wedding day.

Just thinking about this amazing dress filled me with joy, almost as much as the realization that this miserable week was nearly over, or picturing the look on Logan's face when Justin arrived.

The dress revealed as I unzipped the garment bag did not have lacy straps. It was not a gorgeous sheath that hugged my curves before flaring out above the floor. It did not fill me with joy. This was not my dress. Not even close.

The bag contained the dress I'd absolutely, one hundred percent, refused to wear. The very first dress they'd brought to me that day in the salon: a poufy, whipped cream–looking bottom with sheer lace on top—and not much of it. This wasn't the dress I'd picked. It was a monstrosity.

Rachel came over to see what had upset me, and her face went pale. "That's not your dress."

"No." My voice sounded strangled.

"It has to be a mistake."

I couldn't speak, just pressed my lips together and looked at the ceiling, willing myself not to cry and ruin my makeup.

Rachel patted my shoulder. "Don't worry. Your dress must be

around here somewhere. Even if it's still at the store, someone can go get it."

"It's such a stupid thing to be upset about, in light of everything else." I sniffled. "But my dress was basically the only okay thing in this entire fiasco. They pulled a bait-and-switch on me. I can't appear on national television wearing this."

"You won't have to. If all else fails, we'll swap. You can wear my dress instead."

Rachel's legs were about four inches longer than mine, but what the hell. I'd still look better tripping over her dress than in the nightmare the Network wanted me to wear.

My first instinct was to race down the stairs and raise a fuss, kicking and screaming until they brought me the right dress. But I didn't want to do it in the panties and button-down shirt I wore while getting ready. It didn't even conceal as much as the body paint. And I knew, if I put that dress on, the Network wouldn't let me take it off until after the ceremony. Rachel took it and left, promising to see what she could do.

With nothing else to do, I paced the room, texting Ed. By the time Rachel returned, I was too emotionally exhausted to care that she still carried the same awful dress. She held it out, apologizing profusely. I shook my head sadly.

"Maybe it's not as bad as I remembered? Help me get it on?"

"Of course. Do you want my dress?"

The gesture touched me, but I couldn't do it. It didn't matter, anyway. "Nah. One of us should look good."

As she helped me get dressed, the only sounds in the room were the swishing of fabric and rubbing of buttons through buttonholes. Neither of us spoke until the last fastener closed. I avoided her eyes and my reflection on the wall behind me.

Then Rachel pulled out that dreadful headpiece, and my stomach revolted.

"I'm sorry, I just can't do it." I said.

"I don't blame you," she said. "Want me to accidentally drop it in the toilet?"

I shuddered. "Please don't. They might make me wear it anyway."

"Good point. I'll hide it in the laundry room. No one ever goes there."

"Do you know where it is?" During our first stint in the Fishbowl, Birdie and I wound up doing most of the laundry for the house. Rachel, on the other hand, had brought so many suitcases, I didn't think she ever needed to wear the same thing twice.

She put her hands on her hips and cocked her head. She would've looked indignant if she hadn't had to clamp her lips together to keep from giggling. When I raised my eyebrows at her, she lost the battle and doubled over.

"Oh, this has been so much fun," she said when she got control of herself. "Don't make me cry, you'll ruin my makeup."

"Then we'll both look awful!"

She blew me a kiss. "Not if I can help it. This nightmare is going in the garbage disposal. I'll see you down there."

"You're the best!"

After she left, I stood in the center of the room, examining myself in the full-length mirror. Angela, while apologizing profusely, had slathered so much makeup onto my features, it held my face in a smile. They'd have to chisel it off when this day finally ended. My hair looked awesome. Angela used enough hair spray to drown a horse, so at least I didn't have to worry it would get messed up. But the dress... Oh, the dress.

Nibbling on one thumbnail, I paced back and forth, wondering if I wanted to wear my panties and button-up shirt after all. Then I started to think about all the other things that could go wrong. So many questions, no way to answer any of them. When the curtains parted, I breathed a sigh of relief.

Mom showed up in the opening. When she saw the dress, she burst out laughing. "Oh, Jen. I'm so sorry! But...that dress is just the icing on the cake of a terrible week. You might as well go to Vegas and ask Elvis to marry you."

Her laughter was infectious. There was no point in crying. This wasn't my real wedding. Once I started laughing, I couldn't stop. I fell onto the couch, stomach heaving, until my sides hurt.

"Thanks, Mom. I needed that."

"Any time." She pulled a small jewelry case out of her purse and held it out to me. "I brought you something old. And borrowed. I need it back."

The case creaked open, revealing a stunning heart-shaped sapphire pendant on a chain, matching dangly earrings, and a gold diamond-encrusted wedding band. My grandmother's jewelry.

"It's beautiful," I breathed. "Help me put it on?"

"With pleasure. I can't believe my little girl is getting married today! Possibly. To a guy you barely know? You're not going to marry him, are you?"

It took me approximately a quarter of a second to decide to spill my guts. I'd been holding in the truth about our wedding so long, afraid she'd be mad or hurt, but baring my soul made me feel a thousand pounds lighter. When I finished my story, she looked more relieved than anything else.

"Thank goodness," she said.

"You're not mad?"

"No. I'm proud to have such an intelligent daughter who is good at preparing for the unexpected and the completely ludicrous. I love you. But I want to see Sarah's video."

"Sure thing."

She kissed the air near my cheek, careful not to leave a lipstick print. At that point, it didn't even matter. We held each other for a long moment and promised to talk later.

"Knock, knock." Ed stuck his head through the gap in the curtains. He wore a shimmering rainbow-colored tuxedo. It didn't even faze me at that point. "Rachel said you were ready? I'm here to escort you down to the wedding."

"I'll tell them you're on your way," Mom said.

"Actually, can you stall about twenty minutes? Ed's going to help me with something first."

"No problem, dear."

The curtains fell shut behind her, leaving me alone with Ed.

"How are you doing?"

"I've never looked worse in my entire life," I said with utter certainty. "The designer must've paid them a fortune to put me in this getup."

"Don't worry about it," Ed said.

"I appreciate how you don't bother to pretend I look good."

"It's my sworn duty as your best friend and as a gay man never to tell a woman she looks good when she is dressed like a trussed-up piece of cotton candy. From the neck up, you're a knockout."

I groaned. "You, on the other hand, look fabulous. What happened to the black tux?"

"That was boring. This is much more me. I figured you wouldn't mind."

"Maybe people will be blinded by the sequins and they won't be able to see me," I said with a wry smile. "Have I mentioned how much I hate this dress? I can't even look at it."

"Look at the bright side. At least it's made of actual fabric, not paint! Even though it's see-through fabric." He studied me carefully. "Do you want to cover the front with one of my aprons?"

I burst out laughing at the image of Ed's statue of Michelangelo's David apron on top of this hideous dress. The Network would love that. One of the producers would rip it off me before I got halfway down the aisle. "No, thanks. But please tell me you brought the sewing kit."

He reached into the pocket of his jacket. "I did! And I snuck the real scissors out of the kitchen for you."

"Awesome."

Taking the items Ed held out, I got to work. No one would be using the Chapel again until after the ceremony, so I ducked in and started cutting the blue-green satin fabric covering the walls. Ed unzipped the back of my dress while I cut the cloth to fit the front. Then we each took a needle and thread and created a liner for the top of the dress. Less than fifteen minutes later, Ed was zipping me back up.

"Please tell me you can't see my nipples?"

"I can't." Ed planted a kiss on my cheek. "It's not terribly bridal, but also not pornographic."

"Sounds perfect."

"Come on, gorgeous. None of this shit matters. We've got a show to film. Then you can go home with your real husband."

He was right, of course. I held his hands and gazed into his eyes for a long moment. Suddenly, I felt calmer. Things would work out. "Thanks, Ed. You're an excellent friend. And you do look wonderful."

"I know."

"Ready?"

I scooped up my bouquet from a chair where one of the production assistants had left it. Since I'd arrived, I hadn't thought about flowers once outside the centerpiece-creation challenge, but the Network had finally gotten something right. I carried a gorgeous bouquet of pink roses, with a couple of larger yellow roses for accents. No fish in sight, thankfully. "Ready."

Once we got outside, Rachel and Joshua walked in first. They looked great together. When his mouth was shut, I completely understood what Rachel had seen in him. But I wasn't remotely sad at the thought of Rachel dumping him and finding someone better ASAP.

Next, Koji escorted Logan's sister, a last-minute replacement for Birdie. Although Sarah was pretending not to have arrived in time for the wedding, we still used Ed's brother as a stand-in to get back up to six attendants. He walked with a girl I'd never seen. She wore what had to be Sarah's dress, and I wondered if she'd been chosen because they were approximately the same size. The Network certainly didn't care if I knew or liked any of my attendants or guests. At this point, I was just grateful they didn't hire random actors to also pretend to be my brother and his girlfriend. Or if they did, I hadn't met them yet.

I would forever cherish the pictures of this wedding party, with one person I didn't like at all, Rachel, and four total strangers. Well, okay, maybe I'd take one or two to hang on the walls at Sweet Reality. Surely, our fame-seeking groomsmen would autograph one for me if I asked.

"Who is that?" I whispered to Ed, nodding at the girl ahead of us. He knew everyone and watched even more reality TV than Sarah and I, if that were possible.

"Connor's best friend," he whispered back. "They've known each other since high school."

Perfect, just perfect.

When they reached the front, the music changed. Instead of the wedding march, they played a slow, instrumental version of "Happy." The song took me back to that day in the courthouse with Justin and his family. Turned out, that really was my dream wedding. All I needed was me, the man I loved, and a few people who cared about us.

Everyone stood and turned toward me and Ed. I plastered a smile on my face, took a deep breath, and put one foot in front of the other. Together, we walked down the aisle, flashbulbs snapping in our faces every step of the way.

Logan stood at the front of the aisle, waiting for me in what should've been Justin's tuxedo, his long hair pulled into a ponytail with a pouf in the front. Connor stood next to him, holding a camera. A sea of people filled the seats, most of them strangers. I spotted Tammy Rae from our reality cruise near the end of one row and Madison sitting a few feet away. Most of the other faces I recognized were from television.

We'd reserved the first two rows for personal friends and relatives, half of whom canceled due to the storm. Sitting beside Mom, Brandon waved at me from these seats. I waved back, not caring that I probably wasn't supposed to. Everyone else was executives, paid actors, former reality stars, assistants, people hoping to profit from the reception, and other Los Angeles types. Not my scene at all. At least I could show my friends I was glad to see them.

Meanwhile, Ed smiled and nodded at half the people we passed. I squeezed his arm. "You know everyone, don't you?" I whispered.

"I may be a medium-sized fish, but Los Angeles is my dream pond," he replied. "That guy over there? Huge agent. I can't wait to meet him after."

Finally, we reached the end of the aisle. The officiant smiled and nodded at both of us. I forced myself to smile at Logan, though my eyes shot daggers at him.

"You were right," he said. "Horrible dress. You look beautiful, though."

As much as I hated to admit it, he did look handsome in his tux. If he hadn't revealed himself to be pure evil, I'd have told him as much. Still, I smiled for the benefit of the viewers. "Thank you."

He reached out and wrapped a loose tendril of my hair around one finger. He lowered his voice and leaned forward. "I love you with long hair. I can't wait to run my fingers through those long locks, feel them wrapped around me."

Resisting the urge to jerk backward and slap him, I calmly smoothed the lock of hair back behind one ear. Through gritted teeth, I said, "The hair is fake, you jackass. Just like anything you ever felt between us. You will never touch me or my hair again."

Anger flashed in Logan's eyes, but his smile didn't falter.

The officiant gave us a worried look, but we just smiled at him. I nodded for him to go ahead. "We are gathered here today to bear witness to the most sacred of ceremonies. The joining together of two television personalities, hopefully with an aim toward creating a new, unified show."

The audience laughed. My stomach lurched, threatening to

spill its limited contents all over the horrible dress. That might have been an improvement.

"Before I get started, is there any reason these two should not be joined in matrimony?"

My hand shot into the air. Another laugh, this one more uneasy. I turned and looked around the church. Leanna's face was unreadable at this distance. Janine's shoulders shook, and I couldn't tell if she was laughing or crying.

The officiant chuckled. "Nice try. Shall we continue?"

"Oh, I don't think so."

Something clanged from the direction of the house. Murmurs rustled through the crowd. Someone shouted my name. Logan and I turned as one.

At the end of the aisle, several chairs lay flat on the ground, knocked aside in the commotion. Justin was running up the aisle toward me.

Our eyes met, and even at this distance, I saw his Adam's apple bob up and down. My heart soared. Even though I'd been expecting this moment, the thrill of watching my husband race to save me from a forced marriage to another man felt ten times better than imagined.

Logan stepped into the aisle, toward the back of the church. "What are you doing here, Justin? You're too late. Jen's going to marry me."

A murmur went through the crowd.

"Sorry to interrupt. Well, actually, no I'm not," Justin said. "This show is called *Jen & Justin's Big Day*, not *Jen & Logan's Big Day*. That's my bride you're blocking."

I stepped around Logan, beaming up at Justin. "Hi. I'm so glad you could make it."

"Me, too. I drove twenty-seven hundred miles so I wouldn't miss this moment."

The crowd *awwed* at his revelation.

For their benefit, I said, "You drove all the way from Miami to Los Angeles in three days?"

"In about forty hours. To marry you, I'd drive anywhere."

"Uh, guys?" Logan said behind him. "I hate to break up this touching moment, but Jen and I are kind of in the middle of something. We've got a marriage license and everything."

"Sorry, Logan," I said, barely concealing my glee. "I was never going to marry you."

"No. Jen, I can't let you do this. Don't marry him. I'm in love with you. I talked the Network into picking me when Justin got delayed. I did everything I could to make you love me."

Beside me, Justin made a noise that probably sounded like anger. I recognized it as the snort he used to cover up his laughter. Darn it, now I owed him ten bucks.

"Logan, stop," I said. "I'm sorry I didn't say anything sooner. I know you don't care about me. I saw you with Janine in the maze. The two of you were plotting against me."

If I'd thought he would appear embarrassed that I caught him having sex, or ashamed, or whatever, I'd have been wrong. He didn't even blink. Instead, he took a step toward me, eyes still locked on mine. "Don't do this. Don't change the conversation. Don't pretend you don't have feelings for me. I felt it when we kissed."

CHAPTER TWENTY-THREE

<u>Confessions from the Chapel, Saturday afternoon:</u>

Jen: I never expected Logan to kiss me. Everything happened so fast after we fell into the pool. But it didn't mean anything. I told him at the time we could only be friends. I don't have any feelings for Logan, and he doesn't have feelings for me, either. It was a mistake. I'm in love with Justin. I don't ever want to kiss anyone else, ever again. Most certainly not Logan, after everything that's happened. We're not friends. We're here to do a show. He played his part, we're done.

Logan: Jen told you we're not friends? That hurts.

Justin: I drove for three days straight to make it here for my wedding, and I'm not about to let this guy ruin it. There's nothing going on between Jen and Logan, I promise. I have one hundred percent faith in her.

J-dawg: Bro, Jen is freaky, am I right? I was so sure this wedding would be a snoozer, but it's totally epic.

EVERYONE GASPED, except me. Of course he brought up the kiss. Part of me was surprised he hadn't done it earlier, but what better time to drop that bomb than in the middle of a wedding ceremony that may or may not have involved me, Logan, and/or Justin?

"She kissed another bro right before your wedding? Buuuuu-uuuuuuuuuuuuuuuurn!" Joshua said behind me.

I resisted the urge to turn and kick him.

They stared at each other. Justin's jaw clenched. Logan's hands balled into fists.

"Shut up, J-dawg," Justin said, his eyes never wavering from Logan. "You don't know what you're talking about."

"And you do? W-T-F, bro? I'm the one who's been here all week."

Finally, I found my voice. "Logan, stop. This is ridiculous." Then I turned to the audience and raised my voice. "Yes, I kissed Logan, but it wasn't real. It was all staged by the Network. Last night, one of the production assistants came to me and told me she'd quit because the producers played tapes containing subliminal messages that would endear Logan to me."

The crowd gasped. At the back of the room, Leanna's face grew red. She moved toward the end of the aisle, holding my gaze. But then she stopped and gestured as if to say, "Go on."

Of course. This was prime drama, and that's what the Network liked. I searched for Janine to see what she thought of this turn of events, but couldn't find her in the sea of faces.

I turned to Justin, who'd been watching this entire exchange silently.

"You kissed him?" Of course, he already knew the whole story, but the viewers didn't know that.

"We were in the pool," I said. "He was drowning, and I pulled him out. I had to give him mouth-to-mouth."

"She didn't have to give me tongue-to-tongue," Logan said.

"Shut up, Logan," I said. "Justin, it wasn't like that at all. I can explain."

"You know what, Jen? There's no need." Turning to the audience, Justin said, "I already know everything. I know the Network paid Logan to flirt with Jen. I know he wore pheromones as cologne. I know the Network played subliminal messages to increase her attraction to him. I know he pretended to drown. He slipped her the tongue when she gave him mouth-to-mouth."

I stepped up beside him, slipping my hand into his. Connor stepped close with the camera, while I addressed the viewers directly. "What the Network doesn't know is that Justin and I aren't getting married today. We never were."

The audience gasped as one.

Behind me, the officiant cleared his throat. "I hate to interrupt, but should I go? Is anyone getting married?"

"Yes, someone is," Justin said.

"Someone *absolutely* is," I said. Turning back to Ed, I kissed his cheek. He pulled me into a tight embrace.

"Are you sure about this?" he asked.

"I've never been more sure about anything."

Pulling away, I moved to the left, taking my place in the matron of honor's spot. Across the aisle, Justin moved into Connor's spot and took his camera. Logan backed toward the side aisle, realization slowly dawning.

Ed and Connor now stood together, in front of everyone, grinning and holding hands. A wave of whispers flew through the crowd. Someone started to clap, and others quickly followed suit. Brandon stood, then Mom. Next thing I knew, the entire audience gave the grooms a standing ovation.

Janine was still nowhere in sight. Leanna moved from the end of the aisle to stand beside the archway Justin and I would exit through when the ceremony ended. She must be furious. It was too late to do anything, though. I'd promised her a reality star wedding, which I'd delivered. I'd also given her a gay, interracial wedding on a major network, which made her the first reality television producer in history to air such a show.

The ratings would be off the charts, and I wouldn't have to compromise who I was. Or commit a felony. No breach of contract penalty. And Justin probably wouldn't get fired. We hoped. Everything was working out, after all.

The officiant recovered quickly, getting names from each of the grooms and whispering briefly with Ed before projecting his voice over the crowd. "Honored guests, thank you for coming today to witness the union of these two men, Ed and Connor, in marriage. After two years of dating, they are delighted to have all of you come together at the very place where they first met."

Throughout the crowd, heads nodded here and there. The whispers slowed.

"Love is a glorious thing, isn't it? It transcends many barriers, including minor issues like being invited to one wedding and finding yourself attending another." The audience chuckled. "Although I just met Ed and Connor about thirty seconds ago, their love shines out of them, and I couldn't be happier to share in this day with all of you. Ed, Connor, please face each other."

The grooms turned, love shining in their eyes. I wiped a tear from my cheek. Behind Connor, Justin grinned at me, his own eyes glistening with happy tears.

The officiant leaned forward, lowering his voice. "Do you have a marriage license?"

"We do," they said. They'd picked it up at the courthouse on Friday before going to get coffee.

"Excellent! Then we'll continue." He raised his voice. "Ed, Connor, do you come before me of your own free will, asking to be married today?"

"We do."

"Do you swear that you are aware of no lawful impediments to your union?"

"We do."

"Great! I don't suppose either of you had time to prepare some vows?"

"Sure, we did," Ed said, pulling a piece of paper from his pocket. "We've been planning this."

If possible, Leanna turned even redder at his words. At some point, I'd have to talk to her. But she'd never storm down the aisle and interrupt the wedding while the cameras rolled. For now, I focused my attention on the grooms.

As they exchanged vows, happy tears slid down my cheeks. When the officiant asked for the rings, I stepped forward, pulling two platinum bands from where they'd been hidden inside my bouquet. And when they were officially pronounced "spouses for life," I clapped wildly, grinning so broadly, my cheeks hurt.

Before they greeted the crowd, Ed turned to me. "Thank you so much."

"Yes, thank you," Connor said. "Especially after everything you've been through."

I pulled them both into a hug. "None of that matters now. We're so happy for you. Thank you for saving me from Logan."

"He *is* rich and handsome," Ed said. "You could do worse."

"He's also basically evil."

"It's Los Angeles," Connor said. "Everyone's a little bit evil."

They both kissed my cheek before turning toward the crowd. The officiant introduced "Mr. and Mr. Silva-MacLaren," and everyone stood, clapping and grinning. The agent Ed pointed out when we walked in held his thumb and pinky finger to the side of his head in the universally recognized "call me" gesture.

Once they reached the end of the aisle, Justin stepped forward, still holding the camera aloft with his left arm and offering me his right. "Mrs. Reid?"

"Mr. Taylor. Lovely to see you."

At the back of the crowd, Leanna strode toward the center aisle. Apparently, she wasn't going to give us time to make a getaway before she swooped in to voice her displeasure.

"Are you ready to face the music?" Justin asked.

"Sure. After all, I've got a great lawyer."

CHAPTER TWENTY-FOUR

<u>Confessions from the Chapel, Saturday evening:</u>

Justin: This wedding wasn't about us. It was never about us. All our ideas, everything we wanted, went right out the window. But as long as Jen and I have each other, that's what matters. And look, I brought a picture of our wedding certificate, in case there were any questions.

Jen: I'm ecstatic for Ed and Connor. They're the most amazing couple. I couldn't believe when Connor told me the Network refused to let them do the show, so Justin and I decided to help their dreams come true.

Sarah: If Jen and Justin agree, sure, you can see the video. But you'll have to get in line. Talky Ted wants it, too, and he's a persistent guy.

LEANNA GRABBED my elbow as soon as I reached the back of the church, speaking in a low voice. "We need to talk."

Heart in my throat, I nodded, gripping Justin's hand harder. She steered us toward the screened-in porch that served as the secret smoking area during filming.

Facing away from us, she gazed out across the grounds,

watching the people mill around. "I'm not even sure I know what to say. I can't believe you guys did that."

Assuming she had quite the rant planned, I crossed my arms and leaned back against the wall. No need to interrupt until she got out everything she wanted to say. Justin stood, hands at his sides, also waiting.

Then she spun around, a wide smile obliterating her face. "That was amazing!"

I did a double take. If I'd been drinking something, liquid would've spewed out everywhere. "Really?"

"Oh, absolutely," she said. "The ratings will be off the hook. People will be talking about this wedding for years! I was planning to move to a new network, but I'll be able to leverage that episode into a huge raise. Thank you so much."

"You're welcome, I guess," I said. "You're not mad?"

"No way. After this, the Network will put me on whatever show I want. Less drama, more gritty reality. Real shows. The type of thing I got into this business for."

She sounded like Vera. And Connor. How many people walking around reality television started with big dreams of changing the world?

"We thought you liked the drama," Justin said.

"I liked the paycheck. I did my job, paid my dues," she said. "I'm very sorry about everything you two went through. Janine kept pushing things through without telling me, and I had to act like I had it under control so the Network wouldn't give her my job. But she's done."

For a heartbeat, I almost felt sorry for Leanna. But it was tough to forgive everything Justin and I had been through. She should've been on it, not letting Janine run wild. Instead, I made a clucking noise with my tongue and let her interpret it as she would.

"Jen, I talked to Vera this morning."

The hair on the back of my neck stood up. If that whole

conversation was a setup, I was walking out here and now. Not wanting to give too much away about our talk, I said, "And?"

"First, I'm not the one who talked to Justin's boss. Yes, I dated his daughter years ago, but I don't even know how Janine found out about that. She emailed him from my account and set everything up. I never would've blackmailed you into coming onto the show. I originally pushed to let Connor and Ed get married live. I'm sorry the show steamrollered you."

"Thanks." Justin spoke dryly, the tic in his jaw betraying his true emotions. "What about brainwashing my bride into marrying someone else?"

"That was Janine, too. I was giving Jen lots of time with Logan, sure, told him to pile on the charm, but I never wanted to take it this far. Janine's been fired. And when I'm done with her, not even Fox News will put her on another TV show. No way. I'm so sorry."

"Thanks," I said. "I'm sorry we thought we couldn't trust you."

"I don't blame you. In your shoes, I wouldn't trust me, either," she said. "Anyway, guys, America loves you. I'm going to want to talk to you about a follow-up to *Jen & Justin's Big Day*."

"Some other time," I said. "It's been quite a roller coaster."

Justin wisely changed the subject. "Do you have to change the title of the show, since we didn't get married after all?"

She waved one hand dismissively. "It works. It's still your big day, in theory. I can talk to the powers that be, but I don't see any reason to change it. The other nine episodes are all about the two of you."

"So you're not mad at all about what we did?" I asked.

"Honey, I'm ecstatic. Not only did you deliver the reality show wedding you promised, you added drama, plus a twist no one will see coming. At least not once I'm done editing it. You've more than earned everything we promised." She pulled an envelope from the pocket of her green day-dress. "Here. I've got something for you."

"Is it a summons?" Justin asked, still wary.

"Don't be ridiculous," she said. "It's the itinerary for your honeymoon. Take a vacation, on us. You've earned it."

I took it hesitantly, still expecting some kind of trick. This wasn't the Leanna I'd come to know during *Real Ocean*. It was, however, reminiscent of the friendly, overeager production assistant I'd first met two years ago on *The Fishbowl*.

Inside the envelope, I found two tickets from LAX to San Juan, Puerto Rico, plus an itinerary confirming our stay at an all-inclusive resort, prepaid. "Not to look a gift horse, but what's the catch?"

Justin nudged me with one elbow, speaking out the side of his mouth. "Shut up."

"No catch, I promise," she said. "I have to be the hard-ass sometimes, because it's my job to make a good show. I have to answer to the network executives. But every single person in attendance signed a confidentiality agreement when they got here. As long as I can keep this twist from a couple of the more conservative bosses until the show airs, we're golden."

Justin and I exchanged a look. I nodded, guessing what he was thinking. "I feel weird going on this honeymoon when we're not the ones giving you the huge ratings on the final episode. Shouldn't you give it to Ed and Connor?"

"No need," she said. "As soon as you switched places, I texted my assistant. They're going with you. I booked a room near yours, but not too near, if you know what I mean."

To my surprise, I hugged her. To my even greater surprise, she hugged me back. "Now get out of here, you two, and go enjoy the party!"

THE RECEPTION WAS ABSOLUTELY LOVELY, despite the gluten-free, all-vegan crap they served on the buffet. Instead of eating anything, Justin and I danced and danced, lost in our own world. After everyone finished eating, Sarah pulled me to the dessert table, revealing the cake she'd made of me and Justin kissing in the driveway. I clapped one hand over my mouth, too moved to speak.

We gave the cupcakes she'd also brought to Ed and Connor, since they deserved refined sugar for their help. I glanced around, but Logan was nowhere to be found. Neither was Janine. Perhaps they'd gone back into the now heart-shaped maze to celebrate Logan's freedom. I didn't care. If I never again saw Logan Cassidy again, it would be too soon. Justin and I moved quietly around the room, talking to Danielle, Brandon, and the few other guests in attendance who were there to see us. It was the first time I'd managed to truly relax since landing in Los Angeles.

After the toasts, Justin and I said our quiet goodbyes, made Mom promise to come to Florida for Christmas, and slipped out. For the first time in ten days, no cameras followed me. A thousand-pound weight fell from my shoulders.

We wheeled our suitcases to the end of the driveway to wait for a cab. We probably could have asked the Network for a ride, but neither Justin nor I wanted anything else from the producers. In my hands, I cradled a small box containing two slices of Sarah's cake.

"Are you sorry we didn't get married on national television?" Justin asked.

"Not even a little bit. Our wedding last week was perfect, and it was us. This circus would've been neither," I said. "Besides, you saw how happy Ed and Connor are. The Network refused to give them a wedding, you know. Connor offered, when Braden and Amanda first broke up."

"Yeah, he told me." Justin shook his head. "Think about all

the drama we could've avoided if they'd just gotten their wedding in the first place."

A taxi pulled to a stop in front of us. We stood quietly while the driver loaded our bags into the trunk. Behind us, music from the wedding played.

"Sounds like a fun party," the driver remarked.

"It's a good time, with some great people, but it's not our scene anymore," Justin said. "We're ready to head home."

After we settled into the cab, I said, "Imagine if we'd just been regular wedding guests. That would've been nice. No one would've tried to make me attend naked."

"No forty-hour drive across the country in two days."

"No Logan trying to seduce me purely to bump the ratings."

"No actor pretending to be your father."

I sighed and shook my head. "The things we do for money."

"Not anymore," Justin said. "My boss emailed me about an hour ago. The Network signed the retainer agreement, and I've got a job in the pro bono department for as long as I want. I start interviewing interns when we get back."

"What happens if the Network cancels the deal and claims we breached by not getting married?"

He leaned over and kissed me. "Then we deal with it. You and me. Together, we can get through anything."

I leaned my head on Justin's shoulder, and he put his arm around me. My eyes fluttered shut. The rest of the trip passed in silence.

Half a mile from the airport, my phone rang. Leanna's name appeared on the display.

"Why do you think she's calling?" Justin asked.

"They probably want to film our honeymoon baby's conception or something," I said. "Let me turn it off."

He caught my eyes as the phone rang again. "Come on. You're not a little bit curious, after the things she said earlier?"

"We said after the cruise we were done with reality TV. It almost broke us up."

"And today, it brought Ed and Connor together," Justin pointed out. "She did say she's going to have full creative control over her next show."

"Less drama, right? Shows that people can learn?" A third ring. If I didn't answer soon, the call would roll to voicemail. "I suppose it can't hurt to hear her out."

From the front seat, the cabdriver said, "Hurry up, answer it! Even I can tell you want to."

Justin nodded at the phone in my hand. "Go for it. My wedding gift to you."

I mouthed 'I love you' to him while lifting the phone to my ear. "Hi, Leanna. What can we do for you?"

EPILOGUE

Shocking Entertainment News Online

REALITY ROYALTY SAYS "I DON'T"
Last-minute wedding switch = gay ratings bonanza
by Talky Ted

The finale of *Jen & Justin's Big Day* was shrouded in secrecy.
Everyone turned in their cell phones at the front door, no media
allowed, guests were required to sign lengthy nondisclosure
agreements. When the show aired last night, viewers across
America finally understood why.
As the sun set over Los Angeles, *The Fishbowl*'s Jen Reid walked
down the aisle on the arm of handsome fellow contestant Ed
Silva. However, when the two reached the front, Ed didn't hand
Jen off as expected. Instead, Jen stepped aside, and the groom's
spot was filled by Connor, one of the show's producers. Ever
since *The Fishbowl* ended, Ed and Connor have been seen around
town.
Rumors of an upcoming engagement have circulated for some
time, but swapping in a gay wedding was unprecedented for
television, which can be oddly conservative at times.

The groundbreaking episode will re-run Saturday night at 10:00 pm. As of this writing, more than ten million people had streamed the episode live via the Network's app in just one day after news broke. Trust me, this is one show you don't want to miss!

Neither Jen nor Justin responded to a request for comment. However, a lovely source close to the couple revealed that the two may have actually tied the knot before filming began. They intended to repeat their vows in front of the audience, but discord arose when a canceled flight stranded the groom in Florida.

According to my source, the Network insisted that the wedding must go on, with or without a love match between bride and groom, which is when Jen threw in the towel. Producers allegedly had no idea what would happen until Jen reached the officiant and stepped out of the way.

So now the real question: who gets to go on the show-sponsored honeymoon? And what do I have to do to convince Justin's sister to go out with me? Call me, Sarah!

For a full recap of the episode, <u>click here</u>.

Related Stories:

- **Spin-off Series for Fishbowl Baby?**
- **The Network Declines to Renew *Love with Logan* After Maze Sex Tape Surfaces**
- **Rachel Dumps J-dawg on Instagram**

ACKNOWLEDGMENTS

Somehow, writing acknowledgments for the end of a series seems even more daunting than for the first book. As if this is my chance to fit in everyone I may have forgotten along the way. I'm so very grateful for everyone's support, and I apologize to anyone left out.

First and foremost, thank you to my husband for your unwavering love and support. Thank you to Stephanie Thornton again for inspiring this series. None of this would be possible without you, Marie, and Michelle. Go Team Steph!

Thank you again to my wonderful agent, Michelle Richter, and to the Kensington team, especially Wendy McCurdy, Norma Perez-Hernandez, Lauren Jernigan, and Lulu Martinez. Thank you also to the copy editors (and I'm sorry I can't use hyphens). Marty Mayberry and Kara Reynolds, thank you for being the absolute best. Thank you to K.D. Proctor and Elizabeth Newmann for your valuable feedback and insight. Thank you to Karen Sargent and Kari Lemor for your first-chapter critiques. A special thank you to Lex Leonov for your help with the LGBT+ characters. I apologize for any mistakes that crept in due to my ignorance.

Thank you to all my friends and family who've supported me.

You've been amazing, and I'm incredibly grateful to have you all in my life. Thanks, Adam, for telling me how to pasteurize eggs to make cookie dough and fuel this book. Oh, and thank you to my local gym.

I hope you enjoyed REALITY WEDDING. Writing this series was a privilege. The best thing for a writer is to know when readers liked their book. If you did, please consider leaving an honest review.

Find me on Twitter @LH_Writes

or at www.facebook.com/lauraheffernananbooks.

ALL'S FAIR IN LOVE AND BOARD GAMES

Read on for a preview of

She's Got Game

now available from your favorite retailer.

Part I: Boston

Gallivanting Gwen
    June 9

wan-der-lust: /n/ a strong, innate desire to rove around or travel

If home is where the heart is, my home is an airplane. Crisp, clean sheets in an unfamiliar room. Finding the hidden gems in a new city. I've had this blog for almost a year now, and the most common question I get is: why do you do this? Where's your home base?

Well, readers: I do this because I love it. Nothing makes me as happy as strapping into an airplane seat, leaning back, and dreaming about where I'll land. I can recite the safety demon-stration along with the flight attendant. I've touched down in thirty-eight states (including Alaska and Hawaii), and I can't wait to see the rest. My best friend Holly doesn't understand how I can stand airplanes, because the coffee's so gross. Here's the secret: coffee's always gross. Diet Coke tastes the same up in the air as on the ground, even if it pours slower on a plane. (See? I'm full of fun facts, thanks to my travels.)

As a kid, we never went anywhere. Dad worked all the time, and it was just the two of us. We didn't have a lot of extra money. He never wanted to take time off. If I had to name a home base, it would be his place. A couple of boxes with my name on them are currently living in his basement. But I have no interest in owning a home, and there's no lease with my name on it.

Someone pass the avocado toast, please. This millennial has no problems with her life. The American dream, it's a-changin'.

This week, I'm back in my old stomping grounds. Ever since the year it rained 28 out of 30 days, I've avoided Boston in June. However, I'm excited to be participating in the annual American Explorers of Islay Board Game Competition. Love this game.

The conference center buzzed with anticipation. Palpable excitement filled the air. Some of the other participants fidgeted. I stood alone, an island of calm in the sea of activity. Nerves were for the less prepared. I'd done my homework, I'd played endless games, and I planned to make it to the final table in Las Vegas, where I'd win the $10,000 grand prize.

In about six months, anyway. One thing at a time.

My first game started in about twenty minutes, leaving me plenty of time to sip my Diet Coke and survey the competition. If someone said "I'm going to the local American Explorers of Islay Competition," most people would picture a room full of pasty twenty-ish guys with glasses and high water pants, living in their parents' basements. We had those types, sure, and my collection of geeky t-shirts fit in perfectly with that crowd. But the room also contained people of all shapes, sizes, genders, and colors, ranging from eighteen to about eighty. We hailed from all over the region, possessed a variety of interests.

And one of us was a very good-looking guy with curly brown hair, surveying me over his coffee cup with gorgeous chocolate brown eyes. He wasn't pasty at all, with a deep tan and lean muscles making his jeans and black t-shirt look a lot more exciting than they sounded. When I met his gaze, he smiled, flashing beautiful teeth, the kind typically found on the wealthy and children of dentists.

Although I'd never seen him before, he chatted with a guy who showed up at these things every now and then. Tall, with thin black braids trailing down his back, the most beautiful light brown eyes I'd ever seen, and dimples. The two of them upped the hotness average in this room by about thirty percent, but both were unfortunately off-limits to me. I didn't date gamers. Don't poop where you eat and all that.

"Not bad." My former roommate, co-competitor, and close friend Holly appeared beside me. "Looking for a little after-competition action?"

I rolled my eyes at her. "Whatever. I won't have the energy for hooking up after I kick butt."

Participants in the American Explorers of Islay Competition competed in a popular resource-sharing board game. The original game accommodated three or four players, and the expansion allowed for more, but the tournament assigned everyone to tables of four. This morning, everyone would play three games and receive a score based on their final rank in each. Table placement was determined in advance by a random draw.

Holly and I weren't playing each other in the first round, but it wasn't a big deal. At some point, we'd inevitably face off. And if we didn't, well, the trash talk would still kick into high gear. The way the tournament was set up, we could both move onto the next round. After three years of grad school and playing together, we'd still be friends after the final scores were announced. It didn't matter whether one of us got knocked out on Sunday or the two of us made it to the final table.

"*Almost* everyone here. I personally plan to wipe the floor with you." Holly corrected me with a wink and a smile. Trash talk and "game hate" ruled at these events. No one meant anything they said. Usually. "Oh, hey, I forgot to mention–last year's winner is here. I talked to him when he transferred his registration from Florida."

With her background and tech know-how, Holly helped set up the registration database for the competition. After years of acting as tech support and back-up registrar, she knew practically everyone's name. We weren't a large community, at least not locally.

Playfully, I swatted at her arm. "What? I can't believe you didn't tell me!"

Last year's winner was a legend. He'd won four years in a row, more than anyone except John, the current competition host. Rumor had it he was calm, collected, and dominated the table during games. Many a gamer imagined testing our skills against C. McKay. The thought of getting to play him here made my mouth water.

Unfortunately, he lived in Florida, so our paths had never crossed. I'd never been able to afford go to the finals. Usually, I volunteered at the local and regional competitions, then dreamed about the rest. But not this year.

"Sorry. Things have been busy with the wedding planning and everything. But there he is."

She pointed at the list of first round match-ups on the wall behind me. Directly below H. McDonald, also known as Holly, the sheet said, C. McKay. A name I'd never seen on the lists in this state, but sent a little thrill through me. Was he as good as everyone said? I couldn't wait to find out.

"Excellent! I can't wait to scope out the competition, find his weak spots, and destroy him."

"You were checking him out a second ago," a voice said behind me.

John, the only person who won more tournaments than C. McKay, stood behind us. He was medium-height, medium-build, probably around my dad's age, with close-cropped, curly dark hair and a salt-and-pepper goatee. Only his whistle and clipboard made him stand out from the rest of the crowd. And the twenty years he'd been around, playing with everyone, making friends. He and his wife Carla co-owned the local game store with his parents, so I'd known him since I was a baby. "That's him over there. Cody."

Following John's finger, my eyes once again landed on the hottie. So that was C. McKay. My number one competition. My ridiculously buff number one competition. My stomach dropped. Why did he have to be an excellent player *and* totally hot? He reminded me of my very first crush as a child, Jonathan Crombie from *Anne of Green Gables* (who reminded me of my second crush, Megan Follows). Those crushes may have played into my utter fascination with the entire series.

He winked at me. For some reason, winking always weirded me out. Maybe because it was mostly old men who did it, looking at twenty-something women. I'd never seen anyone my age do it. As I rolled my eyes, he flashed a grin. My stomach flip-flopped.

Mentally, I revised my assessment: a good player, hot, and a shameless flirt. He probably thought that made him a triple threat. Whatever. I'd been one of only about a dozen females at these events for years: There wasn't a single pick-up line my friends and I hadn't heard. This guy didn't have as much game as he thought.

"Did he wink at you?" Holly rolled her eyes. "Like he's gonna win because he's cute?"

"I think he did."

"If only he frosted the tips of his hair or wore a popped collar, he could be a total walking cliché."

"Or both," I agreed.

A high, clear tone filled the room: the bell, alerting us that we only had ten minutes to get to our tables and settle in before the first game started. The guy started toward us, eyes still fixated on me, and I groaned.

"Ugh. I'm not up for introducing myself."

"I'd love to say hello," Holly said, "but I need coffee before we start."

"Yeah, I've gotta go, too," John said. "Talk to you later."

"You don't want to say hello yourself?" My question went to both of them, but John had turned away, tilting his head the way he did when someone spoke into the earpiece he wore during these events.

True friends wouldn't abandon me with this guy. If he opened with "Hey, is your name Sonic? Because you've been running through my dreams," I'd never forgive them. And, knowing Holly, she'd be sorry to miss such a horrible line. She'd been attached to her fiancé for so long, most everyone around here knew not to bother trying their luck. Every once in a while, though, a newbie got sucked in by her perfectly polished sorority girl look and decided to make a move. Usually with amusing results.

Holly grinned as she stepped away. "Not with the way he's looking at you. See you later."

Before I could argue I wasn't here to flirt, she vanished back into the crowd, and C. McKay arrived in front of me. He looked even better up close, if possible. A wave of disappointment hit me. Part of me hoped he was like a Monet–beautiful from afar, but a total mess up close.

"Carrots?" he said.

As pick-up lines went, this one stumped me. It beat the Sonic line some creeper tried on me a few months ago, but largely because it made no sense. With no idea what he was talking about, I said the first thing that came into my head. "Squash? Rutabaga?"

He chuckled and pointed at my chest. Oh, right. My t-shirt: *Don't Keep Calm, He Just Called You Carrots.*

My face grew warm. "Sorry, I forgot. It's an *Anne of Green Gables* reference."

"I got the reference. I was trying to be funny. Sorry." He held out one hand. "Cody McKay."

In all the times I'd worn this shirt, no guy my age had ever caught what it meant. Of course, I'd never met a guy who looked like Gilbert Blythe. Under other circumstances, I'd have been impressed. But now I was mostly intrigued to meet the guy I'd heard so much about. Not that he could know. "Gwen Williams. I'll be kicking your ass here shortly."

"Gwen? That's a pretty name." He smiled. "Think I prefer Carrots, though."

My stomach fluttered traitorously at the way he looked at me. My hand tingled where our fingers still touched, but I quashed those emotions. If this guy thought he could charm me to throw me off-guard, he had another think coming. Just because he was better-looking than the average gamer didn't mean I'd fall at his feet once he flashed those gorgeous brown eyes. I came here to win games, not to hook up.

Hoping he couldn't see how flustered he made me, I said, "Then maybe you should hit up the snack room. They've got plenty of carrots for you."

"Sorry. I didn't mean to offend you. I'm usually much better at this."

"Well, if you're not great at playing games, you're in the wrong place." I flashed a broad smile at him to take the bite out of my words. "Excuse me, I've got a tournament to win."

"Actually, *I've* got a tournament to win," he said, smoothly maneuvering around me. Still walking, he turned to look back at me. "After all, I'm the four-time American Explorers of Islay Competition champion."

"That's because you've never played against me." The parting shot had the desired effect in that it made him pause for a second. He shook his head, grinning, which left me dying to wipe the smug look off his face.

So that was the guy I needed to beat. He apparently thought charming the other players gave him an advantage. Little did he know, I'd had plenty of experience with silver-tongued gamers who relied on their good looks to get girls. They didn't impress me. Our interaction only made me more determined to hand Cody his ass in a game.

With a small smile, I tugged at my t-shirt, bringing the v-neck a bit lower. My boobs couldn't compete with Holly's, but I could give him something to look at. Then I shook my long hair out of its braid and pressed my lips together to redden them. Two could play Cody's game. But only one of us would win, and it was going to be me.

BOOKS BY LAURA HEFFERNAN

The Reality Star Series

America's Next Reality Star

Sweet Reality

Reality Wedding

The Oceanic Dreams Series

Time of My Life

The Gamer Girls Series

She's Got Game

Against the Rules

Make Your Move

Push and Pole Series

Poll Dancer

The Accidental Senator

Finding Tranquility

Anna's Guide to Getting Even

INTRODUCING ADA BELL

Welcome to Shady Grove...

Aly doesn't believe in psychics. Too bad she just had a vision.

Future scientists don't have visions. Aly's got enough on her plate, with finishing her degree and taking care of her nephew and starting her new job at the antique store while drooling over the owner's gorgeous son. No visions.

Alas, the universe doesn't care what Aly believes. When she turns 21, she starts to feel psychic impressions left on objects. A disorienting power for someone surrounded by antiques. Then cranky customer Earl is killed, and Aly's new boss Olive is the prime suspect. Who hated Earl enough to kill? Police would rather make a quick arrest than investigate, so it's up to Aly to clear Olive's name.

Shady Grove is reeling from the first murder in decades. If Aly can get her hands on the murder weapon, she should be able to solve the crime. Can she learn to control her visions before the killer sets their sights on her?

Mystic Pieces
The Scry's the Limit
Sight Seering
Seer Today, Gone Tomorrow